THE
SECOND SISTER

BY

RAE D. MAGDON

Desert Palm Press

The Second Sister

Copyright © 2014 by Rae D. Magdon

ISBN-13 9781499127065
ISBN-10 1499127065

Desert Palm Press
1961 Main Street, Suite 220
Watsonville, California 95076
www.desertpalmpress.com

Editor: R. Lee Fitzsimmons
Cover Design: Rachel George http://www.rachelgeorgeillustration.com

Printed in the United States of America
First Edition - April 2014

Acknowledgments

I would like to thank all of the amazing people who helped me through the thrilling but exhausting process of writing this novel. Without you, none of this would have been possible.

First, I must give a big thank you to Lee, my editor, who has stuck with me through the entire series and removed all of my extraneous dialogue tags. You helped put the sparkle and shine on the scribbles I came up with, and I can't begin to express how much I appreciate it.

Thank you to The Royal Academy and The Athenaeum for giving my story a home, and all the readers who sent me messages or commented on my work. You gave me the courage to do this. Also, thank you to the wonderful people at Desert Palm Press for guiding me through the process of getting my first novel ready for publication.

Most importantly of all, I have to thank Tory. Without you, I would be completely lost. You encouraged me to follow my dreams, and because of that, I have you.

Dedication

To Tory, the love of my life.
And to the writers who came before me, offering the priceless gifts of inspiration and self-confidence.

Contents

THE
SECOND SISTER

Part One,

As Recorded By Eleanor Baxstresse

CHAPTER 1

I PEERED OUT of the rain-streaked windows, searching for green as the carriage jolted over slick cobblestones. Sandleford had been filled with it. The rich smell of wet earth and fresh leaves would have blanketed the entire town after a spring rainstorm like this, but Sandleford Manor's gardens and forests were miles away. I would never see them again.

There was no green at Baxstresse. There were no ancient oak trees, no flowering orchards, and hardly any bushes. This was farm country, near the heart of the kingdom of Seria, and everything was flat. Fields with churned-up clods of mud stretching out in every direction. The gray of the skyline blurred into the landscape, and I could scarcely tell where one stopped and the other began.

"Ye can see the manor ahead now, Miss," the carriage driver, Matthew, called back. His voice was pleasant, but I was too busy feeling sorry for myself to appreciate his attitude. I pressed my cheek against the cool window and looked down the road where Baxstresse Manor waited for me. The manor towered over everything else, the only break in the monotonous view. There were no trees or hills or mountains to detract from its height. Blurred by rain, I could still make out the dark points of its roof.

The manor's high walls were built from gray stone. Since there was no quarry nearby, I wondered if the builders had paid mages to move the stone blocks. My father had told me the inside of the manor was grand, but the outside only seemed cold and lonely. Baxstresse was far too barren to compare with Sandleford. I would never be able to call this place home.

After my father's marriage to Lady Kingsclere, he had insisted on moving to Baxstresse, claiming it would be a relief to escape my mother's ghost. Memories of her saturated our old home, but I had enjoyed them. Sandleford's white roses reminded me of how my mother used to weave blossoms into my hair, and the old wardrobe in her room brought back long afternoons of hide and seek. My father had left my mother's spirit at Sandleford, and a piece of my heart had stayed behind with her.

My mother was not the only person I had left behind. I missed the laughing village children, the dogs I had raised from pups, the horses, and old Father Matthias, the local priest. The familiar faces were already fading in my memory. What if I began to forget my mother's face?

A closer view of Baxstresse only made me feel more alone. The carriage rolled to a stop at the end of a long gravel drive. The high double doors loomed above us, dissected by heavy iron bars set in the shape of a cross. A pair of servants rushed out to meet me, throwing a warm cloak about my shoulders as I stepped out of the carriage, and hurried me inside before the rain could damage my traveling dress. It was a wasted effort. Mud stains already dotted several inches of the hem, and the material was bunched and wrinkled from hours of sitting still. It would need a thorough washing before I could wear it again.

We scurried into the entrance hall like a group of mice running into a bolthole, tucking our arms close to our bodies to keep warm. One of the servants, an overly dressed dandy with thinning hair, walked over to the door and held it partially open so the shivering Matthew could carry in my trunks, his thin brown face dripping at the nose and chin. The dandy almost closed the door on Matthew's heels. His coat was stylish, but it had far too many buttons. He took great care to keep it dry as we passed him.

"Af'ernoon, Jamison," Matthew said politely.

The man, Jamison, stepped back, his mouth twisting into something I did not recognize as a smile for several moments. His curled, puckered lips showed he was unaccustomed to the act. I decided I did not like him. "Both trunks need to be taken to the far room."

Matthew's thick eyebrows lifted several inches on his forehead. "Well then, you'd best get a boy to take 'em, aye? Got to see to the horses." Jamison gulped like a fish at Matthew's retreating back, but shook himself and hurried off, not wanting to stay in an embarrassing position. I watched him go until a voice interrupted me.

"You'll be young Mistress Eleanor, then?" said the other servant who had remained beside me. She was a plump woman with an ample chest and big rosy cheeks, stout and broad shouldered. Her hands were large and calloused, swollen at the joints. A servant's hands. "I'm Mam, Lady's chief cook, and I'm to get for you whatever you might be wanting while Jamison collects your things."

"Thank you," I said. My mother had always been polite to the servants, and my father was away too often to protest. I wanted to follow her example.

"You're most welcome." Mam put a hand on my arm and guided me toward a great stone staircase that curved up toward the second floor. "I'll be taking you to Lady Kingsclere now, and afterwards, I'm to show you to your room."

I gazed up at the high ceiling in wonder, scarcely hearing her. An enormous chandelier arched above me, hundreds of candles reflecting their light onto its soft golden body. The room was enormous. Although the manor was built of stone, the windows were stained glass, and the walls were hung with fine tapestries. My father had been right. It was grand, but the rich decorations did not please me. They only stunned me. I knew I would tire of them quickly. I remembered how large the manor had looked from outside and wondered whether I would lose my way after Mam left me.

"Aye, Baxstresse is a large enough place," Mam said as she shepherded me up the staircase, reading my mind. "Don't you be fretting about losing yourself here, though. I'll make sure you get your bearings. If you turn yourself around in the halls, ask a servant to set you right. They'll like you, what with you being polite and well mannered." Her Amendyrri grammar was very down-to-earth and quite charming. Although her hair was silver instead of red, her nose and chin had something of the western country in them. Her sentence structure certainly did.

I lifted the skirt of my traveling dress so it did not trail on the stairs behind me. "How did you know I was worried about getting lost?"

"It's what everyone is thinking when they see the entrance hall. Come now, Mistress Eleanor, Lady Kingsclere will be wanting to see you." Mam's conversation was comforting. She spoke enough to steady my nerves without chattering to fill the silence.

At the top of the stairs, Mam took me past a grand row of stained glass windows, pointing as we passed a large set of double doors. "That's the library. Mistress Belladonna spends most of her time in there, reading. She's a poet and a musician. Both of Lady's daughters are."

I had met Luciana and Belladonna only once before, at my father's wedding. At twenty, Belladonna was a few months older than me. Luciana was a year older, ready to marry. Both were painfully beautiful, with clear, pale skin and thick hair that curled down their backs, although Belladonna's was much darker. Both of them were tall, thin, and covered in sleek sheets of muscle. There was something primitive about them, something attractive. The pair unsettled me, but I had never been able to figure out why.

Again, the perceptive Mam sensed my thoughts. "As to Lady's daughters, I have a small piece of advice, if you won't mind my giving it."

"Yes, of course," I mumbled, still wrapped up in memories of my stepsisters and what had disturbed me about them.

"Keep your pretty head low." It was several weeks before I realized what Mam's warning had meant.

Lady Kingsclere's suite of rooms included a study. Both of us heard voices floating from that room as we approached the door together. Mam paused, her hand raised to knock, listening for a break in the conversation. The voices speaking inside were low and harsh, far too soft for me to distinguish individual words, but the meaning behind them was clear. At least one of the Kingsclere sisters was being scolded.

When the voices quieted, Mam rapped sharply on the dark wood of the door. "Come in," someone called from inside, and Mam turned the knob. She was clever, I thought as I entered the study. A good servant knew when to keep out of the way. As soon as I had slipped into the study, Mam bowed herself out, leaving me alone with my new stepmother and my two stepsisters.

Lady Kingsclere was seated at her desk with a daughter at each shoulder, her hand resting on a piece of stationary. Her hair, just as lustrous and thick as her daughters', was swept up fashionably on top of her head. The streaks of gray running through it only added to the impressive sight she made. She was still beautiful, and I could see, in a detached sort of way, why my father had wanted to marry her.

To her right, Belladonna was studying me. Her hand rested lightly on the arm of her mother's chair, and her long, white fingers curling around the polished wood. She was wearing a fine dress of green brocade that tapered at the waist just above the slight flare of her hips, but her neck and wrists were bare. Her hair washed about her shoulders in loose curls, and her expression was unreadable.

Luciana was just as well dressed as her sister in a gown of dark velvet, but unlike Belladonna, her face was all too easy to read. Her lips were drawn up in an insolent, satisfied smile, and I knew which of her daughters Lady Kingsclere had sided with this time. Her hair had been combed back, and like Belladonna's, it was thick and wavy with curls. The sight of the pair made my cheeks flush. I gazed down at my feet, hoping that they would not notice the mud stains on the hem of my traveling dress.

"Ah, Eleanor, welcome to Baxstresse." Lady Kingsclere gave me a genuine smile. Although I had only met her daughters once, she had visited Sandleford several times, and we were on friendly terms. I had no reason to dislike my stepmother. Rather, it was my father I disapproved of for taking another wife. She did not try to stand in as a substitute for the mother I had lost and struck me as a regal, fair woman who was used to handling things herself.

However, I had overheard a great deal of gossip about her from the servants. After the death of her first husband, Lord Alastair, she had become a recluse, hiding away in her rooms for five years. She allowed no one to see her but her daughters. Finally, she had gathered her wits enough to make public appearances. That was when my father met her. They said that he reminded her of her late husband and that he had given her back her sanity. If such rumors were true, I thought, I was seeing my stepmother as she had been before her illness, intelligent and capable.

I curtsied, lowering my eyes. "Thank you, Lady Kingsclere."

"You may call me mother, but only if you wish." There was kindness in her voice, a tentativeness that took any hurt out of the words. She knew before I answered that I would not call her mother. I took the offer for what it was, a welcoming gesture instead of a threat.

"Thank you, but I would prefer Lady Kingsclere." I lifted my gaze to my stepmother's face, but I saw no disappointment or anger there. A silent understanding passed between us.

"Of course, Eleanor. You have my permission to change your mind, if you feel comfortable. Has Mam shown you around the manor?"

"She helped give me an idea of the place." Something warm brushed against my leg, and I looked down. A plump cat with a beautifully patterned black, brown, and cream coat was rubbing her chin just below my knee. I smiled for the first time in several days and bent to scoop up the cat.

"You're lucky," the cat said, narrowing her eyes at me and lashing her tail as she settled against my chest. "I could have scratched you." My experience with cats told me she was bluffing. She was just as interested in me as I was in her.

Lady Kingsclere's head lifted up. "Well, Jessith seems to fancy you. She's usually not very sociable with strangers."

"Animals are friendly with me," I explained. My strange affinity with animals had been noticed when I lived at Sandleford, but the reason behind it was kept secret. Speaking with animals was not unheard of in Seria, but it would be foolish to advertise such a gift. Although magic flourished in Seria's capital city, particularly at the Ronin College of Magic and Sorcery, it was viewed with suspicion throughout the rest of the kingdom, especially in the upper classes.

Serians with magical aptitude often changed the weather, healed the sick, or grew food, but such favors were quickly forgotten. As soon as the latest catastrophe had been averted, we were back to being Ariada—witches. The word was taken from Amendyrri, the language that had been spoken here before the Serian settlers inhabited the continent. The native Amendyrri still lived in the west, across the Rengast Mountains, but their kingdom was only half of its previous size. In Amendyr, Ariada was not a curse.

I scratched Jessith along her jawbone. She yawned, displaying the pink ridges that lined the inside of her throat. I decided that Jessith, like most cats, was probably very full of herself. "She is a very beautiful cat."

"Jessith is one of our Baxstresse Tortoiseshells," Lady Kingsclere explained proudly. "Our family breeds them. See the unmarked white chest?" Jessith graciously moved her paws so that I could see the puffed white fur around her breastbone. Maybe, I thought, it was not completely Jessith's fault that she was conceited, even if she was a cat.

"It's cold in here. " Jessith nudged my hand with her chin when I stopped scratching. "I didn't tell you to stop, but take me somewhere warmer."

Thankfully, Lady Kingsclere understood that I was tired after my journey and allowed me to make my excuses. She turned me over to Mam, who had been waiting a respectful distance from the door. I tried to remember the halls that she led me through, but I was so tired that I was hardly aware of myself when I collapsed onto my new bed with Jessith cuddled against my chest.

CHAPTER 2

IT WAS RAINING when I woke up the next morning. Yesterday's gray downpour had continued through the night. It was a relief to find myself relaxing in a mountain of soft covers after several days of traveling, but the manor's cold and unwelcoming stones were still unsettling. One of the servants had left fresh undergarments at the foot of my bed. A shy knock came from the other side of the door just as I finished putting them on. "Come in, please," I called out.

The door opened part way, and a thin girl with red-gold hair slipped inside, her eyes on her shoes. Her flaming hair and freckles had me wondering if she was Amendyrri. "Good morning, Miss Eleanor," she said, her soft lips mouthing the words more than speaking them. Obviously, if she was from Amendyr, she had grown up in Seria, or she was a very good mimic. Unlike Mam, I could detect no accent in her speech. "My name is Cate, and I'm to help you dress and get you anything you'd like before breakfast." The proud Jessith, who had decided to bless us with her company, opened one eye and rubbed her jaw against the covers.

"If you would help me with my corset, please," I said. "I am not sure where..." Cate was already hurrying over to the wardrobe in one corner and pulling it open. After I chose a corset, underlayers, and dress, she helped me to put them on. I tried to ask her about the manor as she did up the hooks and eyelets, but her answers, when she gave them, were soft, short, and uncomfortable, though always polite.

"You won't have much luck getting talk out of that one," Jessith said throatily, uncurling from her sleeping position and stretching across most of my bed. She lifted her head to watch Cate adjust my skirts. "Don't look so disappointed. She's like this with everyone, even the other servants. You're getting more out of her than most people would." I ignored the irritable cat and continued trying to engage Cate in conversation until she was finished brushing my hair.

Although Jessith elected to stay behind in the bedroom and sleep, Cate led me down the grand staircase, which impressed me even less the second time I saw it. She seemed cautious as she showed me the way to breakfast, though not flighty, and I noticed her glance over her shoulder several times and peer around corners before she turned them. I suspected it was a habit. I gave Cate a smile when she left me in the company of my stepmother and stepsisters, and she smiled back, a little surprised. I watched her as she left on silent feet, reminded of a frightened dog that was used to dodging kicks.

Still thinking about Cate, I sat down and began a quiet, rather unpleasant breakfast with my new family. Apparently, last night's wounds were still fresh. Belladonna and Luciana spoke as little as possible, giving each other cutting looks when Lady Kingsclere's attention was occupied. I wondered what they had fought about, but knew there was no polite way of asking.

Jamison, the steward, bowed himself into the room as I was biting into a piece of sausage. "Lady, your husband, Lord Roland, is here," he announced, tugging at one of his shiny buttons and puffing up his chest with self-importance. He stepped aside, and my father walked in, fresh from his latest journey. He was a stranger even to me in his long black traveling cloak, and his thick shoulders hung limp with weariness. He looked older each time I saw him. The lines cut into his face were deeper.

He stumbled forward and kissed my forehead with cold lips. I lowered my eyes to his fine black boots, the ones with the bright buckles. Somehow he had managed to keep most of the mud off of them even though it was raining, or perhaps he had asked a servant to clean them before he came in. His pride would never have permitted him to ruin his precious new castle with muddy boot prints.

"Welcome home, Father." I felt my lips move, but I was not consciously aware of speaking. The greeting was automatic, like most of our interactions.

"Thank you, Eleanor. I trust that you have settled in comfortably." He went over to Lady Kingsclere before I could answer, kissing her chastely on her small mouth. I hoped that he loved her, but knew he did not. He had not loved my mother either. Perhaps he had liked her, maybe he had even been fond of her, but his real love had always been money. My mother had been rich when my father married her, although he had made her richer. But now, his new wife had given him something even better—a title to go with his wealth. Having 'Lord' added to his name, I suspected, was a large part of the reason he had married again.

My mother had loved him, though. She had not complained about the long trips he made. She had ignored his cold, dispassionate personality. She had put aside his obsession with money. I did not know if my father stayed faithful during their marriage, but I suspected he had. He was far too concerned about his money to pay attention to such trivial things as women. My mother had admired him because he was a hard-working gentleman, a refreshing change from her other suitors. Boys that were given everything they asked for did not interest her. Perhaps she married my father expecting him to change, and was too in love with the dream she had of him to let go as the years passed.

I could tell that Lady Kingsclere was still in love with Lord Alastair, her first husband. For her, this second marriage was bittersweet. My father reminded her of the love she had lost. That comforted her, but then she would remember they were not the same person, and the ache would return doubled. After she pulled away from the kiss, her face was a tapestry of smiles, worry lines, and unshed tears. I noticed Belladonna's gaze was fixed on Lady Kingsclere's face, too, and I knew she understood.

I looked away from Belladonna when I realized that my father was addressing me again. "...only staying for two days, I'm afraid. I have to travel to Ronin and meet with another dealer."

"Two days? I thought you wanted to see more of Baxstresse before you left?" I hoped this would gain me an extra day, at least. If anything could keep my father behind, it was his beautiful new house. He shook his head, and I stared at my plate, dejected. Though I was used to this, a small part of me was always sad when my father left. I wished he would realize how much I loved him and wanted him to be near me, despite his faults.

"I have no choice. Amendyr's closing its borders has upset all of Seria's trade. I have to sort out another mess in Ronin." Amendyr had caused quite a stir when their queen had halted all trade for the first time in centuries. Diplomats had been traveling back and forth between the two countries for months, but even the aristocracy had no idea what was happening. Information had a difficult time crossing the Rengast at our western border.

"But I promise to make it up to all of you," my father said with false cheerfulness. He gave Lady Kingsclere, her daughters, and me a friendly smile. I was familiar with this game. He often used presents to buy our affections and soothe his own guilt. I wished I had the strength to tell him that his company would have been a far better gift. "I will bring back a beautiful present for each of you, if you tell me what you would like. What about you, Luciana?"

Luciana lifted one shoulder becomingly so that the sunlight bounced off of her light brown hair. She was uncomfortably pretty, even in her high-necked morning dress. I crossed my legs underneath the table and squeezed them together, hard. Something felt unnatural about her smile. It made my stomach twitch. "Father, I would like a new evening dress. In red, if you can find a suitable match."

My face tightened as I heard her say 'father.' No one else seemed to notice what she had called him. They were distracted by the rest of her request.

"Red, Luciana?" Lady Kingsclere raised her eyebrows in disapproval.

"Perhaps something in pink," Belladonna suggested, almost mockingly. Luciana did not even look at her, but I sensed the scowl that lurked behind her smile. "Yes, I think you would look adorable in pink."

"I would really prefer red," Luciana said, softly but firmly. Something dangerous lurked just behind her eyes.

"If I can find something appropriate," my father said, ending the discussion. Merchants, I had learned, were very good at turning conversations away from dangerous subjects. "What would you like, Belladonna?"

Though just as charming as her sister, Belladonna did not try to win my father's affection with smiles. I was strangely pleased. "A necklace, I think. Linked gold, with a pendant, perhaps. Something that can be worn with many different kinds of gowns. I would be very thankful."

Luciana glared so sharply at her that even Lady Kingsclere noticed. I did not understand why their faces were so drawn as they looked at Belladonna, but I knew there was something between them. Belladonna's request had a deeper meaning than I realized.

"That should be easy enough to arrange," my father said, still oblivious. "And you, Ellie? What about you? Would you like a dress or a necklace, too?"

I forced a smile. He should have known me better than that. "If you can manage, I would like you to bring me a hazel sapling." Everyone at the table looked at me, obviously confused. But if my father had thought about it, he would have understood. Sandleford, and its trees and flowers, had always been a part of my life—of my mother's life. Since I was to stay at Baxstresse against my will, I might as well plant at least one tree to help me remember. I had brought some of Sandleford's white roses to plant this spring as well. I worried, though, that planting a tree would do to me what marrying again had done to Lady Kingsclere. It would soothe me for a while, but then the ache would grow.

"I suppose that I can find you one," my father said, "but such an odd request." One last piece of sausage was left alone on the edge of my plate. I frowned at it.

Luciana's eyes settled on me for the first time, and I felt my blood beating in my ears. My pulse throbbed in my neck and my heartbeat quickened. She was not just looking at me, she was almost staring through me. Her eyes seemed bright enough to burn my skin away. Something about the look she gave me felt horribly wrong. I buried my hands in my skirts to keep them from shaking.

While Luciana stared at me, Belladonna was watching her. There was hatred in the thin set of her lips and the stiff way she tilted her jaw. Lady Kingsclere and my father were focused on each other, totally unaware of what was going on. How could they not see? The strange sense of unease filled my chest and cut off my breath. Later, I would look into the relationship between Belladonna and Luciana and find out why they seemed to hate each other so much. Until then, I would tread carefully around my two new stepsisters. Perhaps they could be dangerous.

The arrival of the final course broke the spell that hung over the table. The rest of the meal was finished in a silence that seemed uneasy only to me.

***

True to his word, my father brought me a small hazel sapling when he returned home. Luciana received a stunning red dress that she exclaimed over beautifully. Belladonna got her necklace. As she held it for the first time, I saw her white hands tremble. There was obviously a reason she had requested it, but I was not about to ask her what it was. We were not very friendly with each other, although she was not rude to me either.

While no one questioned my own choice out loud, I started getting strange glances from my new family and the servants. I wondered if Lady Kingsclere and her daughters thought I was touched for asking my father to bring me the sapling, but I did not care.

The afternoon that the tree arrived in a clay pot filled with soil, I took it out to a small mound of grass just before the fields started. Fortunately, the rain had stopped for a few hours and the sun showered the soggy fields with pale light. At my request, Cate brought me a shovel and watched from several yards away as I dug a hole for my tree. Despite the offers of help from the field workers, I finished the hole myself. I made sure that my father was taking his afternoon nap while I dug so that he would not stop me. My mother had done most of her own gardening, and I wanted to be just like her. I would remember her every time I came to visit my hazel sapling.

As soon as the tree was planted, I patted the earth back into place around it and studied my present. It was small and weak looking, but I knew it would grow. Hazel trees needed a lot of moisture, but since Baxstresse always seemed to be raining, I was not worried. Afterward, Cate helped me clean myself up and change my clothes so I would be presentable for dinner. My new family had no idea I had planted the tree by myself.

CHAPTER 3

AFTER I PLANTED my hazel sapling, I turned myself to the problem of understanding my stepsisters. To make sure I did not put them on their guard, I only questioned the most discreet informants. At Sandleford, the animals had kept me as well informed as the most talkative servants. I knew that the animals of Baxstresse would never be able to repeat our conversations to anyone else, and I learned a good deal about my new family from them.

Jessith's keen sense of observation made her an excellent choice for questioning, but the tidbits she chose to drop at my feet did not always fit together completely. Even though she pretended not to care about the goings on at Baxstresse, her instinctive feline curiosity made her a natural gossip. If you know how to talk to a cat the right way, they will tell you almost anything, even if they refuse to explain themselves afterwards.

"I am sure you have noticed how false Luciana seems, especially around her mother," I asked her one afternoon as I sat beside my new sapling. The spring planting had not disturbed the grass around my little tree.

Jessith stretched without worrying about dirtying her fine tortoiseshell coat. Her eyes were closed, and she was trying to soak in as much of the weak sunlight as she could before the gray rain came back. "Clever girl, aren't you, to have noticed that?" Jessith drawled.

I ignored her barb, as I was used to cats. "I wonder why Lady Kingsclere has not noticed. She seems so sensible."

"You're underestimating that woman's cunning." Jessith rarely called Luciana by her name, referring to her as 'that woman' instead, and sometimes just 'her.'

"Cunning?" I pressed my hand against the wet bark of my new tree. My palm remembered the familiar texture.

Jessith arched her back, extending her claws and stretching sleepily into a more comfortable position. "Yes, cunning and hungry for power. The Kingscleres seem to have more than their fair share of greed, don't they? Yourself not included, of course," she added at the last second.

"I am not really a Kingsclere," I said, surprised at the hurt in my voice. I had not meant to put it there. "Besides, even though Luciana is obviously a fake and Belladonna is bad tempered, Lady Kingsclere seems remarkably well adjusted."

"When I said greedy, I meant self-indulgent. They take what they want, even when it is bad for them. Watch yourself around Luciana, Ellie. She hates competition."

"Why would she think of me as competition? I would never try to take her mother—"

"Don't be foolish," Jessith interrupted. "Not her mother, her money! She wants as much inheritance as she can get, and that includes your share."

Perhaps that news astonished me more than it should have. I rarely gave my inheritance any thought at all. After my mother died, my father had become the sole owner of everything at Sandleford, with the exception of a few dresses and jewelry that had been passed down to me directly. Aside from that, inheritance and what it meant had hardly entered my mind.

"If Luciana wants Baxstresse, she can have it. I certainly have no claim..."

"But you do," Jessith insisted. "Your father and mother own everything here jointly. As your father's only heir, you are legally entitled to a third of the estate."

"Luciana does not seem to like sharing. I have no desire to live here any longer than I have to. I would expect some of my father's money, of course, but only so I could move away and live somewhere else, somewhere that at least has a garden." My shoulders sank as I stared at my little tree again. Its branches were short and brittle against the colorless sky and its tiny leaves seemed fragile enough to blow off in the lightest breeze. "Do you really think Luciana feels threatened by me?" I asked, softer than before.

"It's obvious. Her sister is, too, unless I miss my guess, but for different reasons. I can smell her when she looks at you." I decided not to ask Jessith what this meant. "You should avoid both of them. Let them battle each other and try not to get involved."

"So that is why they hate each other? All that, just for money?"

"Not just for money. They have made it personal. Both of them are always looking for opportunities to put the other out of favor." I nodded, remembering the night that I had overheard them arguing from outside Lady Kingsclere's study.

"Belladonna seems introverted, but at least she is sincere. Luciana's fake smiles make my blood freeze, but no one else seems to notice them."

Jessith looked up from bathing her side and twitched one ear. "So you haven't figured that part out yet, then?"

"What are you talking about?" I asked, but a passing robin distracted Jessith before she could answer. She flipped onto her paws and her spine settled between her shoulder blades, her hindquarters twitching. I knew she was refusing to answer me on purpose, but I what else could I expect from a cat?

***

My other primary informant was just as reliable as Jessith, and he was certainly much easier to talk to. I met him at the beginning of my third week at Baxstresse, when the weather finally cleared enough for me to go riding. Baxstresse's horses were even more famous than their tortoiseshells, and the thought of riding one of them lifted me out of my steady depression.

On a surprisingly clear day, as early as it was proper, I asked Cate very politely if she would show me to the stables. After she helped me out of my morning dress and into my riding habit, she led me out across a short stretch of field. I noticed that all of the stiffness left her body as soon as we were outside, although she remained quiet. She even gave me a smile as the sun hit the side of her face. I decided to ask her to accompany me to the stables more often.

Cate helped me pick my way over the wet mud and held my weight easily when I stumbled, even though she was hardly taller than me. I heard her breath hitch when she caught my elbow. She shrank back as I steadied myself, her face turning as though she was expecting a blow. "Sorry, Miss Elea —"

"Ellie, please," I said. "And there is no reason to apologize. It was my fault."

Cate blushed, biting nervously at one corner of her mouth. "Very well, Miss Ellie." She was quiet for a moment. "I would apologize for

apologizing, but you probably wouldn't like that, either." I saw her
retreat back into herself, questioning what she had just said.

I laughed. "No, I wouldn't."

Cate brushed her hair back over one shoulder and my eyes lingered
on a set of ugly, purple-yellow stripes puffing out from the pale curve of
her neck. I continued toward the stables at a brisk walk so Cate would
not catch me staring at them. "Ellie, wait," she called after me, holding
her skirts in one hand as she hurried across the uneven ground to catch
up.

"Someone out there?" a voice shouted from inside one of the stalls.

I peered through the door. "Yes. Where are you?"

After a few moments, a familiar man with a thin, tanned face came
out of the stables, pulling his straw hat down over his brow as he walked
into the pale sunlight. His wide smile carved deep lines in his nut-brown
skin. He offered me a short, polite bow.

"Hello again, Matthew," I told him, returning his smile.

"And a good morning to ye." Matthew's thick, rustic accent made my
smile bigger. "Yer here t'see the horses, then?"

"Yes, please."

The happiness on my face must have been obvious, because
Matthew laughed under the brim of his hat. "Right, miss. We got plenty
of those, so we'll be picking you one and you can be on yer way."

I turned to Cate, brushing my hair out of my face so I could see her
clearly. "You are more than welcome to come with me, Cate, but if you
would rather go back to the manor, I am sure that Matthew can watch
me if I stay nearby."

"I have chores to finish, Miss Ellie, but thank you," Cate mumbled.
She gave me a short curtsy and scurried back toward the dark shape of
the manor, her red-gold hair whipping against her shoulders. I watched
her until Matthew cleared his throat and I remembered to turn around. I
had already decided that while I was questioning the animals about the
Kingsclere sisters, I would ask after Cate. Someone was obviously
beating her, and badly, if the bruises on her neck had been any
indication. I was determined to put a stop to it.

"We got here some of the finest horses in Seria," Matthew said
proudly as he led me into the stables. They were well kept. The smell
was hardly as overpowering as some I had been in. "We've raced 'em at
the Palace fer over a hundred years, and win more of'en than not."

A beautiful white mare on my left stuck her gray nose out over the
stall door and nuzzled my shoulder as I passed her. I stroked her face,
petting the velvety tip of her nose as she snuffled around my fingers.
"That's Corynne d'Reixa. She's a fine girl, Cor. Sweetest horse I got, but

fast as a falcon af'er a sparrow. She's won us the Ronin Cup six times, not countin' the race a few weeks ago when she worked up 'er hind leg. She'll be racin' again next spring, mayhap."

"What does it mean in Amendyrri?" I asked. All great racing horses were named in Amendyrri, a smooth, low language with lots of open vowels. Serian was much harsher sounding, and the Amendyrri always complained that there were far too many duplicate words and spelling changes.

"Queen o' the Wind," Matthew said.

Corynne nosed at my wrist, perhaps hoping for a hidden lump of sugar, but I had nothing to offer her. I patted her snout. "Sorry, girl. I don't have anything for you to eat."

"Matthew has some carrots in his pocket," Corynne said. "You could ask him."

"Are you supposed to have them?"

Corynne tossed her head, but like most animals, she was not surprised that I could understand her. They always seemed to know that I was different as soon as they saw me. The Ariada in me could not be hidden from them.

"No," she admitted. I got the feeling that Corynne was not a very good liar.

"Well then, you will have to ask Matthew later." Corynne huffed, but continued being friendly while I patted her until I looked over at the next horse. "Who is this handsome one?" He was thick chested and tall, obviously not a racing horse.

"That's Sir Thom. He's my own horse, helps me with my work." Sir Thom snorted when I reached out to touch him, not as trusting of strangers as Corynne, but he allowed me to pat him anyway. Matthew raised his eyebrows. "Well, then, look a'that! Thom don't take to just anyone."

"He will take to me. Most animals do."

"Corynne likes carrots too much," Sir Thom said. "She don't understand she has to work fer 'em."

I laughed and moved on to the next horse. The hide over his shoulders rippled as he sniffed at my hand, but he moved in to my caress without fear. "That's Brahmsian Synng," Matthew said. "He's Corynne's younger brother. We'll prob'ly race him next spring. Corynne's still got one more year left in her if her injury don't flare up again, but we're hopin' Brahms'll take the Cup a fair number of times when she's done."

Brahms's ears twitched at the compliment, and then he refocused his attention on me. "I'm just as fast as Cor is. I could beat her." His nostrils flared. Corynne tossed her mane a few stalls away, indulgent of her sibling's comment. "Do you want to ride me?"

I nodded my head and turned to Matthew. "He seems like a fine horse. May I ride him?"

"A'course, miss. I've heard tell yer a fair rider. Spring weather's been nasty, an' he hasn't been getting out as much as he likes. Don't push him too hard, though. We got to have him in good condition when we train him fer this fall."

Matthew saddled Brahms for me and helped me up onto his strong back. The feeling of a powerful horse between my legs again made me smile wider than I had in weeks. Brahms shifted slightly, his hooves scraping the ground, obviously eager to be off. With a light slap on his rump, Matthew sent him running as I gripped the reins.

Although I had been riding since I was a little girl, I had never been on a galloping racehorse until I met Brahms. The difference between him and the Sandleford horses was obvious as soon as he started off across the fields. He rolled over the ground like a strong wind, and it was easy to see how his sister had been named if she was anything like him. "What does your name mean?" I panted.

"Meadow Song," he huffed as he pounded across the dirt.

I rode Brahms until lunch. When I dismounted, I had made a loyal new friend.

CHAPTER 4

BLUE PATCHES OF shadow tucked themselves in the wet, muddy grass
as I visited my tree, unwilling to surrender to the morning light.
Baxstresse stood above everything else, watching the small black shapes
that scuttled in its wide fields, but not interfering. Occasionally a farmer
would gaze up at the turrets and rub at his damp brow, tired even at the
beginning of the day.

Birds fluttered over the uneven dirt, tugging at worms and pulling
seeds free with their beaks. The air was wet and heavy as it settled into
the gutted field, drying and thinning as the sun crawled over the horizon.
Spring at Baxstresse was melancholy. Damp grays and browns
dominated the landscape. No trees, no mountains, flat as a rough-
grained board.

I was picturing the flowers that my sapling would wear in winter
when Belladonna came to me. I had been at Baxstresse for a little over a
month now. Though my sapling had grown taller, its leaves were still
hard green buds dangling on their arched stalks. I rested one hand
against the whitish-red bark and waited as she came awkwardly over
the mud clods. It was one of the rare moments when she did not move
gracefully, like a tall cat.

A single branch from the sapling scratched my cheek, pointing
straight at my stepsister like a dousing rod. I pushed it away, but it
sprang back into position. A sharp wind blew through my skirts and bent
the sapling forward. It almost looked as though it was bowing to
Belladonna in greeting, welcoming her.

"You never told me why you asked for a hazel sapling," she said as she studied my tree. It was one of the only times I had heard her speak plainly, perhaps even kindly, to me. Generally, we gave each other meaningless polite comments when other people were around.

"My mother," I answered. Belladonna smiled as though she understood. Perhaps, I thought, she did understand about mothers. "She loved gardens and trees."

The fresh wind returned, tossing Belladonna's dark curls. "Your mother was lucky, then."

"She died young." I was no longer bitter about it. My tears had scoured most of that away months ago. Visiting the hazel tree to remember her was slowly helping me heal.

"She was lucky even for that, though. Lucky that she had something to love. My mother doesn't love anything anymore. You can see the kind of emptiness that leaves."

I frowned. "Doesn't she love you?"

Belladonna's eyebrows lifted. They were bold and dark, but thin and highly expressive. "She thinks she does, but I have too much of my father in me, and Luciana has too much trickery in her."

I lifted my chin against the wind from the north, gazing curiously at Belladonna's china face. She looked like a beautiful antique doll, the kind you never allow children to play with, and she seemed just as forbidden. She was far taller than I was, and I could sense that she was well muscled through the fabric of her dress. The perfection was almost offsetting. My freckles burned, even in the spring cold.

"And what do you love, Ellie?" Belladonna asked, studying my face as carefully as I had studied hers. A few strands of straw hair blew between my lips, and I pulled them away.

"Everything I left behind at Sandleford. My mother, the animals, old Father Matthias, my friends. And you? Do you love something?"

Belladonna gave a thoughtful pause, staring directly at me. I could not read her eyes. "Yes, I think I do."

"You think?" The wind died suddenly, and my arms tingled as the blood blossomed under the surface of my skin again. There was a slight flush along Belladonna's collarbone, the only imperfection on her clear skin. It crept up one side of her neck, and I could not force my eyes away. I could even see her pulse beating next to the cord of her throat, above the hollow where her neck met her shoulder.

"I think," she repeated. She gave me a fluid smile, her eyelashes brushing her cheeks as she blinked. She turned away, pulling her blue shawl tighter about her shoulders against the biting air. Immediately, the breeze returned, though not as strong as before, as if it knew it was supposed to start up again.

Belladonna took two steps back toward the manor. "You never told me why you came," I said. She turned and looked back over her shoulder, her lips parted.

"I didn't, did I?" Her face told me she was not going to.

Afterward, when I thought about it, the conversation seemed so surreal that I wondered if I had dreamt it.

***

Belladonna usually spent most of her evenings reading in the library, but she began to visit in the early afternoon after our strange conversation. Since that was the time I usually did my own reading, we saw each other more often. Before, my only companion had been Trugel, an old tortoiseshell cat who enjoyed napping by the fireplace. Belladonna and I did not speak much at first, but she never picked a chair too far from mine. I told myself that both of us wanted to be near the fire, but secretly, I wondered.

I learned a great deal about my stepsister by catching glimpses of the titles she read. She enjoyed poetry the most. I often found her with her nose buried in dusty collections older than her great-grandparents. Her tastes were varied, however, and I watched her devour *A History of Seria*, *The Breeding and Training of Racehorses*, and even *Serian Fairy-Stories*. She also was particularly fond of the scandalous romantic poet, Erato.

After a few days of reading silently together, Belladonna and I started sharing small, absentminded exchanges. "Do you really think manticores existed?" she asked one afternoon as she perused *A Bestiary of Magickal and Non-Magickal Beings*.

I looked up from my own book. "I have no idea. The last reported sighting was supposedly hundreds of years ago, wasn't it?"

"Archaeologists have no solid proof, though," Belladonna muttered, flipping her page. She looked up again to ask me something about unicorn tears later, and we had another conversation about astronomy the next day. My stepsister's interests seemed to be completely unrelated. She was fascinated by everything and anything, and she read any book she could get her hands on.

Perhaps our strangest conversation occurred when I caught her curled up with *Queen Toreau's Lover*. I put down my own book of poetry, one that Belladonna had recommended, and stared at the title, quite surprised. I probably should have expected it. Belladonna did, after all, read anything that had words on it, even if it was not particularly appropriate literature for a lady. I wondered vaguely where she had gotten it.

Belladonna looked up, blinking the glassiness from her eyes as they focused on me. I felt a hot blush creep up one side of my neck and flower across my cheeks. I ducked my head to continue reading my poetry. Belladonna laughed. "I knew it," she said, still grinning. My blush was so fierce that it was almost a deep scarlet.

"Knew what?" I asked defensively.

"That you were innocent."

I knew that my burning face had already confirmed her guess. But I was supposed to be, I told myself much later as I paced in my room. I was marrying age, and no intelligent girl would risk her chances of finding a good match for one night. Marriage and the physical aspects of love had never interested me anyway. I did not gush about them like other girls my age. I was naïve and sheltered, but I knew it, and I did not care.

Belladonna was obviously much worldlier than I was, but there was no way for me to know the extent of her experiences. Her teasing might have even been hypocritical. I did notice that she watched my face more after that day. "Your face colors prettily when you are embarrassed," was all she said when I asked her why.

***

While I was learning as much as I could about Belladonna, I was also making inquiries about Cate. The horrible marks that I had seen on her arms and throat made me feel ill. Sometimes they called themselves up again in my mind. The memory of what I had seen when she moved her hair off her neck made my stomach clench with disgust and fear. I was determined to find out what was happening to her.

I thought hard about why someone might want to hurt Cate, but I could not come up with any reasons. She was always polite, quiet, and hardworking, and so I assumed that the marks had nothing to do with an unsatisfactory performance. The culprit was just mean spirited, and had singled out Cate because she was too shy to defend herself. At first I suspected Jamison, the proud steward, but he did not seem like a very physical person. He was all pomp and pride. Getting his hands dirty just to beat a maid did not seem to fit his personality.

There were male servants, of course, but none of them seemed to have the authority or the desire to give Cate the awful bruises I had seen. Even the groomsmen, as lecherous as gossip made some of them out to be, did not seem to treat her any differently than the other women. Finally, I questioned Mam as cautiously as I could. I trusted her, but you never knew who might be listening.

"Mam, do you know if Cate has a lover?" I asked, trying to sound spontaneous. She would suspect me if I acted too casual.

Mam narrowed her eyes suspiciously at me. "Why?"

I was surprised that I had made her suspicious so quickly. I tried to recover as fast as I could. "She is so pretty, but I have never seen her with anyone." I adopted a look of genuine concern, although not for the reasons she thought. "She seems so shy. I thought maybe a sweetheart would cheer her up." Or a jealous one would beat her, I thought.

Mam relaxed visibly. "Aye, Cate's a quiet one at that." As always, her hands were busy. This time she was peeling potatoes and piling the skins beside her. I had taken to visiting Mam in the kitchen when I could, even if it was not really proper behavior. My mother had done the same thing, even though my father had tried to stop her.

"She always looks miserable. I just wish I could do something to make her happier."

"I think you already have. Walking with you to the stables gets a smile out of her if little else does."

"But she never rides with me," I said. "I have asked her several times."

"She's afeared of riding. Had an uncle what died falling off a horse and cracking his head. She likes to look at them, though, and Matthew's pleasant enough."

I felt embarrassed for asking Cate to ride with me after I heard that. "Oh, how horrible. I never should have asked her. I honestly had no idea. She should have told me."

"And how many words has she said to you since you came?" Mam teased, picking up another potato and cutting away at its skin. "Enough to be telling you her entire life's story?"

"Hardly enough to fit in a few lines of print. I'll stop asking her to ride with me, but she may still walk with me if it cheers her up. So," I continued, trying to turn the conversation back to my original topic, "no one has an interest in her?"

Mam's face tightened, but I thought little of it. She often gave me strange, worried glances. "None I can think of."

I knew that talking about Cate would be useless for a little while.

***

Later that evening, I directed my inquiries to Sarah, another servant who had helped me dress on a few occasions. She was of an age with Cate and me, and I knew they spent time together in the evenings.

"Not that I've heard, miss," Sarah said, looking nervously to her left and tucking a lock of brown hair over her ear. She was quite pretty, with a pleasant smile. "But maybe you should ask her."

I looked at her curiously. "Ask Cate? She hardly says a word to me. Is she always like that?"

"Yes." Sarah leaned forward, eager for gossip. "It drives me batty, really, but she's, begging your pardon, Miss, I really shouldn't be chatting with a lady of the house. Please, forget I said anything." It took me several minutes to reassure Sarah that she had not acted inappropriately. I decided to question her further on another occasion.

Jessith and Brahms were not helpful either. Brahms tried to be, but he was not familiar with Cate. He only knew her because she accompanied me to the stables. The other cats that lived in the house were no help at all. There were six in all, including Jessith, and most of them, while polite in their own, distant way, redirected me to her. Apparently, she had decided I was her human. They did not want to interfere.

I was not hopeful when I tried to question Trugel, but she was the oldest cat in residence at Baxstresse and, with luck, might know something useful. When I tried to wake her up, she looked at me with glazed, confused eyes, as if she did not know who I was. Slowly, she raised her head from her favorite rug, purring scratchily as I rubbed her chin. She yawned, and I noticed that most of her teeth were missing. I felt sorry for her and decided to leave her alone.

Rucifee, a fat ginger male that spent most of his time in Lady Kingsclere's room, was slightly more alert. When he finally ventured out for his dinner, leisurely descending the stairs, I walked beside him. "Good evening, Rucifee," I said, trying to be polite.

"They should bring my dinner to the second floor," Rucifee complained, not bothering to say hello. "Really, did they have to add so many stairs?" I agreed with him, but I did not say so. I would have offered to carry him, but cats usually spurned offers of help unless it was their idea.

"Rucifee, do you know Cate?"

"Of course I know Cate. I have been going up and down these stairs for ten years, haven't I? Pick me up and carry me."

Now that he had demanded my assistance, I scooped him up and carried him the rest of the way down the staircase. "Do you know if Cate has a lover?" I persisted, bending to put Rucifee down.

"No, don't put me down! You might as well carry me the rest of the way to the kitchen. And how should I know if she has a lover or not?"

"I thought you had been here for ten years and knew everything," I said, a little annoyed.

"Go ask Jessith. I can't be bothered about servants while I'm still waiting for my dinner." Only slightly irritated, I took Rucifee the rest of the way to the kitchen and went in search of Jessith.

I found her chasing a beam of sunlight in one of the upstairs rooms. She was willing to talk to me, but her answers were too cryptic to be of much practical use. "It takes a wicked person to leave wicked bruises, doesn't it?" she purred when I asked if Cate had a lover among the groomsmen or servants.

"How did you know what I was really trying to find out? Was I too obvious?"

"No. Everyone else is just stupid." Jessith yawned, her eyes following a fly as it wove about drunkenly outside my bedroom window.

"Mam put her guard up when I asked about Cate. Something feels wrong about this."

"I suggest that you broaden your search and keep your eyes open."

"I have been watching for anything suspicious," I said, a little defensively.

"Humans can never watch closely enough. They miss more than they think."

I decided that flattery might be a more effective tactic to find the answers I needed. "Rucifee had no idea what was going on. He told me to ask you, since you notice everything that happens in Baxstresse."

"Don't try and flatter me, silly girl. Rucifee hates me almost as much as I hate him. His Highness would rather die than give me a compliment."

I tried to pull more information out of her, but Jessith was content to sit on my lap and bask in adoration as I scratched her chin and fluffed the fur of her white chest. Soon she was asleep, and I was no closer to finding answers than when I had started.

CHAPTER 5

ONE NIGHT, BELLADONNA joined me as I watched the sky beneath my young tree. "The stars are higher here," I whispered as she spread her skirts next to me and rested her head on the dark grass. "And the ones on the horizon are new to me."

"You are not in the southwest anymore. That group of them just touching the land is Feradith, the dragon." I squinted my eyes, trying to make out the shape of a wing or tail. Belladonna lifted her hand and drew an outline so I could see the dragon's head and three horns. "There is a story about her from Amendyr."

"Please." I turned my head, resting my cheek on my hair. "Tell me."

"Once, a long time ago, there was a horrible drought in Amendyr. Nothing would grow and no one could figure out why. Finally, the king's seer discovered that the drought was being caused by a dragon."

"Is it true that magic is feared less in Amendyr?" I had heard as much, but I was sure that the well-read Belladonna would be able to answer more of my questions about the place. Amendyr had always interested me.

"Yes. In Amendyr, magic is respected. Ariada is an honored title, not a term of hate." I shuddered at the word, even though it was not being used hurtfully. I had thought it to myself, perhaps to take the sting out of it, but hearing it on another person's lips instinctively made me uncomfortable. "Their capital, Kalmarin, is more magical than Ronin twice over. At least, it was..." Belladonna's smile disappeared, and her eyelids fluttered against a small breeze. "Now that Amendyr has stopped trading news and goods with Seria, no one really knows what is happening across the Rengast."

We lost ourselves in thought for a moment, remembering frightened whispers and concerned faces leaning across tables. For over a year, the dark rumors about what was happening in Amendyr had been trickling in to Seria. No one knew how many were true.

After a short silence, Belladonna continued her story. "The dragons usually kept themselves apart from men in those days, before all of them disappeared." Dragons, like manticores, had not been seen in centuries, but there was no doubt they had once existed. There were very detailed writings on them, and they had played a major role in Amendyrri and Serian history.

"This particular dragon, Feradith, had a grievance. The King's mages had killed her hatchling. Feradith did not know how it had died, she just felt its magic go out." Belladonna turned away from me and looked at the stars that made up Feradith's body.

"Why did the King's sorcerers kill the hatchling?"

"To drain its magic. When they tried, some of the mages died. There was too much power for all of them to hold."

I was amazed. I had read of draining magic from people in historical accounts, but never from something as powerful and dangerous as a dragon. Dragons did not just control the bright energy of magic like humans did. They were made of it. Using the energy made us weak, and each of us had our own special ways of channeling it, but a dragon's very essence was said to be magical. Without it, they would not exist at all. "Why would they need that much power?"

"I have no idea. Maybe they were greedy."

We were quiet for a few minutes, listening to the night sounds around us. "Are you going to tell me the rest of the story?" I asked after a moment.

"The king's son, Alharin, heard about what the mages had done. He went to offer his life to the dragon. Alharin told Feradith what had happened to her hatchling, and in gratitude, she refused to take his life as forfeit and lifted the drought."

"So Feradith just stopped the drought?"

"Not quite," Belladonna said. "Feradith did not forgive, she just redirected her rage. Instead of punishing the entire kingdom, she ate the mages. She took little joy in punishing innocents. At least she was fair."

Once the story was over, Belladonna and I stayed stretched out on the dry grass, content with silence. My next memory was of waking up, startled, because I could not recall falling asleep. Belladonna was gone.

***

As Belle and I spent more time together, I began to notice strange things about her sister. Luciana seemed to have some sort of hold over large groups that I could not understand. Only Belladonna, the servants, and I were unaffected. Occasionally, a noble would come to visit, perhaps to court her, perhaps to do business with Lady Kingsclere or my father. Whenever Baxstresse had guests, all of them were enthralled.

Sometimes Luciana wore her red dress at dinner. She smiled and laughed, and her skin glowed. Her eyes held a strange light I could not understand. This same light became a dazzling beacon whenever Lady Kingsclere or my father paid attention to her. Luciana's mother adored her, showering her with affection and praise that contrasted completely with her personality. Her affection toward Belladonna was more serious, although I could tell it was still strong.

Once, while I was exploring one of the many unlearned hallways at Baxstresse, I found Luciana staring out of a window. The room was open and airy, mostly decorative, and it was not used often. I stood just outside of the door, looking in at her from a distance so she would not notice me watching. She turned a little, and I saw a flash of metal in her hand as the sunlight caught it. She stared down at her palm, rich brown hair breaking across her shoulders as her chin dipped to kiss her chest. She whispered something, but I could only see her lips move.

I leaned forward, trying to snatch a look at the thing she held in her hand. I just managed to make out a few links of gold before she turned back fully to the window, watching the darkening sky. She was holding some kind of chain. Silently, I backed away from the door and hurried down the hall, hoping Luciana would stay in the room until I turned a corner. Once I was on the main floor, I relaxed. Catching Luciana in an unguarded moment had been strange. Her light was gone, and the familiar unease that I normally felt around her had not been present. There was only the tightness of my stomach as I watched, hoping I would not be caught.

***

I was settled peacefully in a library armchair with Jessith on my knees when I heard the scream. It was a grating, broken sound, the sound of a woman's sanity snapping. My entire body jerked upright, and my nails dug into the loose skin on the back of Jessith's neck. She leapt off of my lap, hissing and arching her back. "That hurt," she yowled, glaring at me. "If you had been anyone else, I would have bitten you."

"Sorry...it was an accident, Jess," I mumbled, raising my chin to listen. All I could hear was the sound of my own loud breathing. Once I realized that no other screams were coming from downstairs, I looked back down at the unsettled cat. "Did you hear that? Did I imagine it?"

"Of course I heard it. Stop asking stupid questions and get up to see what's going on."

I ignored Jessith's bad mood and scooped her into my arms, tucking her against my chest as I dodged between bookshelves, trying to remember which direction the scream had come from. In my hurry, I nearly stumbled over poor old Trugel, who was sleeping in her usual spot by the fireplace. She hardly stirred, only opening her eyes long enough to glare after me as I ran from the room.

Jessith directed me, putting aside her anger in order to satisfy her curiosity. "Quick, left here. There's a door on this side. No! That's your right, you silly girl. I said left! Here, down this hall..."

With Jessith to guide me, I stumbled my way to the second floor's main hallway, which was lined with stained glass windows. "It came from the entrance hall," Jessith said, the usual dry, bored sarcasm gone from her voice. I couldn't remember her being this interested in anything since I had arrived at Baxstresse. Still clutching Jessith, I catapulted down the large stone steps three at a time in a very unladylike way, rushing to join the crowd that was gathering in the great entrance hall.

One of my father's men was standing in the center of the hall, surrounded by curious onlookers. Cate and Sarah were among them, helping to support his weight. His fine coat and breeches were torn and soaked through with rain. There was blood streaked across his forehead. Lady Kingsclere lay crumpled at his feet, her fine skirts spreading about her limp body. The pallor of her face was a sickly yellow-green that glowed eerily under the light from the chandelier.

Belladonna knelt beside my stepmother, clasping her hand and whispering something in her ear. I noticed that her entire body was trembling. Lady Kingsclere did not respond. She remained completely still, all of the spirit drained from her body. Luciana imitated her sister and bent down at her other side. Someone rested a steadying hand on my shoulder and I turned to see Mam staring down at me. "Come away, child," she said, gently urging me back up the stairs. "You shouldn't be about now."

"But—"

"Hush," Mam said firmly.

"Put me down if you are going," Jessith said, wriggling to free herself from my arms. "I want to stay." I dropped Jessith to the floor and allowed

Mam to pull me back up the stairs by the wrist, tripping along behind her like a limp rag doll. Only my shock prevented me from protesting. The sight of Lady Kingsclere and her daughters kneeling on the floor lingered in my mind as Mam dragged me past the library and Belladonna's room. We stopped at my room, and Mam sat me down on the bed.

"How long were you down there, Miss Ellie?" Mam asked, the sternness gone from her voice.

"Only a few moments." I reached out to stroke Jessith, only remembering that she was still downstairs when my hand touched the bed sheets. I wished she had come back upstairs with me. Something awful had happened, and I wanted her nearby. "Was that one of my father's men downstairs? What happened to Lady Kingsclere? Should someone—"

"Hush," Mam insisted. "Jamison and her daughters will be seeing to her."

"Will she be all right?"

The lines in Mam's tired face seemed to grow deeper. She raised her eyes to the ceiling. "Lord only knows, I'm hoping so..." I shifted uncomfortably on the quilts, thinking about the rumors I had heard. People still gossiped about how Lady Kingsclere had been mad for five years after the death of her first husband...the death of her husband...my father...the man bleeding downstairs. The thoughts collided in my head.

"Mam, where is my father?"

I read the answer in Mam's silence. She put her hand on my arm, but I shook it off. After my mother died, people were always touching me, whispering to me, trying to make me feel better. I did not want anyone's pity, even Mam's.

"Why should I care if he's dead?" I said bitterly, pressing my lips together. "I knew he would die one of these days, wandering off after his horrid treasures...he didn't care about the thieves on the road, he didn't care that he was leaving us behind. His own greed killed him. It was his fault."

I looked up at Mam again, anticipating an expression of pity, shock, or anger on her face. Instead, fear was written there. But what did Mam have to be afraid of? "Miss Ellie..."

"How did he die? Tell me."

"Ellie..."

"Tell me."

"Servants know everything that goes on in a house like this. The buyer in Ronin, he didn't want records or witnesses, I was hearing your father say the other day. Had the stagecoach set upon and lit up in flames. That man downstairs only just got away with his life." Mam glanced toward the door once, checking to make sure it was closed, and leaned in, holding both of my shoulders. "But he—"

"But he wanted the money. He knew there might be danger, but he could never resist the money." My eyes stung and I threw my arms into the air, pointing around the room. "He has all this, and he went anyway. He has a title, a manor, a wife, daughters...Why did he go? He was one of the wealthiest men in the kingdom, but he always wanted more!" I almost dissolved into tears then, but I held them back with the last of my strength. Only my bitter pride dammed them up.

"If you're going to cry for your father, do it now. You won't be having much time to grieve, if I'm right about this household."

"I will not cry," I said, still feeling hurt and rebellious.

"Then don't cry, but you'll be dropping that tone before anyone else hears it if you want to avoid trouble." Something in her voice caught at me, but I brushed the feelings of fear and apprehension aside.

"I would like to be alone, please," I said, carefully removing the quaver from my voice.

Mam picked her heavy body up and walked toward the door, turning back to look at me over her shoulder. "If anything else happens, come down to the kitchen and find me. I'll be taking care of you."

I did not answer, and Mam slipped out of the room, holding the door open long enough to let Jessith in. The cat leapt onto the bed, making soft paw dents in the quilt as she padded over to me. I fell back onto the bed and Jessith curled up on my chest, purring loudly as I scratched her ears. She did not say anything. Cats know that a warm body is more comforting than a thousand condolences.

I fell asleep to the sound of Jessith's light, steady breathing, my hand still resting on her head.

CHAPTER 6

THE FIRST THING I knew the next morning was cold. Someone I could not see had ripped open my warm cocoon of covers, and I threw my arms around myself, squinting up through the dark. The person above me dragged me from the mattress, and my feet burned as they slapped against cold stone.

I tried to scream, but fingers covered my mouth. They did not pull away when I bit down, but I could hear my attacker spit a muffled curse. "Let her scream," said a voice I recognized from several feet away. "No one will interfere with you."

"No one would dare." Luciana removed her hand and I gasped for air, choked up with fear. "I should have you beaten for this," she whispered, her perfect lips pulling back in a feral grin as she held up her red hand. I had not broken skin, but there were purple indents in her fingers.

"You would like that too much," said Belladonna, the other voice from farther away. "Will you let yourself be controlled so easily?" I did not understand what Belladonna meant then, but it became clear later why Luciana tossed me to the floor, bruising my knees and skinning my elbows.

The thought that I needed to do something crossed my mind more than once, but Luciana's actions had struck me dumb. I had never suffered physical abuse before, and I had no idea what to do. It was not that I was cowardly or foolish, even back then, but shock and inexperience deadened my tongue. I would learn how to protect myself later, after many painful lessons.

"Your father is dead and our mother is—"

"Not well," Belladonna sliced in.

Luciana tossed her a piercing glare and turned back to me. There was an unholy flush across her pale cheeks. My heart pounded against my ribs. "And now, our problem becomes how to rid ourselves of you."

That was too much for me to bear, bewildered as I was. "What?"

"Perhaps I should toss you out the window," Luciana purred, caressing the hand I had bitten. "It would be so easy to make it look like a suicide. Poor Eleanor of Sandleford, she threw herself out of her window when she heard her father had been murdered. That would cause quite a stir. Picture their faces when they find your broken body on the ground, with your pretty neck snapped." She reached out and trailed her fingers along the column of my throat, and I jerked away.

Belladonna rolled her eyes, and when she spoke, her voice dripped with disgust. "You're so predictable, Luci. No imagination at all. You can do better than that, surely."

I turned to my younger stepsister, the woman I had begun to trust, and grasped at my last hope of salvation. "But...you hate each other...you..."

Belladonna did not respond. Her handsome face remained still as stone. Even though she had betrayed me, I could not forget how striking her figure was, how commanding she appeared.

"Belle and I have formed a temporary alliance," Luciana explained. "We will go right back to fighting over our inheritance as soon as you are out of the way."

"You...you seriously think you will get away with throwing me out a window? You must be touched." But I knew they probably could. Even if any of the servants suspected that my death had not been a suicide, they would not be in a position to help me. A servant's word against a noble's was worth less than nothing and Lady Kingsclere was obviously too out of her wits to save me. My stepsisters had complete control over Baxstresse, and over me.

Belladonna shook her head at Luciana's heated face. "Disgustingly unoriginal. There are better ways of putting the princess in her place. Changing her identity, perhaps."

Luciana's eyes fired at that suggestion. She did not need much prompting from her sister to latch on to the idea. "That has possibilities. Stripping her of her new title would be a useful lesson in humility. What a pity, after her father worked so hard to get it for her."

I never wanted a title, I thought and tried to say, but the words jarred themselves against my teeth and did not come out. My father was one that had clung to the idea of nobility. Sandleford had not been enough for him. His longing for power had gotten me into this horrid mess.

"No better than a common slut, really," Luciana continued, "grasping at things you have no right to."

"Your mother is the one who married into our family in the first place," I snapped.

Luciana could not hold in her anger. She slapped me across the cheek and sent me reeling. My legs trembled as I touched my face, and something warm and wet ran down my neck. Her nails had broken one side of my mouth and the skin of my cheek. Bright colors swam around my head. I stumbled back against the bed.

"Luciana." Belladonna's voice cracked sharply, refocusing Luciana's attention. Her face quickly relaxed into her usual expression of superiority and disgust. "I was right. You're too weak to let her go." My breath caught at the thought of freedom, but Belladonna's eyes told me that freedom was not what she had in mind. "You want to hurt her so much...tear her...I can see it. Your body is trembling." Luciana flinched. "Oh, you do want her badly...Is torture and sex all you ever think about? You never could resist the pretty ones. Pathetic."

"You're calling me pathetic?" Luciana snarled. "You could never throw her out that window, even if you wanted to."

"And you could never keep yourself from using her and breaking her, like the rest of your toys."

"Couldn't I?"

Belladonna narrowed her eyes. "No, you couldn't."

The argument was quickly becoming too confusing for me to follow, but I could sense that some kind of bargain was about to be struck. I knew that tone of voice all too well from my father.

"I will wager the necklace on it."

For the second time, Belladonna's carefully painted expression cracked. "I will find something to match you with. We have a bet. You will never be able to keep from indulging."

"We can put her in the servant's quarters to keep her close," Luciana said. "Get someone to spread the news that Eleanor of Sandleford has taken ill upon hearing the news of her father's death and can see no one." That part of the conversation, at least, I understood. What I had no way of knowing was how much hurt their bet would cause. At the time, I was grateful they had decided not to throw me out of the window, but later, I almost took my thanks back.

***

I stumbled down to the kitchen in a silent stupor, my mind completely detached from my body. My legs moved, but I was not the one doing the walking. That was some other Eleanor, a little blonde idiot that had been unable to defend herself from her own stepsisters. It could not be Ellie, she would never let anyone strike her, not even Luciana.

I worked some moisture into my dry lips, tasting blood on my tongue. I prodded at the broken side of my mouth. Sticky red warmth coated my fingertips as my mind slammed back into my body. I went from dazed to hysterical in a matter of seconds. The sting reminded me that I had let Luciana slap me. I was ashamed.

Somehow, I found myself in the kitchen. Perhaps my shattered self had remembered Mam's offer of protection, even though I had been out of my head. Steaming heat rose around me and colored my cheeks as I stood there, bare footed and brokenhearted. Mam turned around after taking a hot loaf of bread from the oven and saw me. Her eyes glinted like dark wet stones as she looked at me. The lines etched into her face seemed deeper, stretched and cut with worry. My gut lurched and I slumped forwards, falling into her arms.

"They want me to be a servant." The words spilled through my lips in a stream. "How can she make me? She wanted to kill me...She wanted to kill me! She could have...she tried to throw me out the window."

Mam pressed two fingertips to my lips, covering my soft hands with her rough ones. "Hush, child," she urged, but I was angry at her calmness. She should have been shocked, horrified at what Luciana had done to me. It did not matter that I had not explained my story yet. Mam was supposed to take care of me.

"She wanted to throw me out the window!" I screamed again, stamping my bare foot on the floor with a painful slap. What a sight I must have looked, in my half-torn nightgown with a bloody lip and a bruised cheek. "Why didn't you stop her? Why didn't you—"

"Tell me exactly what happened," Mam ordered, and I obeyed. I told her in breaking sobs, my voice catching as I explained how Luciana had hit me and threatened my life. By the end of my story, fresh tears had burned trails on my cheeks. "Dry your face now, Ellie. You have friends here, mayhap more than you know."

I gave her a blank look. Mam touched my cheek, brushing away a clinging tear. "You're kind and polite when you aren't out of your head, even to the servants. For that, we'll be helping you."

"Can she really turn me into a servant?"

"Until we find a way to help you, aye. Luciana's a bad enemy for anyone to be having. A servant couldn't speak against her. But you're safe for now."

"Safe?" I said, the pitch of my voice rising. "How can I possibly be safe? Luciana threatened to kill me, or have you forgotten that?"

"She made a bargain with Miss Belladonna, Ellie. Luciana's pride is more important to her than hurting you."

"She could kill me anyway."

Mam and stepped a few paces back, turning to the bread she had left on the counter. She held her hand just over it to see if the loaf was cool enough and took a knife to begin slicing. "Miss Luciana likes to win. She'd cut off her arm rather than admit to Miss Belladonna that she was right."

"Why did she do it? She was kind to me at first. We read together in the library. Money never seemed to have that strong a hold on her."

"Only Miss Belladonna could be answering that for you, child. But don't you be looking on her too harshly, now. She saved your life, and she was the only one able."

"Saved my life and sentenced me to the kitchen."

"A servant's lot isn't as bad as you think."

I blushed. "Sorry...I just...I'm not..."

"You're upset. I'll be forgetting all of your screaming after it's over."

I lowered my eyes to my feet. "I suppose I have no choice," I whispered, my anger seeping out of my shoulders and leaving my body limp. "If I ran away or went for help, all bargains would be off and I would be dead before I was saved."

"That you would." Mam took a rag from next to her hand and wetted it before handing it to me. "Clean that pretty face." I wiped the tears and dried blood from my cheeks, careful not to press hard where Luciana's hand had bruised me. "It's still morning and I've got a full day of work. I'll be taking you to Cate and Sarah. They'll be showing you how to get started after we get you some clothes."

And did Cate ever show me how to get started. I saw a different side of Cate that morning, and gained a new appreciation for the timid girl I had pitied so deeply. This time, Cate was the strong one and I was the one that needed shelter and comfort. She was a hard worker, thorough in every task she performed, and she found it easy to instruct me.

We started with cleaning. Usually, Cate spent her mornings in the kitchen helping with breakfast, but Mam had declared that she did not want me anywhere near a stove yet, lest I set fire to something— probably myself. Instead, we went to the library with lye soap, water, and several rags to clean the bookshelves and the floor.

At first I just stared at my palms, pretending to ignore Cate as she scoured the floor, her hair moving back and forth over her shoulders as she worked. Would my hands be hard and calloused from work soon? After a few seconds, watching while Cate worked proved to be too awkward to bear. I lowered myself to my knees beside her, reaching for the spare rag draped over the rim of the bucket. The coarse material of the working dress that I had borrowed rubbed against my skin without the protection of a corset or petticoat. These new clothes were nothing like the gowns I was used to.

Minutes crept by as we worked together to clean the seemingly endless stretch of library floor. The scent of lye tingled painfully in my nose, and my hands were stinging, scraped pink, especially at the heels. If I worked much harder, I thought, I would bleed all over the nice clean floor that I had spent absolutely ages scrubbing, and I would have to wash it all over again.

Cate rested gentle fingers on my arm, perceptive to my mood. "I'm sorry, Ellie. Mam's only doing this for your own good. If Miss Luciana finds out that you haven't been worked hard, she'll hurt you." It struck me then that she had used my name for the first time instead of my title. I smiled a little.

"You should stop calling her Miss Luciana, Cate. She is a horrible snake."

"You shouldn't cross her." I saw a flicker of fear in Cate's eyes, and I felt a sob break in my chest. Luciana probably enjoyed tormenting Cate and the rest of the servants. I was sure I would be no exception. In fact, she would probably single me out for extra unpleasant surprises.

"You know, this is the most you have ever said to me at one time." I thought I saw Cate's face brighten for a moment, but I could not be sure.

"It won't be so bad, Ellie, you'll see. We'll think of something."

I wanted to believe her so badly, but I was unsure. I went back to scrubbing the floor, and Cate did the same. After that task had been finished, we dusted the bookshelves and tried to replace the books that had been left out. The library was cluttered and disorganized, so putting the books away was more difficult than it should have been.

Finally, we went downstairs to the kitchen. I had missed breakfast. The servants had already eaten theirs early in the morning, and I assumed Luciana did not want me to take any more meals with her. There were some leftovers from lunch waiting for us when we arrived, and I ate until my stomach was stretched. I blinked my eyes lazily, wishing I could take a nap.

I looked at my raw, pink hands and frowned. My entire body already ached, and the afternoon had only just started. I was not sure I would survive another week of this torture, or even another day. The food helped, but the tiredness lingered as we cleaned the dishes left over from the afternoon meal. Though they had already been scraped down to a fresh layer of slick skin, my hands still wrinkled as they slopped about in the water. Mercifully, Cate allowed me to rinse and dry so I would not have to touch most of the soap, but whenever any of it coated my palms, the stinging made my eyes water.

Soon, Mam returned to the kitchen and began setting out ingredients for dinner. She gave me a sympathetic smile, but I was relieved when she did not speak. Talking seemed useless after the hours I had spent working alongside Cate.

CHAPTER 7

LUCIANA BEGAN HER game with the lentils on the fourth day of my slavery. I had not spoken with her since the morning she had threatened to throw me out the window, but I had seen her watching me. She looked on as I struggled with my chores, sometimes for a moment, sometimes for several minutes, hungry-eyed and vicious. I was slow and clumsy compared to Cate and Sarah and the other servants, but quick enough to recover from most of my mistakes with their help.

Jessith learned the entire story by the second day without even asking me, and she kept lookout while I worked. When she had to leave, one of the other cats always seemed to be nearby. Even Rucifee gave my hand a friendly nudge when I fed him his dinner.

Perhaps I should have expected Luciana's visit to the kitchen. It was only a matter of time before her sick humor lured her there. I was cleaning while Mam prepared dinner nearby. It would be another week or so, she said, before she would let me help, but she promised to teach me how to cook. Imagining several more weeks of my new life nauseated me, but I steadied my stomach and scrubbed my stack of dirty dishes. Sarah, who had not snubbed me or badgered me for gossip as I had expected, was at the other end of the room, eating a hunk of bread.

As I reached to set aside the plate I had cleaned, the kitchen door swung open. Luciana stood there with her lovely brown hair, wickedly beautiful, and I glared at her with fresh hate. Her eyes were dark and sharp as needle points as she followed the side of a long table. She looked casually around the room, but always returned her gaze to me.

Her smile clawed at my belly, and my face throbbed as my skin
remembered the bruise she had left on my cheek.

She stopped four feet away, resting her arm against a pot of lentils
Mam had taken out for her soup. She studied the fireplace, her fingers
curling over the edge of the table. Her other hand toyed with a pendant
hanging about her throat. It was a golden circle inside a silver circle
inside another golden circle. Three rings. She twirled it with her fingers.
I had to tear my eyes away from the flashing metal.

I set the clean plate to my left and reached for a bowl, but did not
bother to scour it. Across the kitchen, Mam had started chopping
vegetables. Though she did not say a word, I knew she was watching us.
Sarah was much less subtle. She stared openly at Luciana, then at me.
"Oh," she gasped, clapping a hand over her mouth.

Luciana watched me. I held perfectly still. Suddenly her hand shot
out and sent the pot of lentils spinning from the table. The sound of
metal crashing onto the floor made the kitchen ring. Sarah and Mam
flinched. Lentils scattered into the ashes, tiny brown bumps poking out
of the gray white powder. Some were lost from sight at once, others
settled on top of each other, and a few missed the fireplace completely.

"An accident," she said, not bothering to sound sincere. "Be a dear,
Ellie, and gather them up?" It was a ridiculous task. The pot had been full
to the brim, and it would be nearly impossible for me to pick all of them
out from the ashes. The sly Luciana I was used to had never been so
openly cruel, except for when she had hit me. All of her cunning
subterfuge was gone. Lady Kingsclere was sick, and she knew she did
not need to be discreet any longer. She could show her wickedness
openly.

I had no choice. I set the pot upright, got on my knees, and picked a
lentil from the ashes. I dropped it in and listened as it hit the bottom
with a sharp ping. Sarah shot me a sympathetic glance and hurried from
the room as I reached for another one. I did not blame her. What could
she do?

Soon, soot and ash coated my face and hands. My hair was tied
behind my head, but it was dirty, too. Luciana smiled down at my
blackened cheeks and laughed with her eyes. "Look at the princess now,"
she whispered so that Mam, who had remained in the kitchen, could not
hear her. "Back in the dirt you came from."

It took Luciana an hour before she grew bored of her game and left
me. Mam had finished dinner and was helping Sarah to serve it, since I
was occupied with the lentils. I had seen them cast me pitying glances,
but neither had been able to do anything with Luciana watching. I was

left alone in the kitchen, still scraping through the soot and ashes for the lentils. The bottom of the pot had hardly been covered.

Luciana repeated the cruel joke the next day, and the day after that, laughing with her eyes as I bent to pick through the soot at her feet.

***

It was the fifth time that Luciana had spilled lentils in the fireplace for me to gather up. Cate and Sarah, who was turning out to be a very sweet girl despite her talkative nature, helped me gather them when they could, but both of them had their own work to do and could not stay for long. None of us wanted to see what Luciana would do if she came to watch and caught them helping me. Night came and I was left alone, my arms blackened to the elbow, my back shaking with pain and fatigue. I rubbed my eyes and stared up at the window, wincing as I stretched my neck.

I wept, my tears cutting salty lines in the grime on my cheeks. My chest ached, heavy with shame. My humiliation was complete. Luciana had stripped me of my dignity as easily as she had cheated me out of my inheritance. Before, she had dressed me in rags, but I had stayed a lady. I carried myself like one even as I worked. But now, hunched over in the soot, dirty, tired, weeping, I was something less than human, certainly not nobility.

I had never considered myself prideful before, but this new disgrace shattered whatever vanity I had possessed. Part of me screamed that I should not obey her, but I was afraid. If I resisted, she would kill me and say that I had died in my sickbed. The rest of the kingdom, who could not have missed Lady Kingsclere's scandalous wedding to my father—still a commoner in their eyes, despite his wealth—assumed that I was on the brink of death. Luciana made sure I was out of sight when we had visitors. If I ran, she would find me. She needed to keep me close so she could win her disgusting bet and make sure I did not receive my inheritance.

A loud thump against the tiny window above the sink stopped my tears and I looked up. The dark shadow of a bird was silhouetted against the glass, frantically trying to claw its way into the kitchen. I stood up and climbed onto the counter, pushing the window open. The creature tumbled inside and fell onto the floor, its feathered chest heaving as its large black eyes rolled around the room. After I had closed the window, I saw another shadow swoop low past the glass.

"Was it an owl?" I asked the bird.

It lifted its head, surprised that it could understand me. "Ca-roo car-ee, car-oo car-ee. Nightflyer starves, this bird is free!"

I remembered then how awkward it was to talk with songbirds. They always spoke in rhyme, and most of them enjoyed the sound of their own voices too much. Unfortunately, their rhymes were often poor. I pitied the creature, though, and did not regret saving its life. It was a robin, shaking under its coat of ruffled feathers as it huddled against my ankle. I dropped to my knees beside it. "You should stay inside awhile. The owl might not be gone."

"You should ask it to help you," said Jessith, who could move so silently in the shadows that an eagle's eye would not catch sight of her. I started at her sudden appearance, and she lashed her tail. "A bird's beak would be perfect for pecking through the ashes and finding those lentils." The robin flapped into my lap, fear glazing his bright eyes again. "Oh, tell the silly thing I won't eat it. If I wanted to, I would have already."

"Turn and peep, turn and peep, hide until the cat's asleep!"

Jessith gave the bird a wicked hunter's smile. "Horrid creature...I won't eat you if you promise to help this girl. In fact, I'll extend the bargain to every bird at the manor."

The bird looked interested. It hopped forward onto my knee, peering cautiously at Jessith's face. It knew a cat's eyes could cast a spell and freeze it until the death-bite was delivered. "A bargain, cat, you wish to make? No more bird-lives will you take?"

"No. I won't eat any more birds if you pick all of the lentils out of the fireplace whenever my friend calls you. But you have to stop rhyming."

I understood the brilliance of Jessith's plan. A bird would be the perfect creature to help me complete my task. A whole flock of them could get it done in minutes. Luciana would never be able to torment me with the lentil trick again. Soon, Jessith had the robin pecking through the ashes, picking up the lentils with its tiny beak and dropping them into the pot. With its help, the task was done within the hour.

Enlisting the birds as my helpers worked better than I could have hoped. I even grew used to their singing after a few days. One of them invented the rhyme: "The good into the pot, the bad into the crop," and the rest of them picked up on it. Their voices were actually pleasant to listen to if you ignored the bad rhymes and nonsense syllables. Whenever Luciana played one of her nasty tricks—spilling lentils, ordering me to undo long row of stitches in the dark, working dirt into a carpet—the birds helped me. Their tiny beaks and sharp eyes were perfect for all sorts of things. Luciana grew angry that my tasks no longer seemed as much of a burden, but there was nothing she could do.

She could not spend the entire day watching to make sure I completed them without help.

I snuck Jessith some raw fish to thank her for her idea. She gloated over her meal and carried herself smugly for several days afterwards, basking in her own brilliance. Cats are haughty by nature, so I did not mind. True to her word, she refrained from eating any of the small songbirds that swarmed around Baxstresse. Birds are clannish creatures, and many of them came to help me with my work, knowing I would reward them with some grain or breadcrumbs. They had little to fear now, since Rucifee was too fat and dignified to chase sparrows and Trugel hardly ever ventured outside of the library. If they avoided the two tomcats that lived in the barn, they were quite safe.

The strange swell of birds that arrived at Baxstresse did not go unnoticed. "Must be the spring air," Mam commented one morning after a chorus of loud birdcalls had awakened us before dawn. "Gets the birdies up and about, it does. Good for the harvest. They keep down the bugs."

***

A servant at Baxstresse survived by always watching. Watching for Luciana, watching for Jamison. While Luciana tortured for pleasure, Jamison punished for pride. He was our better, and his bright-buttoned waistcoat proved it. If either of them caught us taking a moment's rest, we would be reprimanded.

The hurt he caused was never physical. Too much of a gentleman for blows, Jamison disciplined us with work. He always found the most unbearable tasks to dole out, the worst of which was waiting on Luciana. Jamison chose a girl, usually Cate, to help Luciana with her clothes every morning and evening. If we did something to annoy him, or if he thought we were not working hard enough, one of us would come out of Luciana's room in tears the next day. I had started thinking of the servants and me as 'us'. I was one of them now, forced to complete the same work. I was never chosen to assist Luciana, though. I assumed that she considered me a temptation and did not want to lose her bet.

My opinion of Jamison, already low, dropped like a stone after the affair with the waistcoat. Mam had allowed me to take some carrots to Brahms after lunch. I had not ridden since my enslavement, and she knew I missed the horses. She was always doing kind things like that, trying her best to make my dreary days a little brighter.

Brahms was relieved to see me. "Where have you been, Ellie?" he asked, banging one of his hooves against the door of his stall. "We haven't been running in ages! Can we go now?"

My throat tightened as I held out my hand, offering my friend a carrot. "No, not today." I forced a smile as his wet lips tickled my palm.

"You're sad," Brahms said around a mouthful of carrot.

"Yes." How could I explain to a horse that Luciana had cheated me out of my birthright and forced me to do a servant's work? Most animals were not familiar with the concept of nobility and rank, unless they were part of a pack. Brahms had not been raised in a herd, and had always been doted on. "I have to work in the kitchen now. I am not sure when we will be able to go riding again." I stroked Brahms's soft pink nose, and he huffed appreciatively. I could see myself reflected in his eyes, and I knew he would miss our rides as much as I did.

"Can you work in the stables instead of the kitchen?"

"No. Luciana is trying to hurt me so she can take my father's money." *And because she enjoys it,* I added silently. Luciana could never resist the temptation to harm whoever was closest. It was obvious now where Cate got the ugly bruises that colored her arms and throat, even though she had not admitted it to me yet. Jessith had been right. My search for Cate's tormentor had not been broad enough. Luciana had never even entered my mind as a suspect.

"Luciana hurts a lot of people. Corynne doesn't like her. She hits too hard when she rides."

I gave the horse a thin smile. "Well, horses are excellent judges of character."

"They were talking about her, you know," Brahms said thoughtfully, tilting his head as he focused more closely on the memory that was obviously replaying itself in his mind. "There were two of them that came by here a few minutes ago. One was the girl that used to come with you before our rides. The other had a long brown mane and a round face."

I removed my hand from Brahms' warm nose. "You mean Sarah? What did they say?"

"The girl with the brown mane...Sarah?...said that Jamison should be cooked alive for making the girl with the red mane go to Luciana twice. Then Sarah touched the other girl's face and she started crying."

"Was something wrong with her face?"

"It wasn't shaped right and it was the wrong color."

I exhaled and closed my eyes, knowing what I would find when I went after Cate, but hoping I was wrong. "Brahms, I should go after Cate. I think something happened to her."

Brahms sniffled understandingly and tossed his mane, the bands of muscles across his sides rippling as he backed up a few paces. "Will you come visit me again? I've missed you."

"Of course. I've missed you, too. I'll bring you some carrots or maybe an apple if I can steal one." Brahms flicked an ear, obviously pleased with that thought, and I hurried out of the stables, wondering where Cate had gone.

It did not take me long to find her. She was out in the open, sitting underneath the hazel tree I had planted for my mother, her beautiful red-gold hair caked with blood next to her cheek. Her lip was split and half of her face was swollen. There was an ugly gash next to one eye, and horrible yellow bruises fingered around her throat. Sarah was sitting beside her, trying to comfort her. "Oh, Cate," I said, sinking to my knees in front of her and cupping her chin in my hands. "What happened this time?"

"Jamison," Sarah said. I saw that both of them had been crying. Sarah's skin had patches of red across it, and her eyes were bloodshot. Still, she did not look nearly as frightful as Cate. "He made Cate go to Miss Luciana this morning, even though she already went last night. She was in a rage on account of something Miss Belladonna said."

I kissed Cate's forehead and held her as she cried, shedding a few tears of my own into her hair. Sarah held on to her arm, offering more support. "I wish he would send me instead. Luciana won't touch me because of the bet."

"She might anyway," Cate whispered, her voice so soft that I could hardly make it out. It was the first time she had spoken. "She...there's something in her face right before she...She's not in her right mind. Someday, she'll forget her bargain, and you'll end up worse than me. She might even kill you."

"I should get back to the kitchen." Sarah excused herself quietly, getting to her feet and brushing her hair into place as she smoothed out her dress. "You'll look after Cate, won't you, Ellie?" I nodded, and Sarah left for the manor. We both knew that Cate needed some time. I had grown very close with her through the weeks, closer than anyone else had managed to get.

I knew that the real blame for Cate's hurts lay with Luciana, but I knew there was nothing we could do about her. And so, desperate for an outlet, I focused the force of my rage on Jamison once Sarah was out of sight. "What did you do to make Jamison so angry?"

Cate bit the unbroken side of her mouth, stroking her bruised cheek with feather-light fingertips. "His coat," she mouthed, barely breathing out the words. "I dirtied it."

"He had Luciana beat you for that?"

"Luciana would beat me without any reason. Jamison just gave her an excuse."

Cate's eyes were dim, hopeless, but mine were bright and fresh with rage. "He knew how badly she would hurt you. He helped cause this." I looked at her face, not daring to touch it. "He is as guilty as she is."

We studied each other, reading each other's faces. "It's sweet of you, but I don't want you to defend me," Cate whispered.

I frowned deeply. "Cate, I am your friend. Let me." Cate's eyes fluttered shut, her face tight and strained. Her skin, stretched thin and white across her cheeks, lost what little color it had.

"You'll be hurt, Ellie..." Her voice nearly broke, and tears welled in her eyes. I kissed her hair, holding her steady as she shook. After a few long moments, I took her hand and helped her to her feet, steering her toward the kitchen so I could wash the blood from her face. She went without protest.

"I promise not to try anything with Luciana, but will you let me take Jamison's pride down a few pegs?" I asked, a plan already forming in my mind. I was eager for revenge.

For just a moment, Cate's gaze flared. The corner of her mouth twitched. "Only if we do it together. I want to get some of my own back."

CHAPTER 8

AS MY SERVANT education continued, I learned to walk Baxstresse's halls unnoticed, clinging to the walls like a strand of creeper. I kept a close eye on Cate, afraid that Jamison would turn her over to Luciana again. Through the long weeks of my humiliation, Cate's friendship had been my salvation. Although the other servants had been suspicious of me at first, Cate's support and friendship had swayed their opinions. Mam and Sarah had also stood beside me.

I memorized the schedules that everyone in the house kept, and knew when to make myself scarce. This information would be valuable for plotting against Jamison. I also learned everything I could from the servants. I was one of them now, and they included me in all of the manor gossip, most of which revolved around the activities of the Kingsclere sisters. I discovered more about my adoptive "family" after a week with the servants than in all the months I had spent in their company.

I learned that my stepmother was far worse off than I had believed. Luciana and Belladonna attended to most of the manor business themselves. The rivalry between them ran deeper than I could have possibly imagined. Both seemed determined to make the other fall into disfavor with their ill mother, and they quarreled fiercely behind her back. My earlier assumption, that I was the only one who could see the hatred between them, was proven false. It seemed that only Lady Kingsclere and my father, while he had been alive, had been deceived.

Not surprisingly, Belladonna was the general favorite. Most of the servants wanted her to inherit Baxstresse. She was considered to be less cruel than Luciana, and she treated everyone except her sister with the same degree of cold politeness. I could not blame them for preferring a frosty mistress to a wrathful one.

However, Baxstresse had one secret I was purposely excluded from. The others refused to speak of it with me until I discovered it for myself. Later, I found out Mam had asked them not to, attempting to keep me shielded from the ugly truth as long as possible. Mam acted as mother, teacher, and friend to me as I adjusted to my new life, like a protective hen hovering over her chick.

There were several clues. None of the servants dared to enter either sister's room at night unless Jamison forced them. Certain parts of the house were avoided at specific times. When one of the younger members of the staff went missing for a few hours, no one bothered to ask where they were. There were Cate's fresh bruises, too. But I failed to piece everything together until one afternoon in early summer.

A week had passed since Jamison's latest act of cruelty. Cate and I were washing dishes and stacking them while Mam chopped vegetables on the other side of the kitchen. I pulled my hands out of the stinging soap water and dried them on a rag. "We're almost done," I called over my shoulder to Mam, blowing my hair out of my eyes.

Mam did not bother to turn away from her vegetables. "Then you can be about collecting the trays from the serving room to wash, too." Cate and I both groaned, looking at the neat stacks of dishes we had already cleaned. The task had taken all morning, and the thought of washing one more plate almost had me in tears. Baxstresse was starting to grow warm, and the heat from the stove made the kitchen unbearably hot. Summers at Baxstresse were as parched as the springs were damp. It was not a pleasant change.

"Ah, stop your carrying on. If one of you goes to get the dishes and brings them down to me, I'll be finishing the washing myself," Mam offered, pretending to sound irritated as she turned around to face the sink.

"Are you sure?" I asked, looking down at Mam's hands. They were leathery and cracked, swollen at the knuckles from years of cutting and washing and mending. Mam's hands looked at least ten years older than she was.

"I wash faster than you. You might as well be going to help with the cleaning after you bring down the trays. Don't handle the stairs s' well anymore."

"Cate and I will..." I turned and realized that Cate had slipped away from the kitchen while I had been distracted. "Well, I'll go and get them myself. Where has she gotten to?"

"Never mind yourself about Cate," Mam said sharply, but her face softened as she caught the hurt expression on my face. "Off with you, Ellie, and use the back halls."

"Yes, Mam." I scurried out of the room, relieved to be free of the kitchen's heat for a few minutes.

The back halls were the quickest way to get to the second-floor serving room, but I was in no rush. I decided to take the longer route, up the grand staircase in the front entrance hall and past the library. The cold of the stone steps crept through the thin soles of my shoes as I made my way up to the second floor. The drafty halls were a welcome relief from the boiling heat of the kitchen. I felt my skin tingle as the thin layer of sweat along the back of my neck dried in the cool air.

At the top of the stairs, I listened for the severe click of Luciana's heels or the soft tapping of Jamison's fine boots, not wanting to become a target. When I was sure it was safe, I slipped down the wide hallway that led to the upper dining hall. Pale sunlight filtered through the stained glass windows, casting red and blue patterns across the floorstones. I stopped to admire one window in particular. Saint Eugiers of Maveria was fighting with a great black dragon, his golden sword glinting as he swung it toward the beast's writhing coils. Inaccurate as the sword was, since gold is a soft metal and completely unsuitable for a weapon, the picture was still striking.

I was about to continue on when a soft sound came from across the hall. I started, fearing that Jamison had caught me, but only the great double doors of the library stood before me as I turned. The sound had come from inside. It came again, a sort of gasp or whimper of pain, and I inched the library door open and peered inside.

At first I only made out the shadows of the high backed wooden chairs, but a slight movement drew my eyes to one corner of the room. An arching, smooth, muscled back shifted against a wooden shelf. Naked except for the delicate silver chain about her neck, her soft white skin had been rubbed red by the discarded tight corset. The thick brown hair was unmistakably Luciana's, but she was not alone. Pressed between her lean body and the stacks of books was Cate, shuddering and trembling.

At first, the scene was strikingly raw and intimate, until I saw the glassy tears tumbling over Cate's cheeks. Suddenly, the flash of beauty was gone. I saw the tightness of Cate's throat as she choked back sobs. This was not a happy coupling. I stared for an eternity until nausea struck, tugging at my stomach and pounding across my forehead. It was dizzying, numbing, and I bolted away from the library, staggering and zig-zagging through the cramped servant's hallways.

Baxstresse's oddities suddenly made sense. Cate's extra bruises and disappearances were clearly explained. But what could I do? Who could save her? Not Lady Kingsclere, who was out of her senses, but perhaps Belladonna. Would she even believe me if I told her? I had once considered her a friend, but would she side with Luciana as before? Mam was the only other person I could think of that held some sway with Luciana. I turned in the middle of the hallway and ran to the kitchen for help.

She was there in her faded apron as I ran past the stove, waiting. I half collapsed in front of her and she gathered me in her arms, wiping away tears I did not remember crying. "You never listen, child," she fretted, smoothing back my hair.

"But Cate, we have to..."

"Cate can take care of herself. She's a strong girl, that one."

"You knew? You knew and you let it happen?" The nausea was gone, dissolving into a furious energy. I was sure my grip would leave bruises on Mam's tired arms, but I did not care. How could she let something so ugly happen right above us? But...I had not stepped in to stop it immediately, either.

Mam did not pull away. "You'd rather Cate was dead? Because that's what she'll be if anyone tries, her and whichever fool got in the way."

She let me cry myself out, not even leaving me to stir her precious vegetables or check the bread in the stove. Pain clawed at my chest and throat. My eyes stung when I finally pulled away from her, and my face and neck were covered with bright red blotches. I could not hate Mam. Luciana was the one I hated. I thought I had hated her before, when she had forced me to become a servant, when she had spilled the lentils, when she had beaten Cate, but that hatred was nothing compared to the rage and disgust I felt now.

"Cate was crying. I never learned...about things like that..." Mam's rough hands made soothing circles on my back as she helped me into a chair. I was silent again for several moments, but finally had to ask, "Is it...always so horrible?"

Mam kept a firm hand on my shoulder, her touch drawing out all of my emotions and leaving me empty and exhausted. "No, Ellie, it's not always horrible. If you're in love, it can be one of the most beautiful things in the world."

But I could not imagine it. I only saw Cate crying. I tasted the pain. "If she ever touches me like that, I'll kill her. And then I'll kill myself."

"You won't. You'll find you've got more to live for than you think." Mam lifted her hand and hurried over to a wooden corner drawer I had never seen her open before. Her large, bent back hid what she removed until she turned and placed the familiar large healing basket on the table in front of me. "Cate will be needing a friend soon. Now that you know, you might as well help me take care of her bruises. You'll do a better job of it than any of us. She'll take comfort from you."

"I...I can't bear it." I sobbed, pushing the basket away. "Not me..."

"If Cate can bear the pain, you can certainly bear to take it away," Mam said, although her words were not without sympathy. I was silent for a long time, staring at the woven basket. My anger was drowned in a wave of helplessness. I could not protect Cate. I could not even protect myself. That stupid bet was the only reason I had escaped the same fate.

"I'll help her."

"She won't be down for a while more. Go and see to the bread, and be taking care not to burn yourself."

I was grateful that Mam had given my hands something to do, but they fidgeted anyway as I fetched the bread and set it on the counter to cool. The seconds stretched by until Cate shuffled in through the door, tugging at her skirts uncomfortably with her left hand, her face and neck freshly marked. When she saw I was still in the kitchen, her eyes took on their familiar dead glaze. Now I knew why she had needed to learn it. I walked over to the basket and pulled out bandages while Mam went to boil water. None of us spoke.

After Cate had been bandaged and kissed, washed and soothed back to us, Mam left, sensing that we needed time. I knew that Cate, who was never fond of speaking, would be too frightened to start. "You should have told me. I thought we were friends." I had not, until that moment, realized how betrayed I felt. We had only known each other for a short time, but Cate was dear to me.

"I never told anyone. The others just knew."

My eyes itched again, blurring at the corners. "I would have helped you. I could have found a way..."

"There isn't a way." Cate's expression was vacant, but her words were bitter and cold. It was the first time I had seen her angry, and I was so surprised that I nearly knocked five of the extra bandage strips from the kitchen table. "She first took me when I was fourteen. She'll have me again and again until she gets bored or she kills me."

I opened my mouth, trying to speak, but no words came. "If I run away, she'll hunt me. If I hide, she'll find me. If I fight...Luciana has killed before. I'd rather live in pain than not live at all. Maybe a miracle will happen and she'll die or leave Baxstresse. Perhaps when she marries."

I knew that Luciana would never leave Baxstresse for any suitor less than Seria's prince. Cate understood, but neither of us could bear to consider the alternative. "Ellie," she whispered, all of her anger gone, "you...do you think any less of me?"

I was astonished. "Of course not. Why would I?"

"Because I'm not..." And then I understood. I forgave her a little for keeping her secret. Of course she would feel ashamed to talk about it with me. I was glaringly naïve. Belladonna had picked up on it immediately and I supposed that everyone else had done the same. Perfect virgin, innocent lamb. It all made sense.

"I would never think less of you, Cate. The only person I think less of is Luciana." Cate's lips curved quietly, a soft smile. My right hand reached out, stroking her left cheek. "You have done nothing wrong. Will you remember?" My fingers combed through her tangled red hair as we gazed out of the window instead of at each other.

"I will remember."

CHAPTER 9

THEY SAY THAT giants fall from great heights, and Jamison's ego hovered somewhere near the stars. We were eager to bring the purple-faced dandy crashing back down to earth. All the hatred Cate and I felt for Luciana, all the pain we had suffered, all of our helplessness and frustration was poured into our revenge. Neither of us had much experience with hatred. We hoped that by doing this one bad deed, we could purge most of our black feelings. Neither of us wanted to let them fester and become like Luciana.

Several times, Cate tried to put a stop to our plans. I pushed on for her sake. Cate needed to do this if she was ever going to heal. She had to understand that her honor was worth defending, and that Luciana and Jamison were not untouchable. I needed this victory as well to prove that I was not a silly, helpless fool.

It was easy to see what we needed to do. Jamison's formal waistcoat with the large, bright brass buttons had to go. Coming up with a way to ruin the waistcoat was more difficult. If one of us stained the waistcoat, we would surely be turned over to Luciana, but if Jamison stained it himself, perhaps with wine, we would not be punished.

"Maybe one of us could make a loud noise while Jamison drinks his evening wine in the dining hall," I suggested. Jamison always took his wine in Baxstresse's formal dining hall. It was no secret why. He enjoyed pretending that he was the lord of the manor.

"It might work..." Despite her words, Cate's expression was doubtful. "But what if the spill doesn't catch his coat?"

"It's worth a try, anyway. The library's right next door. One of us could push something over, and if the cup was filled to the brim..."

Finally, Cate agreed to fill the glass. Without discussing it, we both understood that I would be the one to make the loud crash. We hoped that Jamison would exclaim over his coat instead of chasing after the noise, but if he did catch me, I would take the punishment. The bet would protect me from the worst of Luciana's abuse. Cate's poor body was in no condition to take any more.

That night, I waited in the library while Cate brought Jamison his wine. I listened for the large grandfather clock to strike seven as I examined the long rows of bookshelves. Most of the shelves were too heavy to push over, but there were smaller, half sized shelves at the ends of each row that I could just move. Positioning myself behind one of them and kicking aside the feather duster I had brought as my excuse, I rested my hands against the shelf.

We needed to time it perfectly. I had to push the shelf before Jamison drained his glass too low, but if I pushed too soon, Cate would still be holding the cup. We had decided that she would hand Jamison his wine at exactly seven o' clock, and I would push the shelf over three seconds later. Luckily for us, he always kept to a strict schedule.

My eyes rested on the smaller clock pushed in to one corner of the library. Its beautiful face was hardly aged at all behind its shining glass mask, and it was perfectly aligned with the one in the dining room. As I watched, the tall hand pointed to the twelve, and the old clock chimed the hour through the quiet room, its voice strangely muffled by the chairs and shelves crammed together. The echo of the larger, booming grandfather clock in the dining room rang in time with its smaller brother. I counted to three and shoved.

The bookshelf tipped, landing with the echoing crack of wood on stone. I had left the large library doors open, and I was sure that the noise could be heard from several rooms away. I bent over to pick up my duster, not wanting to leave any evidence, and tried to hurry deeper into the library, but I tripped over a pile of scattered books and fell to my knees.

Grudgingly, I stumbled back onto my feet, not bothering to run. It was too late to escape anyway. Too many precious seconds had been wasted. Instead, I picked up one of the books that had fallen in front of me, scanning for a title so I could reshelf it. At least I would look busy if Jamison did decide to investigate the noise. To my surprise, the book's spine was blank, and there was no title on the first page.

I ran my fingertips over the soft leather cover. The book was obviously well loved. The pages were creased, not yellow with age, but smooth with frequent use. The handwriting was varied—usually neat, but occasionally larger, smudged and frantic, as though it had been written in a moment of desperation.

It was obviously a diary of some kind. Not wanting to intrude on someone's personal thoughts, I started to close the book when a few words caught my attention. My name was written several times on one of the open pages. Setting my morals aside, I started to read. Although the page was littered with ink stains and the lines spilled out of their orderly rows, the words were clear enough.

...so beautiful, my sweet obsession. She has no idea how much I want her. I wonder how the liquid satin of her would feel around my fingers, or against my mouth.

In her innocence, she stirs me more than any other woman I have ever taken. She is a complete virgin in both body and mind. She blushes so prettily, my beautiful Ellie. I can hardly stop myself from drawing her into my arms and never letting go.

Such a tender heart should be cherished and protected and loved. I only wish I could be the lover she needs. I need her to need me. I want to be everything for her—a lover, a friend, a guardian. I desire her because she is beautiful, but I love her because she is kind and good. I have seen how protective she is of Cate and how gently she treats the horses.

I love you, my infatuation, my Ellie. I will never have you, but the softness of your mouth is tempting and I wonder at its taste. I have given my heart to you already. The guilty whole of it is yours.

Before I could read further, Cate hurried into the library, worry lines tightening her forehead. "Oh, Ellie, I heard the crash! Are you all right? Why aren't you hiding?"

I searched for my voice, but was unable to form words. The mystery writer had wiped everything else from my mind. I stood there, flushed and frightened and overjoyed all at once for reasons I could not understand, trying to remember what Cate had said to me.

"It was brilliant, though!" she continued, the worry lines easing a little. "Jamlson's precious coat is ruined. I was so afraid for you...you never came out after you knocked the shelf over." Cate looked at the book in my hand curiously, but I snapped it shut. I pressed my lips together, swallowing to loosen my throat. I had no choice. I needed to lie.

"Oh...I was...reading something. Poetry."

"Poetry, at a time like this? It must have been good poetry," Cate joked. I was too distracted to take pleasure in her unusually good mood.

Jamison's defeat had lifted her spirits considerably. "If it's really that distracting, you'll have to read some to me later."

"Not from this one. It's handwritten, and I can barely make it out." I gave her a quick flash of my admirer's messy handwriting. "I was going to see if there was anything in it worth copying over before I threw it away. Mam has been after us to organize this place anyway."

The lie was surprisingly easy to tell. Afterwards, I realized just how strange that moment had been. It was as if I knew I had to keep the diary safe, even from Cate. It was one of the only successful lies I ever told. Perhaps that was why Cate believed me so easily.

I opened the book again as soon as I had smuggled it away. Whoever had written the diary was clever. Hiding a book in a library, among hundreds of others, was a brilliant idea. Curious, I flipped the pages, looking for a name. Soon, my eyes settled on a page that caught my attention. It told me quite plainly who had poured their heart into the journal.

My heart was torn in two today. I betrayed my Ellie. It was hard, so unbelievably hard, to talk Luciana into keeping her on as a servant. I saved her life, but for what? From now on, she will be treated little better than a slave. I bargained with my sister to keep her from using Ellie like the rest of her toys. It is not nearly enough, but her body, at least, is safe. I can do nothing for her heart.

I know what I did was right, but the ache in my chest remains. Luciana would have beaten her, stolen her innocence, and thrown her out of the window, unless she devised another cruel death sentence to use instead. Thankfully, Ellie is alive.

Strangely, the thought of Luciana breaking her body hurts me more than the thought of her death. My Ellie deserves to be taken willingly, worshipfully, lovingly. Any woman does. I am sure that thoughts of Luciana's sick perversions sting the worst only because I cannot imagine Ellie dead. My heart will simply not accept the idea of losing her. If Luciana had killed her, I am sure the numbness would be permanent.

My chest is heavy with guilt. I have not eaten all day. She looked at me while Luciana tormented her, asking why I had hurt her with her eyes. I had no answer to give her. I still have no answer. All I wanted to do was tell her that I loved her, let her know that I would keep her safe. Someday, perhaps she will understand that I had to do what I did. I only wish I could have spared her the pain. I gladly would have taken it myself.

My throat tightened as I realized who had written such powerful declarations of love for me. "Saints," I whispered to myself, dropping the book onto my lap. My hands trembled as I shut the leather cover. I had never seriously thought of taking a lover before in my life, especially not another woman.

Especially not my stepsister.

***

After finding the diary, my mind was not my own. I could barely stomach food, and I spent my nights awake, except for the dreams. I must have looked a sight, because Mam, Cate, Matthew, Jessith, and even the disagreeable Rucifee asked if I was ill. Working as a servant and bearing Luciana's hatred could not ease the intensity of this sickness, whatever it was. I had a guess, although I was afraid to consider the word at first. The closest I could safely come to approaching it was infatuation.

The morning after Cate and I played our trick on Jamison, I carefully returned the diary to the scattered pile of books on the floor. When I checked the library that afternoon, the shelf had been straightened and the diary was still there. Only Trugel, the ancient library cat, watched me as I took it from the shelf, enjoying the weight of it in my hand. I just knew that Belladonna had put it back herself to keep her secret safe. She must have decided that the shelf had fallen by accident and that no one had noticed the diary. Since she was not suspicious, I started to steal it whenever I could.

I was always cautious when I took the diary to read. I counted the books on either side to make sure I put it back exactly where I had found it, in between *Mountaineering: An Explorer's Handbook* and *A Serian's Guide to Sailing*. Since the nearest mountains and oceans were a week's distance away, it seemed like a good hiding place. The rest of the titles on the shelf were equally useless, most of them travel guides and maps that did not discuss the areas around Baxstresse.

Belladonna was careful in other ways, too. She added entries in the early afternoon while her sister and mother napped and the servants were cleaning the table after lunch. I took the diary at night while most of the household was in bed. I could never let Belladonna know I had learned her secret, at least not yet. As much as I wanted to confront her, something gripped at me. Perhaps fear and uncertainty, but it was probably guilt. I was afraid that Belladonna would hate me for reading her personal thoughts. Until I was certain she would forgive me, I decided I would keep quiet.

Thoughts of my stepsister and what she had written ghosted me even when the book was safe on its shelf. The seeds were rooted deep in my mind. Could this be love? I wondered fearfully as I scrubbed the dinner dishes, numb to the sting of lye against my hands. It was not the romantic warmth I had expected. Instead, it ate at me, a sweet torment, bands of it clutching tighter about my chest with every moment. For the first time, I was consumed with the idea of taking a lover, something I had never wasted my time pondering before. High society's disapproval of such things, especially between two women, hardly registered in my mind. Being related by marriage only made it slightly more scandalous.

The more I read of Belle's thoughts, the more certain I became—I was falling in love. Her heart was layered and complex. Her words were always colorful. On my first night at Baxstresse, Mam had told me that Belladonna was a poet. She was that and so much more—a poet, a storyteller, a dreamer, a lover in the classical sense. It was impossible to see Belle's deepest self and not grow attached. If I let her, I knew she would go to the ends of the earth for me.

I was aware of my body as I had never been before. The slightest brush of fingers on my arm made my muscles seize and shiver. Whenever I thought about Belladonna—nearly always—the space below my stomach would tighten with hurt, and an emptiness ached deep inside me.

I accepted my fate more swiftly than I would have believed possible. It took me a week and a half to admit that I was lost to her, spoiled for anyone else.

CHAPTER 10

"PEOPLE HAVE BEEN taking bets on who your mystery lover is, Ellie," Sarah teased one evening as we sat next to the kitchen's fire, trying to warm ourselves before we went to sleep. "You're so distracted!" Cate was with us, staring into the flames as Sarah and I tried to coax her into conversation. So far, we had been unsuccessful.

My cheeks blazed, and I knew from the curl of Sarah's lips that I was blushing furiously. Thoughts of Belle flooded my brain, crowding out everything else and heating me to my toes. "Not a word of it is true," I mumbled, following Cate's example and watching the logs burn.

"You fancy someone." Sarah reached into her apron, holding her fist closed around something as she pulled it out. "Shall we find out how they feel about you, then?"

I could guess what was in her hand. I did not believe in forest magic. The only real magic was done by mages, usually at the Ronin College of Sorcery. "Do you actually believe in that rubbish, Sarah?"

Sarah opened her fist and waved a hazelnut—I had guessed correctly—in front of my face, grinning madly. "A hazelnut I throw in the flame, and to this nut I give my sweetheart's name...Now, what name is that?"

"Did you get that from my tree?" The tree I had planted for my mother was the only hazel tree nearby that I knew of.

"If blazes the nut, so may thy passion grow, for 'twas my nut that did so brightly glow." Sarah and I looked at Cate, surprised into silence. It was the first time she had spoken, except to greet us.

I took the nut from Sarah's hand and gave it to Cate. "Throw it in for me, Cate," I told her. She took it from me and tossed it into the fire. The nut cracked, sparked, and started to glow brightly.

"Aha!" Sarah crowed, leaning back in her chair as she watched the nut burn.

"She loves you, Ellie." Cate's voice was so quiet that Sarah and I could barely understand her. We watched her face as she turned away from the warm red fire and looked at us with far away, glassy eyes. "She loves you deeply. And that love will have to be enough when you break the chain."

Sarah's expression instantly transformed, all of the joy leaving it. "Ellie," she hissed, grabbing my hand and pulling me to my feet. "Come." I tried to sit back down so I could ask Cate about what she'd said, but Sarah was larger than I was and she easily forced me out of the room. "You can't say anything to Cate about what just happened," she said once we had left the kitchen.

I hugged my arms to my chest, missing the warmth of the fire. "Why not? And why did you drag me out into the cold hallway?"

Sarah just shook her head, clasping my wrist tighter. "You can't. Cate...perhaps you don't believe magic is all that useful, but Cate comes from a long line of seers and fortunetellers. Denari, or something...She's Amendyrri, you know."

Cate's complexion had given her Amendyrri heritage away already, but the information that Sarah had told me about her family history was intriguing. "Do you mean Dan'tari?" The name was familiar.

"Yes, that's it. But how did you know?"

I blushed. "I like to read."

"Never mind," Sarah said, dismissing her surprise with a shake of her head. "Not many people know. Please, don't think any differently about her. She sees things, and sometimes doesn't even remember afterwards, but if she does, she usually becomes ill. If she looks at any of us like that, we don't talk about it."

The look Sarah gave me was threatening and protective, and immediately sobered me. "No, of course not. I would never think differently of Cate. I promise to keep it a secret. She is very dear to me." I understood why Cate had kept her gift hidden from me. After all, I was doing the same thing. However, I was secretly relieved to learn I was not the only Ariada at Baxstresse.

I smiled at Sarah and she smiled back. "Cate should be all right now," she said, turning to go back into the kitchen. "Let's see her to bed."

***

The dream again, always the same...*I was sitting by the fire in the library, my eyes resting shut. I often dozed off in the library next to the red glow of the dying fire, but this time, there was someone else in the room with me. I did not need to open my eyes to know who it was. Her presence was familiar to me. She came nearer and my breath caught in my chest, unwilling to release. I was not surprised when a hand caressed my cheek. A finger trailed down to catch under my chin, tilting it up.*

Soft lips stroked my forehead, moving down to my eyelids, kissing them. They fluttered open, leaving my gaze unfocused as a dizzying face drew close to mine. Finally, mouths met, lip seeking lip. Hard, white heat sparked along soft skin, burning flushed patches over my neck and shoulders. I saw her face. Her wet, full eyes. "Beautiful," she said, "so beautiful."

Time passed too quickly, as though several minutes had been snipped out of the dream's fabric and the two edges had been stitched together again. I did not know where we were. Maybe a bed, maybe still in the library. I only knew her. She was above me, against me, in me. That last was the most distracting. I was full, stretched tight with her. Wonderful. She breathed nonsense words against my ear. I had to shut my eyes against tears. They came anyway, and she kissed them away.

"Open your eyes, sweet girl," she whispered. I clutched her shoulders tighter. "Your eyes, Ellie. Let me see your eyes." I opened them, only for a moment, threading our gazes together as she touched a small star of heat between my legs that made me sob and shake in her arms. "Let go, lover. Let go. Let me catch you when you fall."

But when I opened my eyes, I was in Cate's arms, not Belladonna's. She was stroking my hair, whispering different words than my dream lover. I could not bury the disappointment I felt when I realized it had all been a dream. I had not really been with Belladonna.

I forgot my sadness for a moment when I saw the concern in Cate's face. "Ellie, are you all right? You were screaming and crying. Did you have a nightmare?"

"Yes," I panted, relieved that she had made up my excuse for me. "A nightmare."

"You kept screaming Miss Belladonna's name." My lips shook as I tried to speak, but no words came. Cate was sympathetic, gently questioning me while rubbing between my shoulders. "Was she hurting you in the dream?"

"No. Luciana was hurting me," I blurted out, grasping for a plausible excuse. "Belle was trying to stop her. I was screaming for help." This was the second lie I had told my dear friend, and I regretted it. I hated to deceive Cate, but one lie always turns into two, and two into a thousand. I was getting better at it though, I realized sadly.

To my surprise, Cate looked relieved. Her eyes flicked downward to the sheets tangled about my damp body. "She tries to hide us when she can. Belladonna, I mean. I'm glad you don't think she's...like her sister."

Though it had taken several weeks of service at Baxstresse to teach me how to lie, I had always been good at reading people. I knew that Cate was hiding something. She clutched my wrist with her thin fingers, her mouth set in a stiff line, her brown eyes unfocused, panicked.

"What else, Cate?" Without realizing, our roles had reversed themselves. For the first time, I wondered why Cate had not stayed asleep. Maybe I had screamed loud enough to wake her, but perhaps she had been struggling with her own nightmares when she heard me.

"Sometimes she...what Luciana does, but gentler," she said in a rush, not even able to put a name to the act. "She doesn't hurt you."

I knew I should have been surprised, but mostly, I was jealous. My Belle had been sleeping with the servants, but was afraid of asking me to her bed? There had been references to it in her diary, vague though they were, but I had chosen not to believe them. It was too painful to imagine Belle in someone else's arms. "With you?" was all I got out.

"No." Cate looked slightly embarrassed at that admission, almost pained. "She knows...she knows I don't want anyone to touch me. I can't..." I was not surprised. In Cate's limited experience, physical love only meant pain. I desperately hoped I would not share her fate if Luciana decided to give up on her bet. Although Mam disagreed with me, I was still convinced I would kill myself.

I patted Cate's arm, prying her fingers away from my wrist to let the blood flow back into my hand. "Gently, Cate...I know..."

"But Sarah and some of the others," she continued, ignoring me completely, "they're infatuated with her. They say she's a dazzling lover. I've thought about it, really thought about it, but I just can't..."

This confession had been pressing down on Cate's chest for a long time, and I forgot my jealousy to comfort her. She hadn't been with Belladonna after all. She wasn't a threat, and I scolded myself for thinking badly of her. Cate was my friend. Even if she had shared herself with Belle, I thought, could I begrudge her that small happiness? But I was secretly glad that she hadn't found the courage.

"Do you feel like you have to?" I asked.

"Maybe. Most of them do. I feel...strange. Maybe something is wrong with me because I don't want to?"

"Everyone is different, Cate. Some of them might want to forget with Belladonna, but that does not mean you have to. Maybe after Luciana is gone, you will want to take a lover again. Nothing is wrong with you." There were several things wrong with Cate, but I would never tell her that until she was ready to hear it. Not wanting to take a lover after years of abuse was nothing strange.

Cate fell into my arms and gave me a tight hug. I could feel her warmth through our thin nightgowns, and I flinched. The sweet stabs of pain below my stomach doubled. I tried to put the dream in the back of my mind. "Will you sleep next to me?" I asked, threading my fingers with Cate's. "Both of us seem to be upset." Having a solid, warm body next to mine would be a trial, but I could feel Cate shaking against me, and I knew that she could use the comfort.

"All right." Both of us settled next to each other and soon Cate slipped into an easy slumber, her breathing even and slow. Sharing her fears with me had calmed her down, but my muscles were stretched tight enough to bring tears.

Why did it have to be Belle? I thought. *Why not Cate, who is right next to me?* But as beautiful as Cate was, I did not burn for her. No one could replace Belle in my thoughts. When I closed my eyes and started to fade, I forgot it was Cate pressed against me and dreamed I was with Belle.

***

Talking with Sarah was probably unwise, but I needed to know how Belladonna felt about her. Worry bled my heart dry, and I had to talk to someone before I shriveled away. Belladonna had not mentioned taking lovers in her diary except in the briefest way, and I hoped that she had no real love for them. Still, I had to be sure.

The next evening, while we were polishing the great banister along the main staircase, I spoke with her. Softly but eagerly, I asked her, resting fingertips on her arm just beneath the sleeve. Her hand stilled, holding the rag she was using to make the wood shine. "Do you love each other, Sarah?" I did not need to name her. The words would not be swallowed back.

"So you know. It might be hard for you to understand, but no. I suppose you want to believe we're going to live happily ever after." Oh, how she had misread me. She would have been shocked to know what dear, sweet Ellic really thought of her answer. "All I want is someone kind. I know my real lover is somewhere waiting for me, but Belladonna keeps me satisfied for now."

Bands of tense muscle loosened along my shoulders. Instantly, a heavy weight was lifted. "She doesn't...You don't..." My voice cracked. I dared to hope, but I clung to Sarah's wrist, hardly feeling her skin against my palm.

"Belladonna's heart belongs to someone else. We have an understanding." She smiled, but grief tightened her eyes. "I don't want to be Cate, flinching like a kicked dog at the thought of a kiss. When I find love, I want to be open to it. Belle helps remind me that there is still kindness and decency in the world until then."

"I think I understand," I said, but my head was filled with other words. Sarah had told me that Belladonna's heart belonged to someone else. That someone was me. I knew it. The last of my heart's doubts disappeared.

Sarah looked surprised. "You do?"

"Yes, I do." My smile filled out my face. Any jealousy I might have felt was drowned in love. Belle loved me. Any relationship she might have had with Sarah seemed trivial.

"I always thought you had the kind of heart that felt too much," Sarah said, almost to herself. "I admire that in you." Our hands touched, our friendship solidified.

"Cate was having nightmares last night." I turned the conversation, our intimate connection broken but not forgotten. "I had to hold her until she fell asleep. She was shaking."

Sarah's shoulders dropped as she let out a heavy breath of air. Her hands were clutched tightly in her skirts. "I've seen it, too. She's not sleeping, not eating...By the way, Ellie, you've lost weight." She fussed for a moment, brushing hair from my forehead. I smiled and shut my eyes, thinking of my sickness. Even seeing her in my imagination sent lines of gooseflesh rising along my arms.

"Just distracted from worrying about Cate."

"I've asked Mam about giving her some sleep medicine. I thought it might help with the nightmares."

"Good idea. Maybe I could take her outside to see the horses tomorrow. She is so pale..."

"You would be, too, if you weren't so freckle faced," Sarah teased me. "I think you're just as sick as she is. You aren't in love, are you?"

I knew it was a joke, but I felt my cheeks flare. I willed my face to cool and gave her a weak smile, taking the forgotten rag from Sarah's limp hand and starting to polish. "I wish that was why I seem distracted. I would much rather be in love than afraid of Luciana and worried about Cate." The lie worked, perhaps because there was a kernel of truth in it, and Sarah and I talked of other things until we finished our work.

Part Two,

As Recorded By Eleanor Baxstresse

CHAPTER 1

AS AUTUMN PASSED, my days and nights were haunted by thoughts of Belladonna. In the mornings, preparing breakfast, I imagined how soft her hands would feel against my skin. I stared into empty space, picturing her eyes while the others helped Loren, the crooked-toothed old washerwoman, with her piles of clothes. On my way to visit Brahms in the stables, my skin burned hot even in the cool evening breeze.

Thankfully, I did not have to wait on either of the Kingsclere sisters. Helping Belladonna with her clothes probably would have made my body erupt in flames. I imagined Sarah helping Belladonna out of her nightgown, tying the laces of her corset, seeing her unclothed. Those thoughts drove me wild, and I did my best to bury them. Belladonna's diary said that she was in love with me, and I took comfort in those words.

I was constantly distracted, consumed by dreams I had not considered myself capable of having. At night, after everyone else had fallen asleep, I went to the library to read passages from Belladonna's diary. It was the best part of my day. No amount of work could put thoughts of Belladonna aside.

There were other bright spots in my life as well. I was beginning to get used to hard labor, and sometimes I even took pride in my work.

When I first made a soup on my own, when I cleaned an entire bedroom without supervision and Jamison could find nothing wrong with it, and when I learned how to mend my own clothes, I was filled with a sense of accomplishment I would have believed impossible only a few months ago.

For the first time, I had true friends. Growing up, I had been rich, but not titled. I was isolated from other noble children at Sandleford, and the servants' children never really accepted me as one of them. Cate, Sarah, and I had become closer than sisters, although Luciana and Belladonna were horrible examples of sisterhood, as Sarah often reminded us. Mam stepped into the role of mother and guardian, protecting us from Luciana whenever she could, doing little things to make life more pleasant.

Jessith was also an invaluable friend, checking hallways and rooms to make sure that Luciana and Jamison were not hiding nearby. Sometimes she joined Cate, Sarah, and I while we worked, and her sarcastic commentary made me laugh at the most embarrassing moments. Luckily, Cate and Sarah took it in stride, only pestering me about my strange habits once in a while.

Despite these joys in my new life, Luciana hovered over us like a distant storm about to break, seeking me out to play her nasty tricks and hurting Cate. She directed her cruelty toward me less frequently—she usually limited her games to once a week—but she was no less devious. One morning, she came in to the kitchen while I was preparing breakfast, holding something wooden in her hand. When she came closer, I realized it was a pair of shoes.

I did not speak as she approached. Talking would only make my punishment worse. She was toying with that pendant again, the three-circled one of silver and gold. It winked at me as she spun it on its chain. Smiling snakishly, she stared down at my feet, holding the skirt of her morning dress above the kitchen floor with her free hand. "Well, your shoes look nearly worn through," she said sweetly, gesturing toward my feet. It was true. The brown working shoes I had on were almost ready to fall apart. I needed to ask for new ones in a few days. I studied the wooden shoes. Surely, Luciana did not expect me to...

I glanced over my shoulder, hoping Mam was somewhere nearby, but she was in the hallway, carrying the first of the trays up to the breakfast room. Luciana had cornered me alone. "I was kind enough to have some new ones made for you. Here." She dropped the wooden shoes onto the floor in front of me with a loud crack. One turned onto its side, a light, sand-colored patch against the dark stone floor. "Put them on."

The shoes were poorly made, and far too large for my small feet. The grain was rough on the soles, with several splinters sticking out, and I knew they would be high enough to make me trip and twist my ankles. They were completely impractical for walking in, let alone working, but I had no choice. Swearing I would find some way to get even with Luciana, I kicked off my old shoes and stepped gingerly into the new pair. I felt a piece of wood slice into the sole of my foot and tried not to look uncomfortable. Signs of weakness only encouraged her.

"You know," she said, reaching out to stroke my cheek, "good girls are supposed to say thank you for a gift."

Her touch made my skin burn, and I jerked my face away. "Thank you," I said, trying to kill her with my eyes.

She checked in on me throughout the day. When she was not there, Jamison was always lurking nearby to make sure that I kept the shoes on. The birds that had picked lentils out of the fireplace for me could not help me bear this punishment. My poor feet were swollen, blistered, and bleeding by the time I retired for the evening. Mam, Sarah, and Cate stayed up late to pick the splinters from my feet and bandage them properly.

"Heavens," Cate said as she tugged out a particularly long sliver of wood, "this is about the size of a spear. How did Luciana get these, anyway?" She had become much more talkative lately and I was pleased with her progress. Standing up to Jamison had strengthened her spirit more than I had hoped.

"She probably had someone in the stables cobble them together." Sarah was digging in Mam's healing basket for fresh bandages while Mam heated water over the stove. "There's plenty of unsanded wood in there."

Even Rucifee, who was eating a late midnight snack, decided to be sympathetic, and he padded over to butt his head against my hand. I smiled and scratched under his chin. "Your feet are swollen to the size of bread plates." His long ginger tail lashed as he looked at them. "You know, I'm sure I could arrange to leave a dead present on Luciana's bed if you wanted me to."

I bit my lip to stop myself from laughing. Fortunately, Cate chose that moment to remove another splinter and she assumed that I was whimpering with pain. "I'm sorry, but these have to come out. That's the last one on this foot." She gave my wrist a friendly squeeze and lifted my other foot into her hand.

"Thank you."

Cate smiled. "You're welcome." She stood up to help Mam carry over the metal basin of water. When she was out of earshot, I looked down at

Rucifee, who was still lying next to my knee. "How is Lady Kingsclere?" I asked him. I had not gone to visit my stepmother, afraid that Luciana would catch me, but I worried about her. Rucifee spent most of his time in her rooms. He was very attached to her, as sick as she was.

"Not well. She drifts in and out of memories, mostly, calling for Alastair or one of her daughters. Some days are better than others."

"Here, soak your feet in this," Sarah interrupted as she and Cate set the basin in front of my three legged stool.

Cautiously, I submerged my toes in the water, hissing as the heat crawled over my open cuts. "Did you have to make it so hot?"

"It has already been cooling for a quarter of an hour. Heat first, then ice for the swelling," Mam clucked, reaching for the lye soap that she kept next to the sink. I shuddered, knowing it would sting dreadfully against the bottoms of my feet. Luciana did not bother with the shoes the next day, knowing that my feet would be wrapped, but as soon as the bandages came off, she made me wear them again, repeating the process every time my feet began to heal.

***

One morning, about two weeks later, I woke with my heart crashing against my ribs. My skin was flooded with heat, and my dreams had been filled with Belladonna. Her voice, her touch, her lips. Cate slept beside me, dead to the world. I hoped that her dreams were less torturous than mine. The small room we shared felt warm and cramped, and so I decided to go outside and visit my mother's tree. Quietly, I moved through the still hallways and out into the fields.

The grass was wet and cold beneath my bare feet, which had started to scar from Luciana's wooden shoes. For now, at least, they did not hurt. The sky was still dark and the sun had not broken the blue line of the horizon. It was strangely quiet without the shouts of the workers and the chatter of summer birds and insects. I felt like the only person in existence.

As I sat by my mother's tree, my mind turned to Belladonna's diary and a problem that I had been working on for days. Belladonna had already written several marriage poems for me in her journal, although most of them had been scratched out. I wanted to think of one for her. Villagers rarely bothered with marriage poems, but they were required for any proper aristocratic engagement. Marriage poems were incredibly complex, filled with symbolism and allusions, and Belladonna's were far more sophisticated than anything I had read before.

She used swans often—lasting commitment—and coupled it with water, which I did not remember the meaning for. I suspected that grass had something to do with new life, but I was not sure. The number nine was also fashionable and dealt with the metaphysical. Since I did not understand half of what she had written, although her words were beautifully phrased, I had no idea how to write one of my own. I did not want to copy what she had written for me, I wanted to show her my own ideas. Maybe a poem would impress her. Of course, even if I did write a poem for Belladonna, I would probably be too afraid to show her.

A plump mourning dove settled in the tree's branches, shaking his wings free of dew and bobbing his head to look for predators. "Maybe I should ask him for a poem," I whispered sarcastically. Of course, that was exactly what I needed—bad verse from a bird.

"Ask who for a poem?"

I looked up, startled to see Cate's silhouette approaching, backlit by the morning sun. I squinted my eyes and raised a hand to my face. "Oh, just the bird."

"You think she could give you a poem?" Cate lowered herself to her knees and I turned to one side so I could see her face without staring directly into the sun.

"The bird is a he," I corrected automatically.

Cate raised her eyebrows. "Really? How can you tell?"

"I...er...I mean...It just looks like a he, I guess."

"Fine, the dove can be a he if you want him to be."

I was grateful that birds did not grasp human language, unless I was the one speaking to them. The mourning dove seemed to have no idea we were talking about him. Only more intelligent animals, domestic cats like Jessith and horses like Brahms, could understand human conversations on deeper levels without help from an Ariada. Since Jessith was a spoiled cat with too much time on her hands, I wondered if she knew more than one human language. Belladonna probably spoke several.

"Ellie. Ellie, where did you go?"

I blinked. "Oh, sorry. I..."

"Ah, your mystery lover." Cate gave me a small smile. My blush gave me away immediately. "Is she who you want that poem for?"

"She? Why would you think it's a she?" Cate had referred to my secret love as "she" once before, when she had thrown my hazelnut into the fireplace, but Sarah had assured me that Cate rarely remembered her strange visions, or the events leading up to them.

Cate shrugged and brushed aside her hair. "How do you know that the dove is a he?"

"Do you know what doves mean in a marriage poem? I've seen them in a few, but have no clue what they represent."

"Something about innocence, maybe."

"I thought it might represent death or the soul."

"The death of innocence." Cate could not hide the shadow that crossed her face. She picked a blade of grass between her thumb and forefinger, ripping it into tiny pieces and letting them flutter back to the earth.

"Well, at least our dove is very much alive," I said cheerfully. I felt foolish, but knew that the best way to keep Cate from brooding was to keep talking. "You aren't going to start bothering me, too, are you? Sarah does more than enough pestering by herself."

"Sarah pesters everyone." Somehow, that simple statement had both of us laughing ourselves to tears. Cate's head fell back, her laughter floating up into the blinding morning sky. The dove, deciding we were too noisy, opened his wings and left the tree. This moment was all the proof I needed that Cate was starting to rebuild. For the first time in a long time, she seemed happy. My stomach ached from laughing along with her.

CHAPTER 2

AS CAREFUL AS I tried to be when I stole my stepsister's diary, I knew that Belle would discover what I had been doing eventually. I imagined it often—the angry, hurt expression she would have as she came toward me with her high shoulders—but I had no idea what she would say.

One night, after the harvest started, I decided to read by the fireplace. Trugel rested at my feet and the fire kept the autumn chill to the corners of the room. As I reached to turn the page, the library doors crashed apart and I nearly dropped my book on poor Trugel's head. Both of us started, looking up. Belladonna stood there, motionless, a storm of dark curls tossed about her shoulders.

Her eyes were glassy, frosted marbles of blue, strangely empty. She reached forward helplessly, not seeing me, but the diary spread open on my lap. She took in a sharp breath and stepped back. Her lips parted, but she could not speak. Carefully, I stood and walked toward her, clutching the diary to my chest. Before I could form words to explain, Belladonna pulled it from my hands.

"Belle..." My voice broke as I reached for the diary, but she was a head taller than I was, and she lifted it out of reach. I followed her as she went to the fireplace, reaching up as she held it over the darting tongues of flame. "Please, don't burn it."

Her face was white marble as she lowered the pages to the fire. "Give me one reason to keep something that could ruin me."

"Because the thoughts in it are too beautiful to destroy."

Belladonna pulled the diary back, surprised. Whatever answer she had been expecting, it was not the one I had given her. Light caught her hair, pulling half of her face back into warm brown shadows. An idea struck me, and none of the warning voices in my head could dislodge it. Trembling, I lowered myself to my knees, lifting my chin to look into her eyes. I took her hand in mine and she let me hold it. "Forgive me." She said nothing. "Please, my love."

"My love?" she asked me. Then, softly, to herself, "Love..." She was remembering, I knew, just how many entries she had written about loving me, how many nights she had spent thinking of us together.

"If you will have me."

My lips shook as I pressed them to the center of her palm, asking my bold question in the proper way. She looked down at me, shocked by what I had done. I knew she could not truly marry me, but I would ask her just the same, the way our ancestors had done for centuries. I trusted this hand to protect me, guide me, comfort me, work alongside me, and love me.

She trembled above me, letting me kiss each of her fingertips, each knuckle. I had only meant to kiss her palm as I was supposed to, but now that I had tasted the skin of her hand, I could not stop. A burst of red heat covered my cheeks. She looked at me, amazed, gently pulling her hand away from my lips. At first, I was sure she was rejecting me, and I cursed myself for being so foolish. How could I have expected her to forgive me for reading her private thoughts? But then she took my hand in hers and pulled me back to my feet.

In one graceful, fluid motion, Belladonna hooked an arm around my waist and drew me to her, pressing her lips over mine. It was a burning kiss that rolled over my skin like warm water, dulling and heightening my senses at the same time. I cried out softly against her mouth, closing my eyes and losing myself in the smoothness of her lips. Belle's kiss was the perfect mix of soft and hard. There was a sense of power behind it that left me with no doubt that I belonged to her, but there was tenderness and consideration as well.

I broke away from her, panting lightly, my eyes unfocused. "You accept me?" I asked her, suddenly shy.

"Of course. I have loved and wanted you ever since I talked with you by your hazel tree...maybe since I first saw you at mother's wedding." Her bright smile made my head spin with joy. "This is happening so fast...You were an untouchable dream for me until a few moments ago and now..."

"It hasn't happened fast," I argued. "We waited for months and months, only we were both too frightened to admit it. I have been stealing your diary and dreaming about you for ages."

She leaned in and kissed me again. Gently, her tongue teased my lips apart, the unhurried firmness of her request sending a shiver through my body. I parted my lips for her, and she wasted no time caressing the inside of my mouth. She took the time to explore me thoroughly, cupping one hand at the small of my back and pulling me tight against her warm, lean body as she moved her mouth against mine. Timidly, I captured the tip of her tongue between my lips and sucked, hoping to return to her some of the feelings that she was giving me. This soft, teasing acceptance seemed to drive her wild with desire, and she shoved me backwards against a chair.

"No, Belle..." I said, breaking our kiss and glancing over my shoulder at the closed double doors.

"Why not?" she asked hazily, trying to kiss me again. "Ellie, I'll wait as long as you want if you are afraid of this, but now that I know how you feel..."

"It's not that. Someone could come in." I glanced guiltily at Trugel, who had covered her head with her paws and turned her face away.

Belle jerked away from me like a hand from a warm stovetop, jumping back several feet and stumbling over herself. "Curse me for an idiot." She fixed her wrinkled skirts where my hands had been gripping them. "We have to be more careful."

"Enough talking." I fixed my dress and nearly ran toward the double doors. "Your room has a bolt?"

The heat in Belladonna's dark eyes pulsed to life again as she hurried after me. I showed her the fastest way through the servant's corridors, not worrying about the noise that our feet made.

We stumbled into Belladonna's room, the brushing of our bodies making my heart drum harder. She slammed the bolt across her bedroom door, and it fell into place with a heavy thud. I hardly noticed the large, canopied bed that she backed me toward as she stripped off her outer dress. I fell on the bed willingly, welcoming her weight on top of me. She kissed across the planes of my face, and I leaned against the headboard, hardly managing to whimper. Belladonna sank her teeth into my shoulder, holding me steady as I hissed and arched off of the bed. "Mine..." she cooed, kissing and licking the place she had marked.

I buried my face in her hair. "Yes. Yours..."

"I need to feel you, Ellie, please. Undress me."

My fingers fumbled over the laces of her corset and she had to direct my trembling hands to the right places before I could loosen them.

At last, the ties gave and her torso swelled with air. She tore the corset away and threw it aside, revealing high, firm breasts and the bare expanse of her back. I slid my fingertips over the slick flesh, exploring the red patches where the corset had rubbed against her. She looked much more stunning without it.

"Touch me." Belladonna leaned into my arms. "My body is yours to explore."

I gave her my sweetest smile. Even though Belle's earlier displays of ownership had been exciting, I was relieved to know that she belonged to me just as much as I belonged to her. However, I wanted to be reminded of the longing, possessive entries from her diary that had excited me.

It was easy to draw out the part of Belle that I wanted. "I...I don't know how," I stammered, letting all of my embarrassment and inexperience show in my face. I saw her eyes widen and darken, and I knew I had her. My innocence attracted her.

"Would you like me to show you?" she breathed beside my ear as she tugged herself out of her underskirts. I nodded and Belladonna touched her hands to my flushed cheeks, cradling my face. She was completely naked against me as she started to lift my dress. "I was going to let you set the pace, since this is new to you. Oh, Ellie...I'm so honored that you chose me for this..."

"I read your diary," I reminded her as her warm mouth slid over my neck. Reluctantly, I pulled myself out of Belladonna's embrace and stood in front of her on the cold stone floor. Gripping the hem of my dress with shaking hands, I pulled it up and over my head, letting it fall to the floor beside me. I stood before her while she watched from the bed, naked and trembling, my body and soul bared. Part of me realized that making love to Belle would always have this element of power in it, even after we had repeated it a thousand times.

I lowered my chin and held out my hands to her. "Take me. I could never give myself to anyone else."

The last of the doubts weighing on Belladonna's conscience fell away, and I saw something dangerous rise in her. She pulled me to join her on the bed, biting my chin before she caught my mouth in a bruising kiss. Lips still joined, she pinned my wrists above my head as our bodies touched for the first time. Feeling her stretched on top of me, skin to skin, made my chest ache with sweetness.

"Hmm, what am I going to do with you, pet?" she asked as I panted against her neck. A warm hand crept up my stomach, gently cupping one of my naked breasts. I gasped, shaking, trying to push myself into her palm. My fingers found themselves woven into her hair as she kissed down my neck, tasting an offered shoulder. My eyes closed as she took the rigid peak of my breast into her hot mouth, both of us sighing as one with pleasure. I was too overwhelmed with new feelings to be afraid.

Wanting her to feel this with me, I reached a shy hand between our bodies, feeling the smoothness of a hip, the point of a hipbone. My fingers wandered around her waist, moving lower and squeezing the swell of her backside with both hands. She groaned around the bud she was worrying with her tongue, looking up at me with dazed blue eyes. Releasing her lips with a slight pop, she stroked my cheek with her fingers, pressing the tips to my mouth. I bit at them gently and she smiled.

"I'm sorry. Your touch makes me impatient," I explained, smiling back.

"I imagine it might. But you will only get what you want when I say so. Is that clear?" Sparks shot through my belly, and I nodded my head. Her control was firmly established as she reached a hand between my legs and caressed my inner thigh, not moving upwards even when I pleaded with her. I tossed my head against a pillow as she took my breast back into her mouth, her hands charting my legs and hips, but refusing to explore further.

I was almost in tears when she finally moved her hand up, cupping me and squeezing possessively. A flood of wetness greeted her touch. I blushed and Belle kissed my warm cheeks. "Oh, Ellie...You fit inside my hand perfectly." Her fingertips pressed between my lips, and her bright eyes glistened with tears. "I'm so in love with you..." she said helplessly, kissing a purple mark she had left on my neck. "Knowing I'm the first to touch you is making my heart burst."

I slid the palm of my hand down her slick back, rubbing soothing circles over her warm skin. "You'll be the only one to touch me."

Belladonna caught my chin with her lips, sliding her mouth up to meet mine in our gentlest kiss yet. "You're ready?" she whispered into my mouth.

"I'm not afraid." And now that I was used to feeling her body against mine, I wasn't. I trusted Belladonna with all my heart and trusting her with my body came easily.

At last, she let the tips of her fingers press against my entrance, and her thumb grazed over a spot that made my hips jerk upwards. "Oh," I gasped, surprised by my body's sudden response. "More...I want more of you, Belle. Please..." I opened my eyes and leaned up to kiss her tight forehead. The look of amazement and love on her face put all thoughts of pain out of my mind as she slipped a second finger into place and pushed forward, filling me with a slow, burning stretch. We held still, savoring our joining.

My body offered no resistance as she moved inside of me, curling her fingers. The place where she had touched me before, the star of heat, began to swell and ache. I reached down to try and redirect her, because the feeling was almost too intense to bear, but she used her free arm to lift my hands back above my head. I remained stretched out before her, helpless.

"Oh, Ellie, you're so soft and warm...feeling you is driving me mad." She kissed me again, and I was lost in her lips.

Although I had no idea what I was doing, my body responded instinctively. I rocked against her hand, trying to take her deeper. I did not care how shameless my behavior appeared. My inner muscles clasped greedily around her fingers, pulling tight around them as I gasped for breath.

My responses only seemed to encourage her. After a few testing strokes, Belladonna found a place against my front wall that threatened to unravel me completely. She hooked her fingers against it, dragging a sharp cry from my throat. The pad of her thumb continued circling just above, grinding down firmly against me, and I feared that I might shake apart. I had never known that anything could feel this blissful.

Suddenly, Belladonna removed her hand and shifted her weight. Before I could gather my thoughts and tell her not to stop, I felt lips skim down along the plane of my stomach. A wonderful, white-hot burn folded over the place where her thumb had been moments before, and my throat ached as I let out another scream. Forcing my eyes open, I looked down and realized that it was Belladonna's mouth. Her lips were folded around me, drawing me in as her fingers continued moving inside of me. "I...Belle!"

She looked up and we locked eyes. I could not look away. The picture we made, her tongue scraping against me, my pink folds petaled around her fingers, her dark hair running down her back like wet ink, shattered me. I felt as though I was swelling out of my skin. Tears squeezed from the corners of my eyes as I shuddered and released all of myself to my lover.

Belladonna's voice was somewhere nearby, comforting me with nonsense words as I drifted back to her. "Shh, that's it. I have you, my heart, I have you." She was holding me in her arms, pressing kisses to every inch of skin she could reach. The place where her mouth had been shook and trembled with the memory of what I had experienced. "Are you all right, Ellie? Do you need to rest?"

I shook my head, pushing away strands of wet hair plastered to my neck and cheeks. "Only for a moment. Then, you are going to teach me how to do that to you."

Belladonna smiled. "Anything you wish, my Ellie."

CHAPTER 3

I WOKE WITH Belladonna's arm curved around my hip, her warm breath playing over the soft layer of skin behind my ear. Her breasts were pressed into my back, just above my shoulder blades, and for a moment, I felt the most profound peace I had ever experienced. Then, the fear came. It rushed in as soon as the stone wall of Belladonna's bedroom came into focus, tugging wretchedly at my insides. What if Belle left me now that I had given her what she wanted? What if she decided that I was a horrible lover and did not want to bother with me anymore? What if the diary was some sort of elaborate seduction?

The thought of rejection frightened me. I needed the dizzying possessiveness and control of her kisses, the warmth of her hands against my skin, and the wonderful, stretched fullness of her inside of me. Now that I knew what it was like to love another woman, I was not sure I could live without it, without Belladonna. No one else would satisfy me. But what would happen now? Would she continue her rendezvous with Sarah and the others after we had admitted our feelings to each other?

Belle stirred beside me, angling herself on her elbow and lifting her body to face me. I turned in her arms. Her fingers trailed along the small of my back, unwilling to lose contact with my skin. She looked at me, her sleep-swept hair sticking to one cheek. She must have seen the fear and doubt in my expression.

"Do you regret what happened?" The words fell heavily from her lips.

"No," I said, my voice cracking with sleep. "I was worried that you would have regrets."

"Of course not." She lowered her body back onto the mattress and pressed her forehead against mine. She gently fingered the small bruise that ran down the column of my throat, circling a purple bite on my collarbone. Even the memory of the marks she had left, breaking the fresh landscape of skin, sent shivers of lust along the ridge of my spine.

Belladonna felt me tremble and held me tight against her chest. "Oh, darling..." She wrapped her fingers around my naked wrist, gripping it gently. "I'm so sorry. Are you in any pain? What about here?" Her hand moved from my throat to cradle me between my legs, trying to heal anything she might have torn with her soft fingers.

"No, I'm not hurting. I feel...stretched. And the rest of me feels wonderful, even where you marked me."

Belladonna's eyes widened, and her breath hitched in her chest. There was a faint flicker of hope, and perhaps desire, buried deep in her irises. "I didn't hurt you too badly? I didn't..."

I pressed the pad of my thumb against her cheekbone. "No."

"I've never taken a lover like that before," Belladonna admitted haltingly. "I wanted to, but I was afraid of becoming just like her. She likes to leave bruises and bites all over the skin of her toys. With you, though, it felt so right..."

I covered Belladonna's words with kisses, trying to show her that I was fine. "You weren't like Luciana at all. You didn't hurt me, Belle. I like it when you mark me." I closed my eyes, breathing in deeply through my nose. "Will I be your only lover now?" I blurted out, unable to swallow the question any longer.

Belle's bottom lip dropped, her mouth hanging open awkwardly. She looked shocked. "Why on earth would I take another lover? I thought I made that clear last night." Rolling on top of me, she captured my lips in a slow, deep kiss that had my heart drumming inside my chest. "We might not be able to have a large, extravagant wedding or share our marriage with the world, but when you kissed my palm, you asked me to be your wife, and I accepted. It was a little sudden, but I consider that oath binding."

At those words, I was sure my heart would explode through my ribs. It was lucky I was already lying down, because if I had been standing, I might have fallen over. I was dizzy, happy, immensely relieved. I rolled on top of Belladonna and gave her the most passionate kiss I could, wanting to share my joy with her. Her lips met mine eagerly, and we kissed for several long moments.

Belladonna smiled, her mouth still breaths away from mine. "Well, I'll certainly do my best to keep you happy if kisses like that are going to be my reward."

Briefly, I thought about Cate, Sarah, and Mam. If they hadn't noticed my absence last night, they would surely be missing me by now. But suddenly, the rounds of questioning I would have to endure when I went back to the servants' quarters seemed unimportant. The only important thing was this woman with me, my new lover, my whole world. I gave Belle another kiss, softer this time, just a brushing of lips.

"Can we—"

"Make love again?" Belladonna finished my question for me. Her next kiss served as her answer.

***

They all noticed the marks that littered my neck and shoulders, of course. I saw Sarah first and she spent most of the morning teasing me about my rendezvous. "So, our innocent Ellie isn't quite so innocent anymore," she said loudly as we straightened the library. Of course, we would be cleaning the library after the kisses I had shared with Belle there the night before. I was more than a little distracted by the fresh memories and very embarrassed.

"Sarah, lower your voice," I pleaded, dropping a book that I had been trying to put back. Sarah watched me as I bent to pick it up. I gave her a sharp look over my shoulder as I grabbed the book's spine and returned it to its proper place.

She rolled her brown eyes to the ceiling. "Oh, stop jumping around like a frightened cat."

Jessith, who was curled up on one of the armchairs by the fire, opened one slitted eye and yawned. "I take offense to that remark. Humans are so dense sometimes. I can't believe she doesn't know you were with Belladonna. I can smell her all over you." Even Trugel, who had risen from her nap when Cate, Sarah, Jessith, and I had entered her domain, blinked in agreement. I scowled at both of them.

My cheeks flared, but luckily, my conversation with Sarah was embarrassing enough to warrant a blush. "What are these, then?" she asked, prodding at a bite mark along my collarbone. I didn't answer her, pulling away from her finger and reaching for another book. She grabbed it from my hands, holding it against her chest. "So, you're not going to kiss and tell?"

"No, I'm not." I tried to take the book back, but Sarah held it above her head, keeping her arm locked straight. That is one of the annoyances of being small – people are forever holding things too high up for you to reach. Having played this miserable game many times as a child, I knew that I could not win and picked up a third book. Sarah immediately dropped the one she had been holding, and I picked it up, too, reshelving them both.

"Oh, Ellie, don't be angry with me."

"It's too late, I already am. You're supposed to be helping instead of badgering me about who I might or might not have seen last night."

"I'm just curious. After all, you've always been so modest before. One mention of love and you turn bright red. Now you go missing for a night and show up with bite marks all over you. Not to mention you're walking about a foot off the ground and you haven't stopped smiling all morning until I started pestering you."

Although I was more than a little embarrassed, I wasn't really angry with Sarah. I had hoped that snapping at her would put her off, but she was determined. I had stayed in bed with Belladonna for a few extra minutes after we had explored each other's bodies that morning, unwilling to leave her. We had discussed what I would and wouldn't tell my friends when they asked questions. Since Sarah wasn't going to leave me alone until I told her something, I decided to take a different approach.

"I have to be very careful, Sarah," I said, looking over my shoulder to make sure that we were alone. "I'll admit that I'm...meeting with someone. But I really can't talk about it, and neither can you. Luciana can't touch me because of the bet she made, but she could hurt my lover."

"Perhaps we need to get you a pregnancy charm from the village," Sarah teased, completely missing the importance of what I had just said. I was slightly amused by the fact that Sarah, who I knew had taken at least one female lover to her bed, assumed I was seeing a man. I did not correct her. Revealing that a woman had stolen my heart might have given me away, and many Serians, especially the aristocracy, frowned upon choosing a lover of your own sex.

"I don't need a pregnancy charm," I told her, settling for a half truth.

"Oh, don't you? Haven't let him have his way yet completely, I suppose. A wise choice. Wait until there's a bracelet on your wrist before you give him what he wants."

This time, I was the one who rolled my eyes up to the ceiling, adding a sigh to the gesture. "Sarah! This is incredibly serious. We can't talk about it at all. Luciana would find a way of getting the information and using it. It's not that I don't trust you, but you never know who might be listening in the hallways or what she might do to you to get answers to her questions."

I saw a hint of concern in Sarah's face, and I knew she would accept my excuse. Imagining what Luciana would do to her if she wanted information seemed to dampen her curiosity. I could tell she was disappointed that I had not shared my secret with her, though, so I decided to toss her something and ease her appetite for gossip. "I can't give you details, but—since we're alone—I will say that I had a wonderful time."

Sarah seemed satisfied with that information, and we were able to clean the library without any further problems. She did try and catch my eye more often than usual, though.

***

Cate was much easier to deal with than Sarah. She was much more talkative than she had been a few months before, but she was still shy and not as hungry for secrets. She saw the marks while we were clearing the plates from the dining room after lunch, but was not quite brave enough to approach me about them. I noticed her glancing at my arms, checking for bruises and wondering if Luciana had finally decided to break her promise to Belle.

I felt sorry for her. Unlike Sarah, who had immediately assumed that the marks on my body were the signs of a new lover, Cate was all too aware of another explanation for them. Her fears made perfect sense, considering what she had endured. When she nearly dropped a plate as I passed her on the stairs, I decided to speak to her.

"Everything's fine, Cate, no one hurt me," I said once we had set our loaded trays next to the sink in the kitchen.

Cate's relief was visible in her entire body, which nearly collapsed as all the tightness left it. "Thank the Saints," she said, wrapping me in a soft hug. I felt her tremble and I was surprised to see just how worried she had been. "I don't know what I would have done, if she...if you..." Her face was buried against my shoulder and her words were muffled.

"No, I'm fine. Luciana did not touch me."

With her worries and fears released, I sensed Cate's brain searching for the next likely explanation. "So, you...with someone else?" She looked at me with flushed cheeks and such an embarrassed expression on her face that I was reminded of how I must have looked earlier in the library. Cate was certainly a contrast from Sarah.

"Well...yes."

Of course, the next obvious question was, "Who?"

"I can't tell you," I explained. "Luciana might hurt you."

"You don't trust me?" The muscles around Cate's eyes pulled tight. "I'm used to pain from Luciana. I would never betray you."

"Of course I trust you!" I said, pulling away and looking her straight in the eye. "I trust you more than anyone, Cate. You're my best friend here. I just don't want to give her any reason to hurt you more than she already does. You shouldn't have to bear any pain on my account."

"I'm truly your best friend?" Cate asked softly.

"Yes, you are."

"You're my best friend, too, Ellie. I'm glad Luciana isn't..." Her voice trailed off. This time, I was the one who trembled at the thought of what my first experience might have been like at Luciana's mercy. The idea still made me violently sick, but I had hardened myself to it.

"I'm glad, too." Cate smiled, pulling away from my arms and picking up a stack of plates from the table. I followed her toward the servant's entrance and down the stairs with another stack, careful not to trip as we went down. Someday, I thought, I would make sure Cate found someone to show her the wonderful things I had learned and erase her memories of Luciana.

***

"We need to find a way to stop Luciana from tormenting you, Ellie," Belle said that night as we rested on her large, canopied bed. Cate was fast asleep in the room we shared and Sarah had not said anything as I passed through the kitchen, only watching me from her place by the fire with a knowing smile. Thankfully, the darkness hid my blush as I exited through the far door.

When I slipped into Belladonna's rooms, I had found her waiting for me without any clothes. After staring at her with a mixture of shock and desire for several long moments, I took off my own dress and joined her on the bed, hoping that we would repeat the wonderful things we had shared the night before and earlier that morning. But it seemed Belle wanted to talk instead.

"You've already done that," I said distractedly. I was far more interested in the way that Belle's dark hair spilled over her white shoulders, the ends just brushing the tips of her breasts. "You made that bet."

Belle ignored my eyes on her body, unwilling to leave the conversation. "No, I haven't." Her fingers stroked the underside of my arm. My skin seared under her touch, and I tried to turn closer to her. "Luciana still makes you wear those horrible wooden shoes, and she gives you the hardest tasks to do...Whoever heard of picking out ten yards of embroidery in one night? I have no idea how you did it."

I rested my head on Belle's shoulder and dropping open-mouthed kisses on her exposed neck. "I had help."

"We have to talk about this," Belle said, moving out of my arms.

I had been watching Belle's red mouth move in a daze, when a dim question at the back of my mind grew brighter. "Speaking of the bet, what did Luciana mean when she said, 'I'll wager the necklace on it'? The day she tried to throw me out the window, I mean."

The slow burn of desire on Belle's handsome face cooled for a moment. Instead, I saw something shifting there, and it was almost frightening. "My mother used to have a necklace. She never wore it, but she told me that her grandmother—my great grandmother—had given it to her. She used to say it gave her an odd feeling."

"Why does Luciana have it?"

Belladonna's face sharpened with anger. "She stole it. She tried to play with it as a child once. Mother wouldn't let her have it. She must have gone through the jewelry box and found it again, because I saw her wearing it one day. Later that night Mother mentioned it had been missing."

"She stole it?"

"Probably. It wouldn't have mattered. The three of us share jewelry sometimes. Except that she lied about it. When Mother asked if Luciana had seen it, she said no. I told her I had seen Luciana wearing it. Luciana denied it and said I had probably seen her with another necklace. We almost came to blows over it. In fact, it was the night you arrived here." Suddenly, Belladonna's anger dissolved, leaving her face clear and bright again. Her blue eyes were sad as she finished, "I suppose that's rather foolish. All that trouble over a silly necklace."

I shook my head against the bed sheets, making them rustle. "No, it's not foolish. What did the necklace look like?"

She thought for a moment. "It was a silver one, with a queer sort of pendant. A big golden circle, with a smaller silver one inside, and a golden dot inside that, like three different sized coins melted together."

"I've seen her wear it. She likes to spin it with one finger. But why do you want it back?"

"I wanted to show it to our mother, to prove that Luciana was lying. Luci knew it. She knew I would love a chance to catch her. Mother never believed me over her, even when we were children." Belle looked older, and at the same time, younger than her twenty years. There were serious lines in her face, but her eyes were soft.

"You give me the courage to confront Luciana again. I should have done something long ago, but if I tried anything, she took it out on Cate's flesh. She can see how much it hurts my conscience. And now, I'm afraid of risking you. She will hurt you, promise or not, if she thinks it will give her leverage over me."

"I love you. I'm not afraid."

"Go to sleep, Ellie," Belladonna whispered, pressing soft kisses into my hair. My last memory of that night was how wonderful it felt to fall asleep in her arms.

CHAPTER 4

I WOKE BEFORE Belle did the next morning, so used to rising early that even my new lover's warm body could not lull me to sleep. Belle shifted beside me in the comfortable bed, rolling onto her back and sighing deeply as her dark hair spread itself over the white pillows. She had tossed off her blankets sometime during the night, and her pale skin took on a little color in the sunlight that filtered through the bedroom windows. The sight of her body in the light captured me and I was seized by the desire to learn every inch of it.

I remembered vividly how Belle and I had made love two nights before, recalling how she had guided my small hand with her own, shuddering with release under our twined fingers. I had wanted to stay inside her forever, relishing the hot, velvet muscle wrapped around me, but she had turned her attention on me without pausing for breath, not giving me a chance to explore her body further before I was wrapped in my own world of pleasure for a second time.

Studying Belladonna's lovely form proved to be too much for me to bear. I decided to take a chance, reaching out to test the skin of Belle's stomach with light fingers. I waited breathlessly for her to move or open her eyes, but she did not stir. I let my hand creep upward, stopping just under her breast. My mouth spread in a smile as I felt the steady thump of her heartbeat against my palm.

The tips of Belladonna's breasts were a dusty reddish-brown color, and the skin around them looked baby soft. Boldly, I allowed myself to touch one, my eyes widening with excitement as the skin folded and crinkled, the tip extending and turning a deeper shade of red. Without conscious thought, my other hand began to explore the soft landscape of bare flesh open to me.

Shifting until I was hovering over her body, I spent precious moments learning my lover, tracing the line of a leg, teasing the peak of a breast to hardness, reaching under her to feel the strong muscles of her back. I remembered how wonderful it had felt when Belle used her mouth on my body, and I carefully lowered my head to her chest. She stirred slightly as I took her into my mouth, but did not wake up. I was curious to see how far I could go before Belle opened her eyes and, coming to a decision, I reached under what was left of the sheets, gently parting her legs. She made a soft noise in her throat, but her breathing stayed steady and deep.

I held still for a full minute, wanting to discover as much of my lover as I could while she was in such a vulnerable, unguarded state. My lips were still occupied with Belle's stunning upper body, dropping light kisses over her breasts and shoulders as my hand stroked her inner thigh. The muscles in Belle's face were pulled tight, but her eyes stayed shut. Turning her head on the pillow, she let out a low moan and settled back to sleep.

Deciding that feeling all of Belle was worth ending my game, I let my hand go higher, thrilled with the wetness that coated my fingers and proud that I was the cause of it. "So ready for me," I mumbled against her skin as I slipped inside of her, my thumb sliding into place over the hard pearl that rested above.

This time Belladonna moved, and her clear blue eyes captured me. "Ellie, what…" she started to ask, but I nipped at a sensitive spot along her collarbone, silencing her as my fingers probed and traced the slick folds between her legs.

"Shhh…Let me love you." The pad of my thumb flicked over the special spot that she had shown me how to touch. She gave in, going limp underneath me as I took her. I was so enthralled with what I was doing that I forgot to worry about my inexperience. Knowing that I could give my gorgeous Belle pleasure made my heart swell with love and pride.

Carrying my lover higher and higher and holding her as she fell was indescribably wonderful. My eyes stayed locked with hers as I felt her soft inner muscles tighten and flutter around my fingers. She did not cry out or scream as I had done, but I could feel the intensity of her release as though I had experienced it myself. Instead, her mouth fell open and she took in a sharp breath before letting her whole body relax back onto the mattress, her breasts heaving as she tried to take in more air.

"No one has ever made me feel like that, dear heart." She gasped between words, still catching her breath. I pressed a kiss over her open mouth, and her eyes closed in response, smiling into my lips.

"I just tried to copy what you showed me. I had no idea what I was doing," I said, moving my lips to her cheek and whispering the words into her ear.

"Your body knew. Nothing else has even come close to the pleasure you just gave me. I can't explain."

"I think I understand. Our hearts know each other."

Any insecurity I felt about the other women Belladonna had been with left me that morning. On the rare occasions that those feelings returned, all I needed to do was remember that moment, the first time I had really touched Belladonna, and they would vanish completely. The bond of trust and love between us was more powerful than any emotion I had felt before. Sharing our bodies only seemed to make it stronger.

***

Unfortunately, the rest of my day did not play out as wonderfully as my morning. Luciana decided that simply wearing the wooden shoes was not painful enough for me, and she came up with a way to make my work even more miserable.

She found me dusting in a hallway early that afternoon. I was wearing the wooden shoes, which she had taken to leaving next to my sleeping pallet if she expected me to put them on. She liked to check on me throughout the day to make sure I was wearing them, never coming in at regular intervals so that I could plan for her. Fortunately, my skin had grown used to the rough treatment and as long as I removed the splinters and cleaned my puncture wounds and scrapes, they healed quickly.

"Gather your cleaning supplies and follow me," she ordered. Picking up my bucket, I walked behind her down the main staircase until we were standing on the bottom step, looking at the front door. I did not let my displeasure show on my face, refusing to give Luciana any satisfaction.

"You will clean the main entrance hall today. After that, you will dust the chandelier."

I lowered my head, not meeting her eyes, but keeping them high enough to watch her throat. She was wearing the necklace. I bent down to pick up the bucket of soap and water resting beside my feet. Before I could rise again, Luciana held out a hand. "Stop. Don't start yet. Take off the shoes."

I stared openly at Luciana's face, my confusion written clearly in my expression. I was immediately suspicious of her motives. Surely she was not having me remove the wooden shoes to be kind. There must be some other reason. Silently, I kicked off the shoes, not bothering to pick them up and hand them to her. She could bend down herself if she wanted them. Pleased with that small act of defiance, I picked up my bucket and carried it into the entrance hall.

It did not take me long to realize why Luciana had ordered me to take off the shoes. Salt had been spread all over the stone floor, and every step I took with my injured feet sent searing pain shooting up my legs. Tears welled up in my eyes, and soon I had no choice but to let them fall as I worked to scrub the salt from the floor. Luciana was silent as she watched me, but the look of smug pleasure on her face only made me cry harder. It had been a long time since she had succeeded in bringing me to tears, but I could not stop.

The job, and the pain, lasted for hours. I realized that the lye soap cleaned my feet, but stung almost as badly as the salt. There was no blood on the floor from my wounds, since the salt dried all of it up, and for that small blessing, I was grateful. Luciana left me when dinner was served, and I continued my task alone. Mam, Cate, and Sarah would be wondering where I was. Brahms would be missing his apple and his visit. Jessith had probably chosen to avoid me because of her dislike for Luciana. Belle was surely looking for me around the house, wandering corridors and hoping to catch me alone.

My thoughts were interrupted when I realized that I had finished cleaning the floor. I let out a relieved sob, leaving my soap and bucket on the ground and pushing my hair out of my eyes. Since I had no shoes anywhere nearby, I improvised and tied two of the cleaning rags around my feet after shaking them free of salt. I got to my feet and limped out of the front door. Normally, it was not appropriate for servants to use the front door, but since everyone else was eating dinner or serving it, I knew I could get away with sneaking through. I still had to clean the chandelier, and the only ladder I knew of that was tall enough to reach it was in the stables.

I found Matthew feeding his horses supper as well. He watched me tread carefully over the ground, stopping to adjust one of the rags on my feet. He looked at them curiously, but did not ask questions. "Ahay, Ellie, no dinner tonight?"

"Not until I clean the chandelier in the entrance hall. Will you help me get the barn ladder into the manor?"

"A'course, d'be glad to. I'll go fetch it down."

"Hello, Ellie," Brahms said from inside of his stall as I watched Matthew's retreating back. I walked over to him and let him lip my hair, running my hand over his thick neck.

"Hello. I'm sorry I don't have a carrot for you right now. I was working inside."

Brahms snuffled good-naturedly, ready to forgive me for not bringing him a treat. "You're hurting," he said, his large dark eyes studying my face as he shook a fly from his haunches. Animals, I had learned, were more perceptive than humans by far.

"She put salt on the floor, and I had to walk on it with sore feet." As a horse, Brahms was very sympathetic toward anyone with injured feet. A horse's hooves are their livelihood, and if they can no longer walk, they die. He stepped backwards nervously, muscle rippling across his sides and back. Before he could respond, Matthew returned with the long ladder dragging behind him.

"Need ye to help me lift t'other end there, girlie." I limped to the end of the ladder that was still on the ground, bending over to pick it up. Suddenly, Brahms nickered, kicking at his stall door with his hooves. His eyes rolled wildly in his head. Matthew dropped the ladder and hurried over to see to him, whispering soothing words that I could not make out.

"No, don't use that! It smells like her...She's all over it."

"Smells like who?" I asked.

Brahms continued to kick and snort. "Brown mane. Luciana. She touched it."

"Ellie?" Matthew looked at me in confusion. "What's gotten in t'ye?"

"Hold on, Matthew. I need to look at something." I bent down and examined each rung carefully. Luciana had no cause to use the ladder. In fact, she hardly spent any time in the barn at all. If it smelled like her, and I trusted Brahms's senses, then she had probably done something to it.

Near the other end of the ladder, at what would have been the top, I found several rungs at different intervals chipped at and loosened on the edges. If I had stepped on them, I would have been in for a nasty fall. After showing Matthew the vandalized part of the ladder, I headed back for the entrance hall, wanting to get the chandelier cleaned before Luciana finished dinner. Since the ladder was out of the question, I needed a different plan. I saw several songbirds scattered about the fields, searching for their evening meal, and came up with an idea. I was not sure how they would hold the rags, but a few robins and sparrows could certainly fly to the top of the chandelier and get the dust off. I was willing to put up with their rhyming if they would help me get my task done.

I called out to them. "Excuse me, friends, could I talk with you for a moment?" Birds appreciated politeness, which was just one of the many reasons they hated cats. Ten or eleven of them stopped pecking at the ground and swarmed around me, all chattering at once. Because I could talk to them and fed them occasionally, most of the birds around Baxstresse were familiar with me, always willing to help when I asked.

"Ta-whit Ta-whit, if you should call, you have the service of us all," said a particularly fat sparrow whose head barely popped above his swollen belly. I wondered if I was partially to blame for his large size, since I did feed the birds whenever I needed them. Besides, with their mouths full of grain or breadcrumbs, they could not rhyme any longer, which was a relief.

"Yes, please." I glanced over my shoulder to make sure that no one was watching me. They might have found the sight of girl with birds flying around her head strange enough to report. "I need to dust the chandelier in the entrance hall, and since you all are so good at flying and reaching high places, I thought you might be able to help me."

The fat sparrow puffed his stomach out even larger with pride, pleased that he was able to do something that a human couldn't. The other birds agreed to help, chattering excitedly as I led them through the front door, urging them to be quiet and hoping that no one would see them working.

The cleaning rags I had were much too large for them to carry, even with two working together, and so I tore them into very small strips so that the birds could grip them in their small feet and lift them into the air. Somehow, by brushing the cloths through the cobwebs that had gathered on the chandelier, and sending them spinning down onto the floor that I had just cleaned, the birds managed to get the job finished. I made sure to feed them and then picked up a broom to sweep up the dust that had fallen from the chandelier's long golden arms.

CHAPTER 5

THE HARVEST STARTED, and everyone was busy. The fields became deep, golden brown oceans that moved under the cold autumn breeze. The birds were restless, flying in blocks of beating wings, swirling in circles above the ground and settling back down. They would leave for winter soon. I missed the changing of the leaves I had watched every year at Sandleford, but Baxstresse changed for autumn in its own way. It was not entirely unpleasant.

All of these changes, especially Belle, made my life much brighter, but I was not content. Luciana's nasty trick with the salt and her attempt to injure me with the ladder put me on edge. After four months as a servant, I was no closer to freeing myself.

Belle was just as restless. Her temper was on edge. When I told her what Luciana had done, her face turned an angry red color and she stormed from her room to look for her sister. I had to throw myself into her arms and plead for her to stop. Luciana would not hesitate to hurt her, with or without a confrontation. I usually checked Belle's food before it was served to her, just in case Luciana decided that poison would suit her needs.

Belle's mood was terrible the next few days, far worse than mine, and she often made sharp comments, criticizing herself for being so powerless against Luciana. I reminded her that she was not powerless, only concerned for my safety, but I worried that my words did not penetrate her mind. Her conscience was driving her mad.

"I have thought about giving up my inheritance," she informed me during one of our stolen whisper-kissing conversations in an empty room. Seeing her had lightened my spirits, but I could tell how horrible she felt.

"You mean you want to leave?" I leaned on one of the walls to take some weight off my sore feet. Luciana had asked me to wear the wooden shoes the day before, and Belle cleaned and massaged my feet that night. Of course, that gentle, healing touch had escalated into something far more intimate. I flushed at the memory, trying to ignore the heat flooding over my skin.

"I would take you with me," she said. I breathed deeply, relieved. "I just thought that Luciana might leave us alone if I left her the Baxstresse fortune. The money would make finding you seem less important."

"It wouldn't matter. She would assume you were plotting against her if you left and she would spare no expense to find us both."

"Not if we hid."

I sighed, recalling how many times I had thought of the same argument myself. "Do you want to spend the rest of our lives looking over our shoulders for her? That's hardly a life at all."

Belle moved her hand to her slick forehead, pushing back her hair. The thick summer heat still lingered around Baxstresse, even though it was well into the middle of autumn. It permeated even the inside of the stone manor, and we were all dehydrated and tired. The two of us were quiet for a long time and we both listened to make sure we were alone, each with our own thoughts.

"I would rather live peacefully in poverty with you than in luxury with Luciana hovering over us," she said after a time, taking my hand. She placed a gentle kiss on my knuckles, and I glanced toward the door, afraid that someone would see us. "It's all right, sweet girl, no one saw us." Still holding my hand in hers, she glanced down at my feet, which were wrapped underneath the protection of my shoes. "How are you feeling?"

I could not help smiling at Belle, touched by her concern. "Better. My feet are mostly calloused now. I have gotten used to the pain, but I'm worried she will try something worse next time."

It was the wrong thing to say. Belle's eyes clouded, and I felt her hand grip my fingers tight enough to drain the blood from them. "I promise to protect you from her." Looking at Belle's face, the twisted set of her mouth and the moistness of her eyes; I had to take her in my arms, not caring who saw us.

"I love you," I said, stroking Belle's white face with my knuckles, our bodies pressed close.

"I have let her hurt the woman I love for too long. You could have been killed falling off that ladder. I will never let anything like that happen to you." I knew my lover was lost in herself, and I did not try to bring her back. I just held her for the few moments I was allowed, wishing desperately that things were different, but overjoyed that I had Belle.

***

I saw even less of Luciana during the following week, and my world seemed brighter. She did not come to the kitchen to torment me or abuse Cate. None of us saw her except at mealtimes, and even then, she looked strangely pale. Some of the magical glow about her had disappeared.

When I finally saw her alone, the circumstances were so strange that I thought I had imagined them until I saw the proof of the encounter on my hand. I noticed her walking into the kitchen just as I was going out, having washed the last of the plates and silverware. I froze in the doorway, almost knocking into her, knowing that Luciana only visited the kitchen to play her sick games. I looked at her hands, expecting to see the wooden shoes. One was held loose at her side, but the other clasped an object I could not see.

Keeping my expression guarded, I looked at her face, lips parted in surprise. Luciana looked back at me in a daze, her eyes wide and filmed over. Her skin was a strange purple color, enflamed and bruised looking. I could feel heat coming off her body from several feet away. Clear beads of sweat clung to her forehead, streaming down her neck and into the collar of her dress.

I stepped closer to her, and burning energy slid over my skin like scalding water, making me take in a sharp breath. I suddenly realized what was causing the intense heat—magic. I had never felt so much magic! It was thousands of times more powerful than the pleasant flush of warmth I felt when I talked to Jessith or the horses. This magical energy was uncontrollable, leaking out of Luciana and on to me.

Luciana lurched forwards, letting out a hoarse cry as she nearly fell on top of me. I managed to push her weight away, letting her collapse onto the floor. Something bright spilled out of her hand, skittering a few feet from her side. The heat coming from Luciana vanished, and she lay twitching on the floor, shocks rolling through her body.

I bent down to see what she had dropped and caught a glimpse of a silver chain. The three-ringed pendant was familiar. I reached out a hand to pick it up, but the links burned my fingers as soon as I touched it, and

I dropped the chain again. I stared at my palm, which was starting to turn an angry red color, completely shocked. Like a thousand tiny sparks searing holes through my skin, the magic burrowed into the flesh of my hand, humming in my bones. Using the material of my dress to cover the fingers of my other hand, I reached for the chain again, but Luciana was faster. She managed to roll over and grab the chain before I could grasp it.

"Mine!" She clutched the burning metal to her chest, seemingly immune to the heat. "You will not have it." She heaved herself to her feet and ran off like the hounds of hell were at her heels, leaving me alone to pour cool water over my blistered hand, trying to make sense of what I had just witnessed.

***

"She did what?"

"Ran out of the room and left me standing there," I repeated. Belladonna's expression was disbelieving. This time, she had been the one expecting to make love, but I had started talking before she could confuse me with kisses. It had been hard to resist the sight of her stripping out of her dressing gown. The obvious longing in her eyes when she saw me made my heart pound in my head, but the frightening scene with Luciana in the kitchen was still fresh in my mind and my fear overpowered my arousal. My impression of Luciana had changed completely. She was not just cruel, she was insane.

"Let me see your hand again." I heard the concern in Belle's voice, and I wanted to reach out and smooth the worried wrinkle between her eyebrows with my thumb, but I let her take my hand in both of hers and turn it over. I shivered, gritting my teeth as she peeled the dressing away from the raw skin of my palm. "You say the chain did this? The chain that Luciana took from my mother?"

"Yes." Repeating the story did not make me angry. I could scarcely believe it myself, and I could not expect poor Belle to take it all in right away. "What I don't understand is: where was the magic coming from? Luciana or the chain? Luciana felt fevered, but her skin did not burn like the chain when she fell on me."

"I have never heard of an ordinary object burning someone or creating its own inherent magic. Usually, someone has to channel power through it, like a magic mirror."

"Well, this object was far from ordinary." I tried to pull my hand out of Belladonna's grip, but she brought it to her lips and brushed an impossibly light kiss over the skin. It should have hurt, but strangely, the pain seemed to ease.

"How do you know that what you felt was magic?" Belle asked, staring at me curiously. "It's not like you have any experience with it. Neither of us are Ariada..."

For some reason, the word did not seem dirty coming from Belle's lips. I blushed fiercely, not knowing how to explain my secret, but feeling compelled to share it with her. I had already shared my heart and body with Belladonna, and it seemed wrong to keep things back from her.

Surprisingly, Belle guessed before I could tell her. "You are Ariada, aren't you?"

I felt my breath leave my chest. Tears flooded my eyes and I blinked to keep them back. "Would you hate me if I was? Would you reject me?"

"No," Belle insisted. "You think I care that you are Ariada? I could never reject you! But why did you keep it a secret?"

I pressed my lips together, unsure how to answer. "I didn't want you to stop loving me."

"You didn't trust me." Belle's voice was flat and devoid of emotion, and it made my heart tear. She was right. I had not trusted her. Her pained expression made sense.

I stepped forward, taking Belle's wrist in my uninjured hand. She stiffened at the touch, still hurt. "I know it's a little late, Belle, but I want to tell you. I am Ariada. I can talk to animals. That is my gift."

She smiled at me weakly, the fresh pain between us beginning to recede. "You can talk to animals," she said, testing the idea. There was no fear or disgust in her face or her voice, only leftover sadness and perhaps a spark of curiosity.

"Some of them have very interesting things to say. Jessith in particular is always..." I paused, trying to searching for an adjective worthy of my friend, "opinionated."

Belle raised her eyebrows, and her tight posture relaxed. "I should think a cat would be. Is Rucifee entertaining as well?"

I groaned. "You have no idea."

Satisfied with my apology, Belle took me into her arms again. "Of course, now that I know that you can talk to animals, I will pester you and ask what they are saying every time we see one."

The idea actually appealed to me. It would be a pleasant change to share my gift instead of being secretive about it. "Well, right now, Ellie says she would very much like to kiss you." My eyes lingered on Belladonna's lips as I spoke.

Tipping my chin up with two fingers, Belle pressed gentle kisses to the freckles on my cheeks and the corners of my lips before finding my mouth. Several moments later, while both of us breathed heavily, she said, "Belle says that was a good idea."

Relieved that Belle and I were back on good terms, I hurried to show her how appreciated her acceptance was. Thoughts of Luciana were put aside for the rest of the night.

My sleep was not peaceful. I was trapped in a dream, the kind where you know you are dreaming, but cannot escape.

I was standing before Luciana, but she was frozen in time, her shoulders as stiff and lifeless as her face. I touched her skin and it was cold. My eyes were drawn to the chain that hung around her throat. The pendant was on it.

The three circles pulsed and rippled, growing larger until they were the size of my fist, my head, my entire body. Soon, the gigantic pendant dwarfed me, leaving me to stare up at it helplessly. Luciana had disappeared behind it. If she was still there, I could not see her. The flat surfaces of the pendant's metal rings grew dull until they were almost black, and I saw—or thought I saw—movement inside them.

With horror and disgust, I realized what the pendant looked like. It was a huge, bulbous eye, staring ghoulishly at me through the thin metal. I stumbled back, wanting to run far away from this horrible thing. A strange voice, so old that its layers sounded like many voices tied together, spoke through the eye. ***"I am awake. I see you."***

When I stopped screaming, Belle was holding onto me. Both of us were crouched down on the cold floorstones, and the sheets were tangled about our legs. Somehow, I had fallen off the bed. "Ellie?" she whispered frantically, stroking my hair and rocking me like a child. "Ellie, what is it?"

It was a long time before I gathered enough courage to tell her about the dream, and an even longer time before either of us fell back asleep. When we did, my sleep was dreamless.

CHAPTER 6

"YOU KNOW, IF YOU have a question, the most sensible place to look for an answer is in the library."

Belle and I had stolen a few moments together on the second floor, next to the tapestry of King Faron of Amendyr on a wild boar hunt. Running with him were several wild-looking creatures, each more fantastical in appearance than the last. "Sometimes I wonder if you love that library more than me," I complained. The only thing larger than the Baxstresse library was Belle's admiration for it. Occasionally, I found Belle's fascination with the place wearisome, but I could not help being enamored with it, too. So much of my relationship with Belle had been formed there. The companionable hours we had spent reading together by the fire, the secret moments I had stolen with Belle's diary, the first kiss we had shared, which had led to so many more firsts.

"Only a little. You have to admit that it knows more than we will in ten lifetimes."

"And does nothing with that knowledge but collect dust, which I am usually the one cleaning. Do you know how often Sarah and I are in there, keeping things in order?" Truly, I did not mind cleaning the library, although I did have a tendency to blush when I passed the fireplace. Sarah had even asked me if the heat was making me feel unwell a few times.

"Still, it's worth looking, don't you think? There must be a book about magic and burning chains on one of those shelves." I turned away from Belle, whose flushed face was capturing a little too much of my attention, and glanced sideways at the tapestry. One woman—at least, she had the face, shoulders, and breasts of a woman—was piercing the side of the boar with her spear. Where her ribcage ended, a huge, bulbous black body was set over eight spider's legs.

If they truly existed, the Liarre lived on the other side of the continent next to the sea. Since Amendyr rested between Seria and their kingdom, no one I knew had ever seen them. Many Serians claimed they were not real. I never had cause to think about them for longer than a passing moment, and I did not know if they actually existed. I was certain that Belle would know. There were supposed to be many tribes of them—spiders, wild dogs and cats, horses, and even giant lizards.

"...can find it, I am sure."

I blinked, drawn from my thoughts by Belle's comment. "The place is hopelessly scrambled for the most part. If you want to dig through all of those books to find what you want, feel free. No one ever said that I needed to categorize the books. Dusting them takes long enough."

Belle's forehead lifted and she looked almost reproachful as she stared down the line of her nose at me. "I know where everything is in that library. It's perfectly easy to find what I'm looking for."

I almost choked on the laughter that spilled from my mouth. "What? No! Be serious...the place is in shambles. Admit it."

"Never."

"Go and look for our mysterious burning chain, then, and show me when you find it."

"Fine, I will. And when I do, you'll owe me a kiss."

I should have known better than to issue Belle a challenge. Three and a half hours later she was shoving a very thick book with the title *Elementary Majicks* under my nose, somehow managing to wave the heavy thing in my face. "There! Right there, the second paragraph..."

This is what I read:

One of the most difficult objects of power to create, a focus object, more commonly known as a sorcerer's chain, was once considered a standard magical tool for Ariada in the Kingdom of Amendyr, less than half a century before the Serian explorers put an end to most magical development in the eastern half of the continent. A focus object allowed magic to be infused within the object of the caster's choice—usually a thick chain, orb, or ring. This magic could then be recalled instantly at a later time, usually during a duel, without directly draining the magician's energy.

The amount of magic within a focus object depends upon the endurance and experience of the Ariada that has created it. Theoretically, a focus object can be used by anyone with magical ability, although they might easily lose control of someone else's magical energy, particularly if they are inexperienced. However, in reality, almost all focus objects were enchanted with a familiarity spell, allowing them to recognize the original caster and rendering them useless to anyone else. Upon touching a focus object, any living being is able to sense the magical energy, often feeling a strange vibration or slight warmth caused by the agitated state of the contained magic. If unused for a long period of time, perhaps over the span of several years, the magic will gradually leave the focus object and return to the earth, leaving the chosen item in its former state.

Chains remained the most popular form for focus objects until the High Ariada fell after the death of Kamen Thyr, because of their light weight and concealable size, while rings fell out of fashion, as they were easier to misplace and harder to properly fit to the magician's specific finger size...

"Slight warmth?" My voice cracked as I looked up from the book. "My hand is still blistered from touching that thing. Whatever Luciana's got her claws around must have the magic of ten Ariada in it."

Belle's expression turned thoughtful as she examined the page I had read. "Maybe whoever it belonged to was a very powerful sorcerer?"

I shook my head, dismissing the notion immediately. "No human could be that powerful. Besides, this book is talking about sorcerer's chains, or focus objects, or whatever they are, in the past tense. I've read about the High Ariada before, but didn't they exist centuries ago?"

"About half a century before the Serians came. Amendyr was left weak without them. That is why Seria gobbled up half the continent so easily before the Amendyrri Ariada that were left held them at the Forest Pass."

"What about the eye I saw? It must be a part of the chain. Was it just a dream, or was it magic?" Belle looked slightly overwhelmed by all of my questions, but I continued anyway. "Why has this chain suddenly appeared now? If it is so old, why hasn't the magic gone out of it? Why is it so strong? And how did the vile thing get into your great grandmother's hands?"

Belle took the book from my hands, closing it and tucking it under her arm. "I don't know, Ellie. Maybe this book will tell me more. It refers to other texts in many of the chapters, and I might spend some time reading those as well. I want to find out as much as possible about this chain before Luciana discovers a way to use it against us."

***

Two nights after reading about sorcerer's chains in *Elementary Majicks*, another book was waved under my nose as its holder yelled at me. This time, it was Sarah. She was holding a familiar leather-bound journal in her hand. "Ellie, it can't be true," she nearly sobbed, almost slamming the cover of the journal into my face. "Please tell me that nothing in this is true!"

"Where did you get that?" I snapped, trying to grab the journal from her. She was too quick for me, holding it above my head where I could not reach it. We had played this game before, and I knew that jumping was useless. "Give it back."

"All this time, your mystery lover was—"

"Don't say the name! Just give me the book back."

Sarah was nearly crying at that point, still holding the journal over my outstretched hands. "Ellie, I won't let you elope! It's the most foolish thing I've ever heard of in my entire life. If you try, I'll stop you."

"I don't suppose you read the last entry in that diary, did you?" I asked, lowering my hand.

Sarah rolled her eyes. "I couldn't get through the rubbish without wanting to vomit. Of course I didn't read the last entry.

She sounded like an insulted courtier, conveniently forgetting that she had gone through my things and taken the book without my permission.

"Well, since you've already stolen it from me, you might as well read it now."

Sarah looked down her nose at me, studying my face as she considered my suggestion. Tilting her head up so she could see the pages without lowering the book, she flipped to the last entry, a scowl pulling over her lips. Her mouth dropped open. She forgot about holding the book up and let her arm drop to chest level. I took the diary from her and she did not protest. First, she stared at me, loose jawed and wide eyed. Then, she started to laugh. "You almost killed me, Ellie. I can't believe—"

"Exactly," I interrupted, keeping a tight hold on the journal now that I had it back. I could not have anyone else reading it, just in case they misinterpreted. "Cate and I thought you needed a friendly warning before you got all of us into trouble."

It had started because Sarah's teasing about my mystery lover was driving me to distraction. Despite my warnings about Luciana's taste for blackmail and torture, Sarah's curious nature subdued any caution that she might have possessed. As dearly as I loved my friend, she was one of the most indiscreet, gossip-hungry people I knew. Letting her discover my relationship with Belladonna would have been disastrous. Cate was sensible about the whole thing, and so I enlisted her to help me teach Sarah a lesson.

The joke was rather simple. Since Sarah was so eager for information, I decided to give her the most lurid gossip of her life. Belle's journal had given me the idea. Instead of letting Sarah get her hands on that private book, in which Belladonna still wrote entries for me to read, Cate and I had composed our own. My favorite scene was a particularly lustful encounter with Jamison on the stairs.

"I can't believe you, Ellie Sandleford. You had me thinking you were going to elope with that odious Jamison and have ten children with him in Briaridge!"

"On the other hand, I have no trouble believing that one of my best friends would go looking through my things just to satisfy her curiosity." Sarah had the decency to blush. I smiled and put a hand on her shoulder. "It's all right, I'm not angry with you...much. But I'm certainly not helping you clean up tonight, if you catch my meaning."

"I suppose I deserve it," Sarah said, blowing her loose bangs out of her eyes. "I never should have fallen for that rot you put in there. Jamison? You couldn't have picked someone else?"

I grinned wickedly. "Of course not. I wanted to pick the most horrifying, vile person imaginable. Besides Luciana, Jamison was the obvious choice." I offered my hand to Sarah. "All right, if you promise to stop going through my things to learn details about my private life, I promise not to elope with Jamison and have ten children. I'll even keep being your friend. How does that sound?"

"Sounds wonderful to me." Sarah looked relieved. I had a feeling that keeping her nose out of my business was going to be more difficult for her than she realized, but I knew she was a well-meaning girl very deep down. This scare would probably keep her out of trouble for a week or two, at any rate.

***

While Belle was reading book after book on magical objects and sorcerer's chains, I had an idea of my own. The troubling dream did not return to haunt my sleep, but it was with me during the day. When I passed into a shadow, when my mind wandered from Belle for just a moment, when everything suddenly paused and the entire manor stopped to listen to a sound that was not there, I saw the large, burning black eye in my mind. It made my stomach squeeze and my heart curl in my throat.

I decided to ask Cate about the pendant. Sarah had revealed that she was from an ancient Amendyrri family. Perhaps she had lived there as a child. She might know something about dream-telling, especially since she could See. Better yet, she might know of a way to get rid of frightening dreams and visions.

I spent many hours at night thinking of what to say to her, but in the end, I just blurted it out. "I know you can See."

Cate was not surprised. "I knew you would find out," she told me, setting down the load of fresh laundry that she had carried in to our room. We actually needed to take the bedding upstairs, but we decided to stop for a few moments to catch our breath. "Sarah can never keep her mouth shut."

"I don't think any differently of you," I said. Cate looked relieved, and once she had lowered her arms and the bundle of bedding, I could see that her lips were pressed tight. She was calm, but still alert. "Actually, I am..."

"I know, sister," Cate said.

My eyes grew large. "Do you know everything I want to say before I say it?"

Cate gave me a small smile. For a moment, her freckles stood out on her milk-pale skin. "No. But I get strong feelings from you. Also, I've heard you talking to the cats. Rucifee was pestering you the other night."

I scowled, remembering. I had stepped on the fat ginger nuisance's tail. Although I had apologized very politely, he had taken a swipe at my leg with his claws. I shook my head and focused on Cate. "Cate, I had a dream. Have you noticed that Luciana wears a pendant around her neck on a silver chain?"

Cate thought about it, squinting her eyes as she concentrated. It did not look like she was performing any magical actions and I did not feel the pleasant, warm buzz that I had grown to associate with my own magic. A dark look crossed her face and she nodded. "She never takes it off. Even when...I mean...She never takes it off." There was a long pause. "Sometimes she makes me undress her. I tried to unhook it once. She knocked me over a table."

I gasped and reached out a hand, but Cate shied away from my touch. "Don't. Don't touch me right now. I'm all right."

"I'm so sorry, Cate. I didn't mean to make you think about..."

"I'm all right. Tell me about your dream."

And so I told her. She listened with a serious expression on her face, but she no longer looked pained or frightened. She was focusing. She shivered slightly at the part about the giant eye and my bones twitched in response. There was something primal and evil about what I had seen.

"Your dream sounds real. My mother told me that everyone has a little bit of the Sight in them. Before we came to Seria..." She closed her eyes, remembering a time long ago. "We lived in the Forest at my grandmother's house, before the bad time."

"The bad time?"

"Mother was sick. Grandmother sent me away to relatives across the border. When they grew too old, I ended up here. I still miss the Forest."

I was surprised that Cate was discussing her childhood so freely, but as soon as the thought rose in my head, she decided that she was tired of talking. She watched me for a long, tense second. I gave her a smile and she smiled back, slowly and carefully, wondering if she had revealed too much. "Every Ariada has a little bit of the Sight in them. Listen to your dreams."

"I will."

As we picked up the forgotten bedding and walked up the stairs together, most of our discomfort faded and I was left with more questions I could not answer.

CHAPTER 7

SHARING BELLADONNA'S bed could only go unnoticed for so long. We knew that we were taking a risk by being together, but we continued meeting all the same. They say that love is blind, but I know better. Lovers see, but choose to look away. The tears of joy that stained our cheeks at night never blurred our sight completely. Perhaps we stole a kiss more than was wise in one of Baxstresse's many empty rooms. Still, the day came when one of our rendezvous was rudely interrupted.

Belle was busy blazing a trail of dusky purple marks along the column of my throat, bruising my skin with heated lips and tongue, strands of her black hair tickling my bare shoulders. "Mmm, you taste good," she breathed across my collarbone, peppering kisses over the bite marks. I had already stolen an hour in her arms, but I still wanted more. If I had been standing, her kisses would have made my knees weak.

"You shouldn't," I whispered, tugging weakly at her wrist. "Someone will see them."

"Then let them see that you are mine. You belong to me." She left my neck and moved her face over mine, our mouths brushing together without meeting.

"I've been gone too long already..."

"I don't care. I need you again, my beautiful girl. I have to have more of you."

"Yes," I hissed. My eyes fluttered shut as heat blossomed in my chest, beating out to my fingertips. "Belle, I love —" My declaration was cut short as the doors flew open, and my heart skipped. I crossed my arms over my breasts, lips parting in surprise.

Luciana walked casually into the room, the corners of her mouth flickering up with satisfaction. "Good evening, sister," she drawled, her cold voice cutting off my breath. Her gaze dug into every inch of my bare flesh and my skin prickled with fear. I clutched the sheets at my throat, huddling into a ball to hide from her wicked black eyes. Belle did not even bother covering herself. She placed a hand over mine, where it was clutching nervously at her hip, and removed it, pulling away from the safety of my touch and standing up. All the warmth inside me left with her.

"Luciana," she said, challenging her sister with her eyes.

Luciana rested a hand on her waist, tilting her head back proudly. "You know, I hardly believed it when I first heard." She finally tore her eyes away from me and turned to Belladonna. "Taking your own sister to your bed. How shameful." She shook her light hair off her shoulders, her thin smirk broadening.

"Not nearly as shameful as raping kitchen maids and beating your lovers to near death. Ellie gives herself to me freely. I would never take her against her will."

For the first time since she entered the room, Luciana looked surprised. She glanced at me, bafflement breaking through the haughty mask of her face. Was it really so unbelievable that I would make love to Belle willingly? She recovered quickly, returning her attention to Belladonna. "I'm sure you would feel uncomfortable explaining all of this to our mother."

"Blackmail," Belle whispered to herself, glancing at the floor stones. "All right, Luci, mother's favorite. What do you want from me?"

Luciana's lashes lowered wickedly. "Your complete obedience and...friendship." Her eyes rose again to take in Belle's breasts and stomach, her smooth legs. I was disgusted.

"Friendship? That's what you call it, then?"

"Friendship," Luciana answered, enjoying the word on her tongue. "And, of course, the friendship of our dear stepsister. I am sure that Ellie will enjoy herself with me."

The expression of horror on Belladonna's face mirrored the fear collecting at the bottom of my stomach. "You will never touch her."

I wanted to go to Belle, embrace her, thank her for the flood of shielding warmth that her words enveloped me in, but I could not move.

I reached out my hand after several still moments in silent thanks. She took it, brushing her thumb over the tops of my knuckles.

"Who will believe you, Luciana?" Belle was powerful and intimidating even in her nakedness. I shrank behind her, biting at my bottom lip. "No one would accept such an allegation, even from you."

Luciana was unfazed. "Perhaps they wouldn't, if I had no proof." She pulled her white hand from the folds of her skirt and held up a familiar leather-bound journal. My heart jerked out of rhythm for an instant.

Belle's stoic expression faltered. "My diary..."

"Written in your own hand."

Belle was silent again, clearly shaken. Even so, she did not retreat. "Ellie is mine, and as long as I have strength to protect her, I will. You won't lay a hand on her until my death."

Luciana did not take the threat well. The back of her neck straightened and she lifted her chin, revealing the three-circled pendant at the base of her throat. It bobbed wickedly as she breathed, seeming almost alive itself. I could not tear my eyes from it. All I could see was the eye, watching us. I thought I could hear it speak. *'I am awake. I see you.'*

"I think not, sister," Luciana said through gritted teeth. I shot back into the present moment. Red sparks of light crackled and danced around her clenched fist, although the hand holding the book remained dormant.

My eyes widened as the sparks jumped around Luciana's pendant, rushing to her fingertips as she extended them towards Belle. She held her ground, but I caught the flash of nervousness in her eyes.

"No," I said hoarsely, my throat tight with unshed tears, "don't hurt her." I moved to the side, away from Belladonna's protection, still near enough to clasp her hand. "I...I will do whatever you want, but don't hurt her."

Luciana smiled. "Good girl," she purred, tucking Belladonna's diary back into her skirts and silencing the sparks along her slender fingers. The words made my eyes sting with tears.

The thought of what I had said to Mam all those months ago came back to me. "If she ever touches me like that, I will kill her. And then I will kill myself." But could I go through with it now that I had Belle?

"I won't let —" Belle started, but we were interrupted by a knock on the door. "I'm not dressed," she called out, staring at the door.

"'Course you're not," Mam said. I could feel her roll her eyes even from outside the room. Only Mam would dare to sass Belladonna. "Is Ellie in there with you?"

"Yes," I called out. My voice shook.

"Good. You'll be helping Miss Belladonna into one of her evening gowns, then. A messenger with a fine red coat is waiting at the door, and if he don't look a sight! I'm thinking he's from the palace."

Relieved that I had something to do, I bent down properly at the waist and picked up Belle's chemise. Luciana watched as Belle lifted her arms over her head and let the simple white garment settle about her shoulders. I could see the lust in her eyes and it made my chest tighten. I did not want to know what she was imagining. I bent down again to lift Belle's corset. My hands shook terribly, fumbling over the hooks and eyelets as Luciana stared at us.

"She will try to find me next," she said, not looking away. "Neither of you will say a word about this to anyone, unless you want this," she held up the diary, "to be made public."

As suddenly as she had entered, she was gone. I fell into Belle's arms, sobbing against her bare shoulder, leaving her corset half tied. I felt something wet against my forehead and realized that she was crying, too. "What are we going to do?" Belle whispered, tracing my lips with her fingertip. "I will never let her touch you. Oh, Ellie..." She kissed me, and her lips were rough, needy.

"But she will ruin you. She can take away everything with this."

"We can run away. We will go to a place where no one knows who we are."

I shook my head, knowing it was impossible, but Mam entered before I could answer her. "Ellie, finish helping Miss Belladonna." Silently, I finished tying Belle's corset and helped her with her dress. "Now, away with you," Mam ordered, pointing imperiously at the door, and Belle obeyed without protest. Only Mam was indispensable enough to give orders to the ladies of the manor. Baxstresse would collapse in on itself without her steady management.

Belladonna gave me a soft, open-mouthed kiss before she left, giving both of us strength. I was left alone with Mam. We stared at each other silently for a long moment. "You don't have anything to say to me?" I asked. I could not meet Mam's eyes as she lowered her full body and picked up my dress from where it lay crumpled against a wall.

"Better be putting this on." Mam offered me the bundle. I uncrossed my arms from where they had been shielding my modesty and worked my hands into the sleeves. The rough material scraped my skin as it settled across my shoulders. Once, I had refused to consider myself spoiled at all, but I had learned that being a little spoiled is better than suffering poverty. I missed the luxury of comfortable dresses, although the corsets were something I did not miss at all. I would probably not return to wearing them if I ever escaped this hell.

I felt better once I was covered, and was almost able to look Mam in the eye. "Luciana knows. She wants Belle's inheritance out of this." I could not speak of that other horrible thing she wanted, could not even think of it. "She can prove what Belle and I have done. She found a diary."

Mam let her eyes fall shut, lowering her chin and pressing her lips tight. "Oh, Ellie." Her mouth moved, but there was nothing left to be said. I held my wrist with one hand and feared what love had brought me.

***

A little less than an hour later, Belle found me scrubbing dishes in the kitchen. The chores of Baxstresse waited for no one. She walked up behind me so quietly that my breath caught when she finally spoke. "Put that down. I need to speak with you."

I obeyed and put down the plate, still holding the limp drying cloth in my hand. "Is there anything to speak about?" I said softly, afraid that Belle would confirm what I had already been thinking—there was no way to stop Luciana.

"The messenger was from the palace. We have been invited to a ball."

"You mean you and Luciana have been invited to a ball." Like Jessith, I disliked speaking Luciana's name. It made my mouth feel sour.

"No, all three of us. Everyone outside of Baxstresse only thinks you are sick. The invitation was sent out of politeness."

"What does an invitation to a ball have to do with protecting ourselves?" I was irritated with Belle for wandering from the topic I wanted to discuss. How could she think of anything but the disgusting way Luciana had looked at us?

"This is not an ordinary ball. It is Prince Brendan's twenty-first birthday ball. His parents are tired of him gallivanting about the Forest Pass and slaying monsters along the Amendyrri border. They want him to pick a girl to marry. Luciana wants to be that girl."

My heart stopped in my chest. Luciana wanted to be queen? Prince Brendan could not make a worse choice. Having a sadistic, power-hungry demon on the throne would tear the kingdom apart. I did not dare think about what Luciana would do if her plan succeeded. "How do you know?"

"She told me. The snake wants me to watch her at the ball, powerless to stop her, while she seduces him. She thinks I am too much of a coward to interfere." Belle's thin eyebrows furrowed, her lips peeling back in a snarl as she glared at her hands. "But she is wrong. I will not stand by and let her evil go unpunished, not this time. It has to be that chain, the one you felt burning. I am sure it is a sorcerer's chain. We have to find a way to break it."

CHAPTER 8

IN THE DAYS THAT followed, Belladonna spent most of her time reading magical texts in the library. I discussed Luciana's plan with Cate, Mam, Matthew, and even Sarah. I left out the parts about the burning chain and Luciana's attempts at blackmail. Instead, I told them that Luciana wanted to drag a marriage proposal out of Prince Brendan. The possibility that Luciana might become Queen of Seria horrified them, and they were more than willing to help.

"I will ask Miss Belladonna if I can go to the ball with her," I told Cate and Sarah as we were discussing ways of stopping Luciana. "I was invited, after all."

"Do you honestly think Miss Belladonna will say yes? I mean, maybe I should ask her," Sarah suggested. "I know her better than you do."

I swallowed to free the tightness in my throat, staring down at my lap. I did not want to be reminded of how well Sarah had known my lover. "I will do the asking. Belladonna does not want Luciana to be queen. We are friendly enough." More than friendly, but how could Sarah know? "I could follow in a carriage behind them. I can't let Luciana know I am going. Matthew will lend me a horse."

Cate nodded. "One of you should distract Prince Brendan and the other can try and keep Luciana away from him."

I jerked my head up in surprise at Cate's simple idea. "Of course. Luciana will think I am at Baxstresse, so that leaves me to watch the prince while Belle watches her." I hoped that no one noticed the accidental endearment. Sarah was too distracted to care, and if Cate thought anything of it, she was too shy to say. She did give me a contemplative look, however.

Sarah nearly swooned at the mention of the prince, her face turning bright red and her brown eyes shining with moisture. She looked positively ridiculous, but I probably looked just as silly when I was thinking about Belle. "Oh, I would love to dance with Prince Brendan for a night! I saw him once, you know, when I was about ten years old. He was so handsome!"

"If it was when you were ten, then he was only twelve. He could not have been that handsome," I pointed out.

"He was! He had wavy brown hair and the clearest blue eyes I have ever seen." I thought about another pair of blue eyes, more beautiful than Brendan's, and my face grew hot.

"I don't care what his eyes look like as long as he doesn't marry Luciana. Any other idiot would be fine, just not her."

"There can't possibly be anyone worse," Cate agreed.

"I would be a wonderful queen." Sarah waved her hand regally in the air. I rolled my eyes, but Cate smiled, distracting me from my sour mood.

"What would be your first royal decree?" I asked, playing along.

"I..." Sarah paused dramatically. "Would order Luciana to be thrown in the dungeon."

"Or executed," I suggested.

"Or thrown in the dungeon, tortured, and then executed." Both of us stared at Cate, surprised at the venom behind her words. We knew how much she hated Luciana. She had more cause than any of us to despise her, but we had not expected our shy friend to speak so viciously. "It would serve her right."

Without speaking, Sarah and I both put a hand on one of Cate's shoulders in silent comfort. Even though I had not endured as much pain as Cate, I understood her a little better now. Luciana's threat to take me to bed had shaken me. Belle and I did not want to think about the possibility, but both of us were afraid.

The conversation drifted after that. All of us were too stunned by Cate's words to plot anymore, and I could tell that Cate had surprised even herself. I saw it as a good sign. Perhaps Cate's inner strength was beginning to return.

***

That evening, I went to Belladonna's rooms, unable to fall asleep beside Cate. We had not made love since Luciana's interruption, although I had spent two nights sleeping in her bed. Both of us were awkward with each other, consumed by our worries and afraid of intimacy. Part of me longed to know my lover's body again, but Belle had shown no interest in being with me and I was too afraid of upsetting her to be the aggressor.

Belle's door was unlocked, as I knew it would be. I did not bother knocking and let myself in as quietly as I could in case my lover was asleep. She was reading a thick, yellowed volume, shadows bobbing over the skin of her bare upper body. Her legs and hips were wrapped in the bed sheets. I could not help staring at her breasts, longing to stroke the hard tips with my thumbs. Instead, I stripped, folding my dress and leaving it at the bottom of the bed.

Belle shut her book, not allowing me to catch a glimpse of the title before she set it on her wooden nightstand. She held out a long hand to me, and I took it, climbing next to her on the bed and wrapping my arms around her warm body. "I love you," she said suddenly, pulling me closer against her side.

"I love you, too. And I will love you until the stars fall into the sea." I blushed, surprised by my sudden burst of inspired poetry, and more than a little embarrassed.

Belle only smiled, resting a cool hand against the side of my neck. I knew she could feel my heartbeat pounding beneath my skin. "That was very prettily phrased, Ellie. Have you ever thought of trying your hand at poetry?"

I looked at Belladonna uneasily, unsure whether she was joking with me. "Oh, no, I really don't think..."

"Why not? You would probably enjoy it."

"I'm not sure." I blushed bright red to the roots of my hair. "You're a real poet, Belle. I don't understand why someone with such a gift wouldn't share —"

Belle interrupted me again. "But I have shared, just not under my real name. I'm sure that you have read, or at least heard of, Lord Erato's poetry? Probably only heard of...you don't strike me as worldly enough to indulge in such vile, disgusting literature."

"Well yes, I have heard of Erato, but those poems are all about...oh. Of course they are about loving women."

"Not all of "his" poetry is that base, of course. He has written...I have written...about heroes, betrayal, loss...Stuffy society ladies just seem to draw attention to the ones about lovemaking. It's not my fault they are dirty old hags. You and I are the only old ladies I want to imagine in any kind of intimate situation."

The mental image that my lover had given me made me smile. The thought of growing old with Belle made me feel comfortable and happy. "I like picturing us together when we are old. I will still think you are the most handsome creature I have ever seen."

Belle smiled back at me. Although I could still see the exhaustion and worry behind her eyes, her brief expression of happiness was genuine. "And I will still think you are the prettiest woman in the world, sweet girl."

I gave Belle's form an appreciative glance, although my body was so entwined with hers that it was difficult to see all of her. I was unwilling to let her go. "If you end up looking nearly as good as your mother does, you have nothing to worry about."

A brief look of sadness darkened Belle's eyes. "You have been looking at my mother? That is disgusting," Belle said. Her teasing sounded forced and I pulled myself tighter against her, gazing into her eyes.

"Why are you sad, lover? Is Lady Kingsclere worse?"

"About the same," Belle confessed. "At first, I thought it was shock, but now, I'm sure she's tied up in whatever Luciana is doing. On good days, she recognizes me. She tells me about the past, stories I have already heard. I don't think she realizes what time she's in or that my father is dead. On her bad days she won't talk at all, or she screams and tears at her hair, telling something to leave her alone, to stop hurting her."

I could not think of any words to say, so I wrapped my arms around Belle and held her tight. I hoped that the comfort I wanted to give would pass through me and into her. Somehow, my embrace turned into a caress and our lips found each other in the half darkness. I let Belle lead, and her mouth moved to stroke my eyelids, my cheeks, my chin. She kissed along the line of my jaw and I felt her teeth nip at the soft skin behind my ear.

I lifted my eyes, wanting to see my lover's face. The naked expression of need staring back at me made my heart stutter. Belle grabbed my wrists and pinned them above my head, settling her body on top of mine, her thigh pushing between my legs and rubbing against me. I was overwhelmed by Belle's tall, sleek figure, feeling small and vulnerable, but also undeniably safe. My skin flushed and I felt tears rise in my eyes. Making love with Belle touched some deep part of my soul that often made me cry with joy.

The places where Belle's naked skin touched mine burned. She kissed my breath away until I was sure I would drown in her. I lifted one of my hands, weaving the fingers through her dark hair. She recoiled, flinching away from my hand like a nervous animal. "Don't, Ellie. Stop."

I could see the brightness in her eyes, the blood rushing beneath her skin. Her entire body trembled with energy, need, and—fear? I could not imagine this powerful, elemental woman being afraid of anything. Belle's aura radiated strength and control. I knew that she needed me. Why was she frightened?

"Belle," I whispered, reaching for her hair again. "Please. I want to feel you." She held her shoulders stiff, body trembling, fists tight. She allowed me to take her in my arms, and I pressed my face into her shoulder, feeling her heart pound along the curve of her throat. Wanting to calm her, I smoothed my hands over the bunched, chorded muscles of her back. Sometimes, Belle made me feel like I was holding a tiger in my arms instead of a woman. She was all tensed, smooth strength and barely contained energy. But she was also my protector, and I trusted her with everything.

In the safe darkness that was Belle, I found words. "Please. Don't you want to be inside me? Feeling me around your fingers, full and tight and warm?"

She lifted my face from her shoulder, tipping my chin so I was looking into her eyes. A glassy texture clouded them and I blushed, hardly believing what had passed between my lips.

"I was going to take you," she admitted haltingly, her face a strange picture of desire and panic. "I just wanted to slide inside of you, hard. Fill all of you. Make you stop breathing from feeling so much at once. I didn't even ask. I could have hurt you. Just like—"

I cut her off. "You are not your sister. My body is yours. You never have to ask to touch me. I belong to you. You won't hurt me."

Belle hesitated. "But—"

I took her trembling hand and shyly placed it between my legs, holding it against me. "You won't hurt me," I repeated. Her breath shook as she finally gave in, scattering kisses across my chest as she pushed her fingers forward, splitting me open. Her touch was not gentle, but I craved this overpowering connection as much as she did.

She found the spot inside of me that always made me see stars and drove against it again and again. I trembled and shook, spreading my legs wider in order to take more of her. Her thumb rolled over me in hard, wet circles as her other fingers kept thrusting, filling me until everything but her faded away. It burned, even hurt a little, but it was so wonderful that I knew I would not be able to bear it if she stopped.

I whispered words of pleasure in her ear, reminding her that I loved her, that I loved this, to ease her conscience. I could not bear to let my lover feel ashamed of something so sacred.

I tried to reach down once, to give her the same pleasure that she was giving me, but she bit the vulnerable skin of my neck hard enough to leave a large purple bruise. I kept my hands where they were, leaving myself helpless and exposed for her. We completed each other, joining our two souls. A miracle older than we could imagine, but that seemed new and wonderful to us.

My release surprised me. I threw my head to the side, screaming into the bed itself, and my entire body hummed with power and energy. Even though I had not touched her, Belladonna followed me over the edge seconds later, grinding herself just above my knee and covering me with wetness. She claimed my lips in a brutal kiss that made me flood her hand, and I lost control a second time.

"I told you I was yours..." I whispered in between the kisses that I pressed to her forehead.

"Mine," Belle growled, curling her fingers inside of me and making me shiver. We were silent for several minutes. Before we fell asleep, still joined together, I heard Belle whisper something in my ear. "There isn't enough paper in the world to write all the poems you inspire in me."

CHAPTER 9

"YOU ARE GOING TO need a dress."

I turned away from the fire where I was warming my hands and watched Sarah from over my shoulder. It was evening, and we were sitting in the kitchen after dinner, waiting for Cate. She had been gone for almost an hour, and I was worried that Luciana had caught her in some dark corner. "A dress?" I asked. "Why?"

"A dress for the ball, of course. You can't go to Prince Brendan's ball without a dress and jewels."

I felt foolish. A dress and jewels? I had not even considered that. Of course I could not make an appearance at the palace unless I was dressed to out-dazzle the stars. That was what all of the other noblewomen would be doing. Even if I did not look or feel like a lady anymore, I was still one of them.

"How am I supposed to get them?" I was irritated that I had forgotten about the dress. Most of my time had been spent thinking up ways to explain my presence at the ball to Belladonna.

Sarah frowned at me. "You don't need to get angry. We just have to find a way to steal them."

"From who? Luciana and Belladonna are too tall. Their dresses would never fit me." Sarah's thin smile was positively devious, and I shivered. She could be nosy and talk too much, but behind all that, she was sharp.

"Who else is your size, Ellie?"

"You are enjoying this too much. Stop it."

"Lady Kingsclere," Sarah crowed, unable to hold it in. "She's much smaller than Miss Belladonna and Miss Luciana. Still bigger than you, but I should be able to alter one of her dresses. I know she will have something suitable. We just have to steal it."

One of my stool's three legs almost tipped out from under me as I shifted on the seat. I was too surprised to care. "Steal a dress from Lady Kingsclere? You've gone mad."

"Do you have a better idea? The ball is in six days. I need time to alter her dress if you want to go. It won't be that hard. All we have to do is go take her lunch up instead of Nancy. We can drug her wine. The woman's crazy anyway. She won't notice if one of her dresses is missing."

"I am not going to drug my stepmother. What if we give her an overdose and kill her? What if Nancy catches us? So many things could go wrong."

"Fine," Sarah pouted, clearly miffed that I did not appreciate her brilliant plan. "Go to the ball stark naked for all I care. I was just trying to help."

"Trying to help send me to the madhouse," I muttered.

"Send who to the madhouse?" a voice called from behind us. Sarah and I stopped fighting and turned as Cate entered the kitchen. I gave her a quick up-and-down to check for bruises, but she did not seem to be in pain and had no visible injuries. Luciana had not been the reason for her late arrival.

"Sarah," I said, as Sarah answered, "Ellie."

"Should I send both of you there? It would be about time." Cate's smile convinced me that she really was all right. Impulsively, I stood and gave her a tight hug. She returned it, and then Sarah wrapped her arms around both of us. When the embrace broke, I gave Sarah a shove and sat back down on my stool.

"Sarah wants to steal one of Lady Kingsclere's dresses. She says I need something to wear to the ball."

Cate did not look surprised. "I knew she would suggest that. She's the only one close to your size. You really don't have any other choice, Ellie. Buying something so late would be impractical."

"All of the seamstresses are probably up to their necks in orders for the ball. You need something in less than a week," Sarah added, encouraged by Cate's support.

"Besides, where would we get the money?"

I scowled. "And so I am supposed to drug my stepmother's drink without getting caught by guard dog Nancy, steal one of her dresses so that I can go to the ball, and stop my wicked stepsister from taking over the kingdom?" *Not to mention confront my lover about my plan,* I added privately.

Cate and Sarah did not say anything for several seconds. Finally, Sarah blinked. "Well, yes."

"Do you have any idea how crazy this is?"

"It's not crazy if it works," she insisted. "We have to try. If you don't go to the ball, no one will stop Luciana. We can't just let her become queen. We're as good as dead!"

I closed my eyes, knowing I was beaten.

***

Sarah, who enjoyed subterfuge more than I felt was healthy, came up with an elaborate plan to sneak some powdered walnuts out of Mam's medicine basket. She was put out when I simply asked Mam for the sedative, claiming insomnia.

I proved less capable when the time came to put the powder in Lady Kingsclere's drink. It was Cate who measured out a pinch of the stuff and sprinkled it into the bottle, recorking it and fetching a glass from the cupboard. I took them both to Nancy, pretending to smile helpfully. I had become a very capable liar in a short period of time.

She met me on my way up from the kitchen, nearly running into me as I turned a corner. She looked at me disapprovingly—Nancy was always looking at people disapprovingly—and took the tray from my hands. "Thank you," she said coolly, studying me in a way that suggested I might drop the tray if I held on to it.

"Of course. We finished lunch early, so I thought I would bring you the wine and save you a trip downstairs," I explained, keeping my nervous eyes on the bottle.

Nancy grasped the neck of the wine bottle. "Is this the right one?" She shoved the tray and glass back into my hands so that she could hold the bottle with two hands. I watched with horror as she uncorked the bottle, lifted it to her lips, and took a long sip. She lowered the bottle, wiping her lips with the back of her hand.

I grabbed for the wine just as Nancy's knees buckled and she crumpled to the carpet. I looked around to make sure no one else had seen the accident. Assured that we were alone, I dropped to my knees to check on the unconscious upstairs maid. I sighed with relief when I felt her strong heartbeat under my fingers.

Still carrying the open wine bottle in one hand, I ran back to the kitchen to find Cate and Sarah. They looked at me with identical expressions of surprise as I burst through the swinging wooden door.

"Both of you, come with me," I panted, making sure they were following me before hurrying back to Nancy.

"What happened?" Sarah's breathless question came from behind me.

"Nancy...the wine...she fainted dead away!"

"She drank it?" Cate squeaked.

"Right from the bottle." We approached Nancy's curled figure. She was still resting on the floor.

All of us stood silently for several moments, with Nancy's limp form sprawled at our feet. "Well," Sarah said, her voice unnaturally loud in the quiet hallway, "what do we do now?"

"I will take the wine up to Lady Kingsclere. There won't be another chance after this..."

"You're absolutely insane," Cate muttered, but she did not disagree with me.

"She's got to." Sarah picked up the tray and glass, which I had dropped on the floor when I grabbed for the wine. Their fall had been cushioned by the soft carpet, and they were unbroken. "Here, Ellie. Take these." I took them with trembling hands as Sarah prodded Nancy with her foot. "She's well and truly gone."

"Go, Ellie." Cate put a steadying hand on my shoulder. "You need that dress." And so I went, still shocked that we had accidentally drugged Nancy.

Lady Kingsclere's bedroom was cold. The chill ate into my bones and settled there. There was no fire in the fireplace, and the curtains were drawn, leaving the room dark. I could barely see the outline of Lady Kingsclere's body underneath the dark yellow bed sheets.

"Milady?" I called out, keeping my hands tight around the edges of the tray. There was no answer from the bed. As I stepped forward to set the tray on the small table beside the bed, the form under the covers moved. A thin, bony face peered out at me suspiciously like a bird from its nest.

If I studied her closely, I could see traces of the proud woman I remembered my stepmother to be, but with her skin pulled tight over her cheekbones and her once-beautiful hair let loose and wild around the crown of her head, she was almost unrecognizable. "Alastair?" she asked, her voice almost lost in the sheets. "Is that you?"

"No, Milady. I have your wine..."

Lady Kingsclere tossed aside the covers and stared at me with peering eyes. My heart pumped furiously against my ribs. "Oh, Luciana," she said flatly. I could not stifle a gasp of surprise. First she thought that

I was her long-dead first husband, and now Luciana? Lady Kingsclere was worse off than I had anticipated.

My stepmother was beginning to frighten me. I blinked back tears as I poured the wine into the glass that I had brought. My hands shook. *Oh Lady,* I thought, *what has Luciana reduced you to?*

"Why do you hate me, Luciana? I always loved you. I tried to love you."

"Luciana hates everyone, Mother," I told her. I lifted the full glass to her lips, and she sipped like an obedient child. I put a gentle hand on her shoulder, tears streaming down my face. I felt a wave of affection for this woman and a surge of hatred for Luciana.

"I suppose she does," Lady Kingsclere said, her voice surprisingly steady. Her eyes appeared clearer for a moment, and she looked directly into my face before her head fell back onto the pillow.

Setting the half empty glass of wine on the tray, I walked shakily over to the wardrobe, my mind awhirl with the things I had seen. First Nancy, now Lady Kingsclere. What was I doing?

The dress I selected was quite lovely, with cheerful blue fabric in ruffles that complemented my skin well, but I scarcely studied it as I grabbed the neck and hurried from the room. I could not have told anyone what color it was until I saw it again later. I took three steps through the door before I remembered to return for the wine and tray. No one could know what Cate, Sarah, and I had done, and I did not want to get caught because I was too flustered to hide the evidence. Nancy's fainting spell would be difficult enough to explain on its own.

I did not stop to breathe or think until the wine had been emptied outside, the glass and tray had been washed, and the dress was tucked away safely in Belladonna's wardrobe. I assumed it would not arouse suspicion hidden among other dresses.

The sound of footsteps behind me made my breath catch and I clasped a hand to my chest in surprise as I whirled around to see Cate walking toward me. "You're all right?" she asked, concerned.

I nodded. "Yes, I survived. The dress is hidden in Belle's wardrobe."

Cate looked at me curiously. "Belle's wardrobe?" My bright blush gave away my secret and the ever-perceptive Cate's face lifted in understanding.

"Yes," I whispered.

Instead of reacting with confusion or anger, Cate burst out laughing. I watched her, dumb as a rock, as she shut her eyes and howled. "Belladonna is your lover and you didn't think to ask her to get a dress for you?"

I nearly imitated Nancy and fell to the floor. Helplessly, I joined Cate and laughed too, until Mam came in to see what we were up to and scolded us for wasting time in her kitchen.

CHAPTER 10

IT WAS FIVE DAYS before the ball. Belle and I were involved in a newly discovered shared interest—chess. She was a more experienced player, but I was familiar enough with the game to present her with a challenge, and I was enthusiastic about improving.

"Watch your knight," she said. We were sitting at a table in the library, a crowded chessboard in between us. Belle tapped her finger on the head of the piece in question.

I studied the congested center of the battlefield, noting where her pieces of power were positioned. Then, I looked up at her. Thick locks of her glossy raven hair wrapped around the pale landscape of her neck. This was, perhaps, my greatest strategical weakness. Belle was always able to distract me while I tried to play.

"Ellie." Belle's voice intruded on my thoughts. "Ellie. Your move."

"Oh." I shoved a pawn forward. Within two turns, Belle had taken my knight.

"Maybe if you started looking at the chessboard instead of me, you would win more often," Belle teased, covering my hand with hers and rubbing her thumb over my knuckles. I smiled, purposely lowering my eyes and letting them wander over every inch of her upper body. Who could concentrate on chess with such a beautiful sight right above the board?

I turned my hand over, letting her trace patterns over the sensitive skin of my palm. "You are more interesting to look at."

She laughed. "I am surprised you win at all, then."

"Are you implying that I am a poor chess player, Belladonna Kingsclere?"

"I am implying that you are more interested in what is underneath my dress than in winning a game of chess. At least, right now you are." The relaxed, almost coy expression on her face was unexpected, but certainly not unwelcome. I felt guilty that I had to ruin her good mood.

Belle leaned forward to kiss me, and I pressed my fingers to her chin, holding her head back. "No." One kiss from her lips would make me forget everything I had to say.

"No?" She lowered her eyebrows, looking wounded. Perhaps she saw a flash of nervousness in my eyes. "Something bad?"

"If you allow it to be." My voice sounded quiet, even to my own ears. Belle pulled closer to me. Her hand covered mine. "I am coming with you to the ball."

Belle stared at me, setting her jaw. "No."

I stared back. "You need me. Have you even thought about what you are going to do once you get there to stop Luciana?"

"Of course I have."

"And did you come up with any ideas?" She gave no answer. "I thought so."

"How can I make a plan when I have no idea what Luciana is going to do?"

"That is exactly why I need to be there. Two people working together have a better chance —"

"I don't care about our chances!" She stood in a flash, her hands clenched at her sides and nearly kicking over her chair. "I will not watch you go. You're staying here, far away from her."

"Belle..."

"Ellie, I won't let you..."

Belladonna reached out, grabbing my wrist in a tight, frantic hold as she pulled me towards her. I winced in surprise and pain, struggling to pull my wrist out of her grip, but it was too late. Although she let go almost immediately, I could still see lines where her fingers had been.

Belladonna was badly frightened by her own strength, but still furious. Tears of anger welled in her eyes, but I knew she was not upset with me. She was angry at herself. I knew her so well that it was easy to read what she was thinking. If I had any doubts, her next words proved me right. "Oh Saints, I hurt you...Luciana will hurt you...You are NOT going."

I opened my arms, reaching for her, but she pulled away violently, squeezing her eyes shut and storming from the room.

***

I searched for Belle the next day, hoping that a night apart had cooled her temper. I found her in the library, a book on her lap. She rose from the armchair as if she had been waiting for me, but did not reach out in greeting. I took a tentative step forward, watching her face for any sign of fright or anger. To my surprise, she looked defeated, almost cold. I lowered my eyes, unable to stare at that dead expression for another moment.

Belle stepped forward, too, until we were a foot apart. It felt as though there were miles stretching between us. One of us had to cross that empty space. I reached for Belle's hand at the exact moment that she reached for mine. I gave her a hesitant smile.

"I already snuck a dress away from your mother," I said.

"Really? Why? I could have taken one for you."

Belle watched me, puzzled, as I shook my head. Of course, I had to explain the conversation that Cate and I had shared, and soon, Belle was laughing. We did not need to discuss the subject of my attendance at the ball. It had already been decided without words. Belle knew I would go no matter what she did, because I loved her. Just as I knew she did not want me to go because she loved me.

Our hands gripped each other loosely; both of us enjoying the physical contact after our separation. "Would you really have taken a dress for me?" I asked.

Belle nodded. My face broken in a brilliant smile, and I squeezed her hand. Never again would I wonder if Belle respected my ability to make decisions. Perhaps we were not always equals when we made love, but Belle did not see me as a pet or a child, totally dependent on her, completely submissive to her authority.

I threw myself into her arms and held on tight. "Thank you," I said, the words cracking as they scraped through my dry throat. Belle kissed my hair. I felt her heart pumping slowly through the fabric of her morning dress.

"You are most welcome, dear heart." She dropped a second kiss onto the crown of my head. "You promise to be careful?" Belle could not disguise the naked fear in her voice. Her heart thumped faster.

"Of course." I traced soothing circles over her back with my hands. "I have everything to stay safe for. By the way, I had an idea about the ball."

"Really? What is it?" Belle asked. She had not been very successful in her research on sorcerer's chains.

"We should write a letter to someone at the palace. Surely there are people guarding Prince Brendan against magical threats. He is royalty, after all. Perhaps one of them will be able to protect him from Luciana if they are given proper warning."

"I already did. Oh, don't give me that look." Belle stroked my cheek, trying to smooth my frown away. "I was going to tell you, but we started fighting."

I could not blame her for keeping that piece of information from me. After all, I had been keeping my own secrets from her. "Who did you contact? What did you write? Did you—"

Belle's hand moved to cover my lips. "Shhh, Ellie. The High Wizard Cieran and his wife, Cassandra, live at the palace. I have met them before. In addition to being the king's magical advisors, they are some of the most well-respected people in the Kingdom of Seria, even if they are Ariada."

"And?" I asked, my excitement growing. "Did they write you back?"

"I explained that a sorcerer's chain was going to be used to cast a love spell on the prince. I left Luciana's name out of it, but I did put my signature at the bottom. I wanted them to know that the warning was coming from a reputable source. They would never believe me if I accused my own sister outright. They might assume I wanted her inheritance. I received a reply this morning from Lady Cassandra, saying that they were grateful for the warning and that I should try and speak with them near the beginning of the first ball."

I was relieved that someone with proper magical training had been alerted to the situation. Belle hesitated for a moment. "Will you dance with the prince?"

Seeing the frustration behind her eyes, I kissed her gently on the lips. "If he is agreeable, yes. But in my heart, I will never dance with anyone but you. There is no reason for you to worry about me eloping with Prince Brendan or anyone else."

Belle smiled again, and I smiled back. "I know. I just wanted to hear it."

We held hands, leaning against each other. "And I will say it over and over again until you believe me."

Belle and I were much friendlier to each other after our reconciliation. However, sometimes, as she watched me working, or as we rested in bed together before dawn or read together in the library, I caught her looking at me with a curious expression on her face. Her lips would part, slowly, as if she wanted to speak, but she never did. She only stared at me with tortured blue eyes until I kissed her, spoke, or looked away.

***

I told my worries to Cate one morning as we cleared the breakfast dishes. I had forgiven Sarah for reading my fake diary entries concerning Jamison, but I still did not trust her with my secrets. I knew that Cate would listen and comfort me much better than Sarah could.

"She refuses to talk with me." I set my stack of plates down on the kitchen counter. "I think she is afraid of getting angry again." When we had made love the night before, Belle had been exceedingly cautious with me, kissing my wrists over and over again, wanting to heal the bruises her fingers had left. I had enjoyed myself, but I wanted my barely restrained tiger back, the powerful woman who would lose herself in her passion and consume me.

I could not explain this part to Cate. I did not want to frighten her by discussing the subject of physical love. Her broken heart probably could not handle the conversation.

"Perhaps this is a problem that Belladonna needs to solve on her own. She is afraid. I think being afraid of something is a new experience for her."

"What should I do to help?" I asked. I was sure that Cate had gotten it right. Belle was not the kind of woman who admitted that she was afraid of anything. Maybe she did not want me to think she was weak. She already felt weak and guilty for not taking a stand against Luciana earlier.

Cate covered my hand with hers for a moment. Because my friend did not usually initiate physical contact, I was surprised by the touch. I managed to hide my reaction, not wanting to startle Cate. "Just remind her that you love her. Tell her you will always be there. She needs to hear that."

"You are probably right. If I confront her directly, she will only get defensive."

Cate nodded. "I can picture that. Ellie..." She reclaimed her hand, twisting it nervously into the fabric of her dress. I leaned against the counter, dishes forgotten. "Thank you for talking to me. For trusting me. I have never...I mean...you are the first real friend I have ever had."

I placed an affectionate kiss on Cate's soft cheek, and her face flushed a fiery red. "Thank you, Cate. I am glad that you are my friend, too. I have never really had any friends before, either."

We both smiled at each other and returned to the dishes that were waiting for us.

Part Three,

As Recorded By Eleanor Baxstresse

CHAPTER 1

WINTER WAS COMING fast, and soon the fields would be covered in a blanket of snow, but for the moment, there was only a light dusting of frost over the grass. The cold winds from the north brought more strange dreams with them. Plans for the ball and worries about Luciana had pushed them to the back of my mind, where they lingered like the last gray snow, but the sorcerer's chain and the eye were never forgotten.

At least six times I saw the eye, twice in my dreams and sometimes in waking-dreams that fell upon me while I was working. Once, I nearly fell down the stairs. Only Cate's quick grab at my arm saved me from a nasty fall. It was golden and silver, glinting wickedly in a pulsing light.

How could an eye be awake? Why was it watching me? I did not think that these were visions like the ones Cate had. They were a warning. I often felt the strange hum of magic in my skin and blood after seeing the eye. Perhaps it—or someone using it—really could see me? Maybe the eye wanted me to see it? Something was watching me, and I was terrified.

I told Belladonna about the dreams. I did not tell her how frightened they made me, but she could tell. My lover knew me better than I knew myself. Even Cate noticed that something was wrong, and when she asked, I could not lie to her.

"Maybe your magic is reacting to the sorcerer's chain. You said that it burned your skin. Could your magic have made the burn stronger?"

"We are the only two magical people I know of at Baxstresse." I looked at Cate. "You would have to touch it to find out, and I want you as far away from Luciana as possible."

"There is something behind the chain. It is not some leftover relic from the ancient past. If the magic in it is strong enough to burn your skin and give you nightmares, then there is some powerful force channeling through it."

When I told Belle about my conversation with Cate, she did not respond for several minutes. She stroked my hair, a thoughtful expression on her face. I was patient with her, and she finally said, "I wish there was a way to research its history. Maybe I can ask Cieran or Cassandra at the ball."

"It's worth a try. You should discuss it with them."

Belle sighed and pulled her arm tighter around my shoulder. "If they don't know anything about the history of this chain, perhaps they can direct me to another resource. I know how hard it is to get magical books in Seria, but I'm surprised that there isn't more information about sorcerer's chains in our library."

I patted her shoulder, offering comfort. "It's a wonderful library, Belle. Magical books are rare on this side of the border. We can always look for more later."

"Something else to ask Cieran and Cassandra about," she said, but she still looked worried and disappointed.

I decided to give her a kiss to brighten both our moods. One kiss turned into two kisses, and we completely forgot what we had been talking about. My sleep that night was blissfully empty of all dreams.

***

Sarah spent several hours each evening tailoring the borrowed dress to fit me. She used her eyes to estimate most of the measurements, since I was too busy to stand for fittings more than a few minutes long. As the dress took shape, feelings of excitement rose in me. The dress was a link to my old world; the one Luciana had stolen from me. I hoped to return to it, and Belle, wiser, kinder, and humbler.

I was also excited about modeling the dress for Belle. Her dashing good looks and fine clothes intimidated me, even though our relationship was not built on such trivial things. I wanted to remind her that I was a lady, more to improve my own self-image than to change Belle's perception of me.

Proper underthings were borrowed from Loren's never-ending piles of laundry, and Sarah's quick fingers stole several pieces of costume jewelry for me to wear. I could have asked Belle, but Sarah still did not know we were lovers. The only thing I could not find was a pair of shoes. My feet were smaller than Luciana's, Belle's, or even Lady Kingsclere's.

I was considering the problem as I cleaned a spare bedroom. Jessith, who was sunning herself on the bedspread that I had just changed, stretched one paw and batted at my working dress, her claws catching the fabric. I felt the tug and looked down at her. "Ellie? Are you listening to me? I just said that I have a message for you from Belladonna."

"How long have you and Belladonna been having discussions?" I asked. I had not been able to focus all day. I was too embarrassed to admit that I had been worrying about something as trivial as shoes when there were many more serious problems to be concerned with.

"Since you told her you could talk to me. I usually pretend that I am not paying attention. She mostly rambles about you. Human love softens the sharpest minds. Thank goodness I am a cat."

"Jessith, do you have a point?"

But Jessith was a cat, and cats are used to taking their time. Licking her right forepaw was too important an activity to interrupt. "Belladonna told me she wanted you to meet her this afternoon. She has a surprise for you."

Knowing my lover as I did, I immediately interpreted the message as a physical invitation. "I suspect she does," I purred. Jessith ignored me and rolled across the bed to reach her back leg. "No, stop that. I just made that bed and washed those sheets, and you are going to get fur all over them."

Jessith glared at me. "Humans leave hair everywhere, too."

"And I have to clean up that hair as well as yours, so stop making my job harder."

"What job? You haven't done any work all day." I couldn't argue with her. I had been especially lazy today. Thankfully, Cate and Sarah had understood.

"So," I said, changing the subject, "when is Belladonna going to give me this surprise, or did she not say?"

"I told you, this afternoon." Animals experience time differently than people. There are four times of day for them: morning, afternoon, evening, and night. However, their bodies are very sensitive to the earth's physical changes, and they are able to follow their own particular schedules almost to the minute without trying.

"Right now," said a rich voice that made my skin prickle. Belladonna leaned against the doorframe, and I turned to watch as she stepped toward me. Held over one of her arms was something I recognized. My hands flew to my mouth.

"Oh, by the Saints! That was my mother's dress. How did you find it?" The dress was a subtle red, not bright enough to make me appear wanton, but deep enough to bring out the color in my cheeks. It looked more beautiful than I remembered.

Belle smiled, looking almost like Jessith when she had caught a mouse or a spider and was bringing it to show me. "I managed to steal a few things before Luciana got rid of them. Nothing else as big as a dress, but I did find some other surprises for you."

My smile split my face in two as Belle set the dress carefully on the bed beside Jessith, kissing me until I thought I would float from the floor. Even Jessith seemed impressed by Belle's actions, and did not make any snide comments.

"Thank you, but why did you keep it a secret?"

"I like seeing you smile," she said in the dreamy way that we both spoke after kissing. "I have another present for you, too."

"Oh? Something else? Was it my mother's as well?"

Belle lowered her eyebrows mysteriously. "I will just have to show you. Close your eyes." I closed my eyes tight and clasped my hands behind my back, like a child waiting for a treat. Belle pressed her lips to my forehead, and I listened as she moved back out of the room. It did not take her long to return, less than a minute, so I guessed that she had left my surprise just outside the door.

I nearly jumped when I felt soft hands lifting my ankle and removing the worn brown working shoes that I wore when Luciana did not force me to put on the wooden ones. My feet only had one or two small cuts on them, and they were healing, so her touch did not hurt. She slipped something cool onto my foot, and I opened my eyes and looked down.

Instead of my dirty working shoes, delicate silver slippers rested on my feet. They had also belonged to my mother, and they were a perfect fit. Belle pressed her face against my belly, breathing against the fabric of my dress. "Do you like them?" she asked, looking up at me with a hopeful expression.

I was so warm with happiness and love that I might have been glowing. "Belle...thank you, thank you..."

"I would do anything for you. I am sorry I waited so long to give these to you. I planned on doing it before, but then we fought, and I was distracted."

I curled my hands through the soft, dark strands of her hair. "I am distracting?" Belle lifted my ankle and dropped a kiss on the soft skin. "What other things did you take?"

"You." I gasped, heat rushing up to my cheeks and down to pool between my legs. Belle's warm hands explored the skin behind my knee and slid up my thigh. My eyes darted to the door, relaxing when I saw it was closed. "Oh," Belle said casually, "you meant your mother's things. I stole some jewelry, some books, some flower bulbs, a beautiful red shawl..."

I let out a cry of delight just as Belle's lips caught my knee. "That shawl belonged to my mother, and those bulbs are some of Sandleford's white roses. I wanted to plant some here..."

This was too much for Jessith, who leapt off of the bed and crawled underneath it, slightly reproachful that we were not paying attention to her any longer. She was, however, polite enough not to disturb our moment, for which I was grateful. I sat down in her place, certain that my legs could not hold me anymore.

Belle's teasing became more serious as she lifted the skirts of my dress and ducked her head underneath. I giggled as her breath tickled the sensitive skin of my inner thigh and groaned as her sharp teeth nipped me. "My rose," she said, her words muffled by the fabric of my dress. Her lips, hands, and tongue proceeded to drive all thoughts of my mother's things out of my head. Her clever fingers made quick work of my underthings, and I was grateful that I no longer wore layers of petticoats.

She spared no time, possessing me with one smooth stroke of her fingers, and I nearly fell backwards onto the mattress with surprise. She held still inside of me, unwilling to leave my warmth. My hands clutched my skirts to my hips. I needed to watch Belle as she had me.

Belle pressed her face against the fluttering muscles of my stomach, curling her fingers to find me. I cradled her head against my belly, still holding up my skirts with one fist, gasping at the familiar, wonderful stretch. "I can feel how much you need me," she breathed, her voice controlling me even while she was on her knees in front of me. Her fingers moved, leaving me empty and aching until she filled me again, grasping my waist with her other hand.

We fell into an easy rhythm, moving together as one. The pleasant burn I felt as two of Belle's fingers stretched me caused my head to fall back and my eyes to squeeze shut. I rocked hard against her hand with every thrust, allowing Belle to touch me deeper than she ever had before.

"So full...I feel...more..." My hips jerked unevenly as Belle kissed up along my thigh, settling between my legs and leaning forward to taste me. Her lips wrapped around me, tugging at the stiff point just above her fingers, and I whimpered as her tongue began to paint over me in circles.

With her mouth occupied, Belle could only groan against me, and I felt the vibrations in her lips.

My hands flexed, releasing the material of my skirt as her fingers hooked inside of me. They pressed up, filling me with slow, deep thrusts. I was helpless against her hands and mouth. My only regret before colors burst behind my eyes and empty sound roared in my ears was that I could not look into Belladonna's eyes as I gave all of myself to her. I tightened around her fingers, spilling into her hand and twitching wildly against her lips.

Finally, when I could see again, I looked down at her face, blushing furiously when I noticed the wetness smeared across her cheeks and chin. Although it was a sight I had gotten used to, it still made me ache hollowly with want. "I'm far from finished with you, pet," she said after she licked her lips, pulling her fingers out of me and standing up so that she could join me on the mattress. "But first, let's get you out of your clothes. I don't want to ruin them."

***

"Ellie, you look beautiful!" Sarah cried, clasping her hands with delight.

I could see Sarah's reflection in the mirror, but I did not need to look to see how happy she was. I could hear it in her voice. My own reflection was smiling, but I hardly recognized myself. The thin, pale girl that I had seen in warped metal pans for the past months looked nothing like this soft, golden creature I had become. I felt a surge of confidence. I was going to make Belladonna proud tonight, even if I could not walk into the ball on her arm. I was wearing the finished blue dress, which really did suit my complexion well.

"Yes, you do," Cate agreed. I could not see her reflection, because she was still behind me, brushing my hair. She had already stroked it to gleaming with the fine bristles, but was not ready to stop. Around my neck was a piece of costume jewelry that Belle had found for me. I did not explain its presence, and perhaps Sarah assumed that I had taken it with the dress from Lady Kingsclere, but Cate gave me a knowing look as I fastened the catch.

The smell of lilacs still surrounded me from my bath. I had been plucked, rubbed with oil, prodded, and laced into a corset for the first time in months. But I forgot the discomfort now that I was staring at myself in the mirror. I liked what I saw. No one at the ball would ever guess that I had been picking lentils from the ashes and cleaning garbage for the past few months. Only my rough hands would give me away. I would need to wear gloves.

"I'm ready," I said, and Cate helped me gather the layers of my gown as I stood up, tossing one last glance over my shoulder at my reflection. I would fit in perfectly at the ball. The pleasure that I took in my appearance helped me dismiss some of the fear that still clung to me. I had no idea what Luciana planned to do, and could not prepare in advance. Belle and I would leap on Luciana and physically restrain her if we needed to, although we would probably look foolish tackling her to the ground in the middle of the ballroom.

I examined the skirt of my dress, enjoying the movement of the soft underlayers against my legs as I walked down the stairs. "You really did a beautiful job with the waist, Sarah."

"You could work professionally at dressmaking or sewing if you wanted," Cate added.

"You did at least a third of the dress, Cate," Sarah said, blushing prettily. She turned to me. "And I'm sure that you will attract quite a bit of attention at Prince Brendan's ball. I hope your secret lover is not the jealous type."

I shared a quick glance with Cate. Although she was not controlling, Belle was an extremely possessive lover. I was glad that she would be tailing Luciana instead of watching me near the Prince. Even if he showed no interest in me, I could stay near him. It would not look too suspicious, since many other young women would be trailing after him, vying for his attention.

"I have no interest in Prince Brendan," I said firmly.

Sarah smiled dreamily. "He's handsome all the same."

"You can have him. One love is enough for my lifetime." *And for all eternity*, I thought. Of course, the Church discouraged thoughts of reincarnation, but if I did have more lives to live, I would spend them looking for her. If I was only granted this one life, I would follow Belladonna to heaven, hell, or whatever came after death.

As if she could read my mind, Cate stared at me with such a naked longing that I nearly gasped. *Here*, I thought, *is a heart aching, calling to its other half.* Cate had transformed since I first got to know her. She had become braver, friendlier, more talkative, and more confident. If she was not ready to seek love yet, she would be soon.

"I would come with you if I could, Ellie," Cate said. Though her voice was soft, it did not lack support.

"I would, too," Sarah agreed.

Both of them really meant it. My heart floated. A girl could not ask for truer friends. I tucked a lock of Cate's red curls behind one of her ears, leaving my hand on her shoulder. "I know you would. And thank you both again for the dress."

CHAPTER 2

THE PALACE WAS white and gleaming, a miracle of magic and craftsmanship. Its crisp outline stood proudly against the dark night sky. I stared at its painted turrets, watching the long, flowing banners flutter and then fall still. They were all stitched with the same coat of arms: two crossed quill plumes for knowledge, and a sword pointing down between them for strength.

The carriage—the second-best one, since Belladonna and Luciana had used the finest—jolted to a stop in front of a white set of stairs. Since Belladonna knew that Matthew would be driving me, she had arranged for one of the stable hands to drive their own carriage. Luciana had not seemed to notice or care that Matthew was not on the box.

Since Belle and Luciana had taken the matching pair of carriage horses, I had to enlist the services of Brahms and Corynne, even though they were not exactly built for pulling a carriage. Matthew took them slow, which infuriated them, because he did not want to strain the delicate horses with work they were not used to. They lifted their hooves, their flanks twitching as they tossed their thick, corded necks, eager to keep moving.

The main roadways, which had been magicked to allow us faster travel, had them excited. The bewitchment was another example of how hypocritical Serians were. Magic was evil, except when it was convenient. I appreciated the shorter journey, which had taken about two hours instead of five days. It would have been impractical to house all of the courtiers and visiting nobles in the capital for three days and nights.

"The castle, Lady," Matthew said, bounding down from the driver's box and opening the door for me. I blushed in spite of myself. It was the first time I had been treated like nobility since my forced servitude, and I found returning to my status unsettling, almost unpleasant.

"Thank you," I said with my eyes. There were other fine coaches around mine, and the elegant ladies and gentlemen stepping out of them might have heard and found it strange that I was showing gratitude toward a servant. Matthew smiled, and I knew he understood. I gave Brahms and Corynne a silent thank you as well and turned to face the palace. Trying to draw attention to myself so I would not be noticed, I ascended the wide steps in a practiced glide. To blend in, I needed to look like I was trying to stand out. I would surely be noticed if I acted shy or afraid.

Everyone inside was preening and puffing themselves up. The women gathered in groups like colorful flocks of birds in their ruffled gowns, and their men eyed each other in silent challenges for dominance. The crowd had little effect on me, and neither did the grand entrance hall's beauty.

My eyes darted from one side of the room to the other, skipping over the rare decorations that were worth my father's fortune many times over and the impressive spread of food, searching for a head of thick, lustrous black curls. When I did not see Belladonna, I waded my way into the tide of people, hoping to spot either of my stepsisters. I knew if I found one, I would find the other. Luciana would not dare let Belle too far out of her sight.

I caught a glint of lustrous brown among the beautiful ball gowns. There was Luciana, her slender arms curving at her sides, brightening the faces of everyone around her with a false light. As I drew closer to the crowd that shielded her, I felt magic hum in the hollow of my chest. Luciana was bewitching in folds of blood-red silk. For a moment, I felt desire cut quick below my stomach. But then I remembered that she was casting a spell, and I swallowed my guilt. The silver-gold eye of the pendant winked at me, and I looked away.

I had no solid plan, no obvious road to take. I only had a task, and a whole kingdom of people to complete it for. If I had to grab the necklace from her hands and tear the gold apart, I would do so gladly, subtlety be damned. A sorcerer's chain had one weakness: it was easy to break.

For the moment, I chose to wait and watch. I knew Luciana probably would not do anything tonight. Like me, she was observing, waiting for her chance. She would not rush and waste it with a whole kingdom at stake. Belladonna stood only a few feet away, but she could not see me.

I had just lifted my slippered foot to creep closer to Belle and Luciana when fingertips touched my wrist. I held still, turning to look over my shoulder at the person who had tapped me. It was a woman with dark hair that reminded me of Belle's and a thin, attractive face. She was much smaller than my lover, but her entire body was surrounded by magical energy. My head spun. Between her and Luciana, I had never experienced so much magic before in my life, except when I had accidentally touched Luciana's chain.

"Lady Eleanor of Sandleford," she said. It was a statement, not a question. She offered her hand and I took it, surprised at the firmness of her grip. "I believe your lover sent me a note." My mouth hung open, leaving me incapable of speech. The woman paused for a beat before laughing. "Oh, I apologize. My husband's visions, you see...sometimes I forget no one else knows that I know what I know."

I had the impression that this woman was used to talking and being listened to. She spoke with great enthusiasm, even though she was careful to keep the volume of her voice low, adding a great many hand movements to emphasize her point. "I am Cassandra, High Wizard Cieran's wife. I think my husband is cornering Belladonna as we speak."

Still trying to process the fact that Cassandra knew about Belle and me, I gave myself a mental shake. "If you got her letter, than you know what we're afraid of. What are you doing to protect the prince from Luciana?" I saw no reason to hide her identity now. She was positively reeking of magic. Even a poor, half-talent fortuneteller would have been able to sense her.

"We are not concerned about the prince being bewitched. The real danger lies in Luciana physically harming him. She is untrained, filled with stolen raw power from the sorcerer's chain. If Prince Brendan or anyone else does something to anger her, who knows how she might choose to unleash it?"

I looked at her curiously. "Stolen magic?"

"Yes. My husband and I need to do some more research, but we believe your stepsister has in her possession a very old, very powerful talisman that was once owned by the sorcerer Umbra. It is ancient, and its magical fingerprint is unique."

I nodded in understanding. So, Cate had been right. The sorcerer's chain did have an ancient history. I was impressed that Cassandra and Cieran had been able to discover its origin. "I know that it used to belong to Luciana's great grandmother, but I have no idea how it came into their family's possession. A friend of mine with some magical aptitude suggested that something might be using the sorcerer's chain to direct its power."

"It is possible. Umbra has been dead for centuries, so it could not be him. Even a necromancer cannot return a wizard's magic to him once he has died. But perhaps someone else has found a way to break the familiarity spell, if there was one, and use it. Cieran and I will try and discover more after the ball. For now, our priority is to keep Prince Brendan from getting hurt."

"So you don't think Luciana can enchant him?"

Cassandra shook her head. To my surprise, she was smiling. I wondered if that smile ever left her face at all, no matter how dire the circumstances. "No, my dear. In all likelihood, any spell she casts with the sorcerer's chain will fade a few hours after she leaves the immediate area. She does not have the magical stamina or skill to create lasting magic. With the protective signs we have drawn on the prince, he should be mostly unaffected if she tries to bewitch him. However, that talisman is packed full of highly dangerous magic. If she were to use it as a weapon and throw him off the palace roof, for example, I doubt Cieran or I could save him in time."

A thought occurred to me. "Now that you sense the magic surrounding her, couldn't you ask the king to take her away to the dungeon? Waiting for her to strike seems dangerous."

Cassandra shook her head. "No. You and I can sense her powers because we are Ariada, but we have no other proof of her intentions. Accusing a noble of using dark magic is one of the most slanderous accusations one can make, and the Kingscleres are one of the most powerful families in the kingdom. The king can be fair, but he is more wary of magic than his son. Without proof, it's just our word against hers." She gave me a look, and I understood immediately. Despite the wary respect that Cassandra and her husband received at court, they were still Ariada to the king, and not to be trusted completely.

I frowned. "So, what should we do instead if the king won't believe us?"

"All we can do is watch and try to head her off before she does anything too dangerous. But now, I think someone else wants to make your acquaintance..." As suddenly as she had appeared, Cassandra was gone. I looked around for several moments, trying to see her, but there was no one nearby except for a young man approaching me. I ignored him at first, but the sound of a clearing throat drew my attention, and I turned to look at him. Standing at my left side was one of the most beautiful men I had ever seen. His rich brown hair was tied back with a leather cord, his chin was strong, and his bright eyes and smile made the air charge.

I appreciated his beauty, but looking at him left me cold, partly because men could not hold my attention like women, but mostly because his face was not the one seared onto my heart. His lips spread in a smile. "Good evening, Lady." He searched my face, looking for any sign of discomfort, and I knew that he would leave me alone if I asked. "May I ask your name?

I returned his smile, deciding that a version of the truth would do no harm. "Lady Eleanor of Sandleford." It was the first time I had used that name in ages, and it felt uncomfortable on my lips.

I allowed him to place a chaste kiss on the back of my hand. "It is a pleasure to meet you, Lady Eleanor. I must admit, I am surprised to see you here. I had heard that you were ill."

"I am finally recovering, but neither of my sisters wanted me to attend the ball." I glanced over at the last place I had seen Luciana and Belle, but they had moved to another part of the room. "They do not exactly know I am here. I would be grateful if you did not tell them."

He laughed. "I have had experience dodging people at formal occasions, although I usually want to sneak out of balls instead of into them. My name is Brendan."

"Prince Brendan?" I dipped into a curtsy, but I could not bring myself to swoon like some of the other ladies of the court. I decided to try and stay in his company for as long as I could, knowing it would make keeping him away from Luciana easier. He looked different than the child I had glimpsed briefly the few times my family was at court. We were not courtiers, although we had more money than some of the old families did. We had never been formally presented or introduced at court.

He gave me a broad smile, tugging lightly at the cuff of his sleeve. His nervousness was charming, and I hoped he would ask me to dance. It would be simple to keep him far from Luciana if we were on the dance floor, since we could lose ourselves in the crowd.

"Lady Eleanor, would you honor me with a dance?"

"I would enjoy that, Sire, as long as we stay far away from my stepsisters. If they catch me, they will send me straight home to bed like a sick child." Once again, learning how to lie had proved useful.

"Of course. I will make sure they don't see you." Prince Brendan took my hand and led me onto the dance floor. The string orchestra began to play a waltz, and the prince put his hand cautiously on my shoulder. He looked so hopeful that I almost pitied him. The spark he obviously felt did not light in me. "Thank you for dancing with me," he said as we moved across the floor in time with the music.

"Thank you for asking me, Sire. I think I will enjoy myself."

I did enjoy dancing with the prince. He was a good partner, although it was difficult for me to remember the steps to some of the newer dances while sneaking looks at his face and watching for Luciana out of the corner of my eye at the same time. I could not help studying Prince Brendan while we danced. I had never seen a royal up close before, and I certainly had never touched one. Luciana came close to us a few times, but thanks to my warning, Prince Brendan was able to add a flourish or twist to whatever dance we were doing and change our direction enough to avoid her.

Conversation with the prince was pleasant. We mostly talked about the upcoming Prince's Cup and which horses from Baxstresse we expected to race. "Do you really think Brahmsian Synng is that promising, then?" he asked.

"Yes. I have ridden him myself. He is surprisingly sturdy for a racehorse, not as delicate as Corynne. I will certainly be placing a bet on him next year, after he has gotten some experience and his sister is retired."

"Well then, I will have to keep an eye on him in this year's Cup. If he does well, I will consider betting on him myself next year."

I heard the deep tolling of a clock just as our dance ended and decided to excuse myself quickly, before Luciana had a chance to spot me. "Sire, I have had a lovely time dancing with you, but I..." My voice trailed off as I felt hot magic crawling over my skin and I glanced over my shoulder to see Luciana coming toward us. Out of the corner of my eye, I saw Belladonna move to intercept her.

I turned my face away from them so that Luciana would have a harder time recognizing me and bolted for the door, leaving the bewildered prince staring after me. Thankfully, he did not shout my name, which would have revealed my identity to Luciana. He started to run after me, but I was already down the white steps and climbing up into my carriage before he could figure out which way I had gone.

"Hurry, Matthew." I slammed the carriage door shut, kicking off my slippers. "The Prince is after me."

"And you want to run away?" Matthew laughed, urging Brahms and Corynne forward. "Is he that bad looking?"

"Luciana almost caught me. She is a vulture, circling him and waiting for her chance."

"Aye, that'd be her," Matthew muttered. Lost in our own thoughts, we were silent for the rest of the journey home.

CHAPTER 3

THE NEXT MORNING, Belle made love to me as though it was our last day on earth. Every touch of her hands and mouth against my skin burned, every sound that passed from between her lips made my heart stutter. "I love you," she whispered over and over again, in my ear, in my hair, against my neck.

I kissed her furiously, forcing her to remember that I was warm and solid and alive in her arms and that I would never leave her. Her large, powerful hands trembled as she palmed my breasts, rubbing the beaded tips with her thumbs while she suckled a sensitive spot on my neck. I cried out as her sharp teeth sank into my shoulder, holding the skin, but not really hurting me.

She reached between my legs, but I closed my thighs, trapping her hand instead of opening for her. "What is it?" she asked, a crease forming on her forehead.

I swallowed, trying to work moisture into my dry, nervous mouth. A sudden desire had struck me, too powerful to ignore, and I felt brave enough to ask for it. My hands gripped Belle's hips, urging her up along my body. "I want to taste you." She tried to turn us over, reversing our positions so that I could settle between her legs, but I stopped her again. "No. I want you over me."

Belle's smile was fierce, almost predatory as she stalked up my torso, positioning herself above my mouth. I stared at her in wonder. Her soft pink lips were swollen open, glistening with her wetness, red at the edges. I had never observed her this closely before. She was beautiful. Her fine muscles twitched as I traced her outline with the tip of one finger, parting her for me.

After an eternity, Belle lowered herself onto my waiting mouth. I clutched at her hips, pulling her tight against me. I sighed against her warmth, content, but also unbelievably excited and desperate for more. Her taste burst on my tongue, salty, sweet, and almost overpowering. It made my head spin as Belle moved above me, taking her pleasure. At first, the strokes of her hips were long and even. I lost myself in the feel, the taste, the smell of her. All Belle. This had to be the most glorious feeling in the world.

I was eager to please her, and even though she controlled the pace, I explored her as thoroughly as I could. I covered her with flat, broad strokes of my tongue, pausing to flick over the tight bundle above her entrance. That made the sheets of muscle in her strong stomach quiver, and so I dipped lower, swirling around the tight ring of muscle at her opening. She groaned when I pushed inside, rocking even harder against my mouth, and I let out a muffled whimper as more of her wetness filled my mouth.

Unable to decide which of her reactions I liked better, I alternated between the two. Her fingers burrowed in my hair, guiding me up to suck her before pushing me back down to thrust back inside of her. Part of me wished that I could use my hands so that I could pay attention to both places at once, but they were occupied with the sheets.

Gradually, her movements became short and jerking. I sucked the point of her pleasure between my lips, pulling it out of its hood and kissing the tip, trying to push her over the edge. I would not hold her on the precipice for an eternity, not now.

"Yes," Belle hissed, trembling over me, her muscles clenched tight under my clinging hands. "You feel so good, my Ellie."

Her possession of me, her ownership, drove me wild. I captured her lightly with my teeth and tugged. Belle screamed, collapsing on top of me, releasing violently as I continued to explore with my tongue. I did not let her go until she had exploded a second time, and the feeling of her release against my mouth sent me over the edge as well with three quick strokes of my own hand.

***

Wearing my mother's red dress on the second night gave me even more confidence than Lady Kingsclere's dress had on the first. This time, Belle was the one who helped me get ready. "You know," she said as she drew a brush through my loose hair, "running away from the prince worked perfectly. He spent the rest of the night looking for you, and Luciana did not have a chance to dance with him."

I blushed. Belle knew my sudden departure had not been planned. It was only luck that the prince had kept searching for me instead of dancing with his other guests. "It could have turned out badly. If I had stopped to think—"

"It does not matter. Belle dropped a kiss on the top of my head, holding her face against my hair and breathing deeply. "Mmm. You smell wonderful, sweet girl. Why you did it is not important. It worked. Two nights to go."

"What will we do after the ball if our plan works?" It seemed to me that Luciana would have other visits to court in her life. She could easily attempt to bewitch the prince again.

"I had not thought about it. I suppose that we need to trust Cieran and Cassandra." Belle did not sound pleased with this idea. She was an active person who felt insecure leaving problem solving to others. "If we keep her away from Brendan long enough, maybe she will lose her temper and try something desperate. Cieran and Cassandra can throw her in the dungeon to rot." That mental image seemed to cheer her up considerably.

"Luciana does lose her temper quickly, but I'm not sure waiting for her to harm someone is a good idea. I wish there was more we could do."

"So do I. For now, let's just focus on making sure Luciana doesn't harm anyone for the next two nights." I turned to look over my shoulder, but Belle pressed another kiss to my forehead and straightened my head with her hands. "Hold still. I need to finish your hair."

I smiled into the mirror. "It has been finished for fifteen minutes. I just like having you brush it."

"A beautiful girl deserves beautiful hair to go with her beautiful dress." My belly twisted itself into knots. How did Belle's voice have that effect on me? I was not sure, but I knew that my lover's words and touch would never lose their magic. We spent another silent minute together, with Belle brushing my hair as I watched our reflection. We both had talkative personalities, but we did not always need words between us. So much could be shared by just being together.

After a while, Belle offered me her hand to help me out of my chair, and I rose to step into her arms. She embraced me and, to my surprise, pulled me against her chest and spun me around in a circle. Both of us laughed. Only Belle could have made me so happy with such a serious task facing us.

"May I have this dance?" she asked as she set me on my feet. I curtsied, and she wrapped a strong arm around my waist, stroking a possessive hand along the curve of my hip. With Belle leading, we danced in the middle of the bedroom, not caring that there was no music. As I had expected, my lover was a fine dancer, incredibly easy to follow. Belle's smile made me wonder if my slippers had grown wings and lifted me into the air.

"I have never had a better partner," I said as we moved together. It was the truth. Her eyes lit up and her cheeks flushed to match mine. The compliment had touched her. It was the truth. I knew that Belle had wanted to dance with me at the ball, in front of everyone, and that she was jealous of my dances with the prince. I needed her to understand that the best dancer in the world—and Brendan was a good dancer—would never compare with her.

***

The second night of the ball began much like the first. The women swept by in their colorful dresses, leaving traces of perfume where they walked. The men danced with them and stood around the food, talking and exchanging greetings. I weaved through the crowd, looking for Prince Brendan and, secretly, Belle. My lover's absence was a gripping ache in my chest. I would only dance with Belle tonight in my mind.

As I was searching for Prince Brendan, he was also looking for me. It took him only a few minutes to catch sight of me and walk over. "Good evening, Ellie." I curtsied, and he bowed. He was wearing his army dress uniform of red and gold, and he cut a dashing figure. Many girls would have thought him a dream, but not me. My dream had already come true.

"Would you like to dance with me again? If you are not going to run away from me, of course." He took my hand and lifted it to his lips, but he was not forward enough to remove the glove. I was relieved. I did not want him to notice my rough hands.

"Of course. I ran last night to avoid my sister, and could not find you afterwards." As the orchestra struck a pavane, I silently thanked my father for insisting on dancing lessons. He had claimed that I would have to dance at my wedding. Secretly, I wished Belle and I could share that special dance. I remembered what Belle had told me the morning after we had made love for the first time. "You asked me to be your wife..." That helped to fill the small, unsatisfied corner of my heart.

A strange heat on my face told me that several pairs of eyes were watching me. My smile faded as I noticed the unhappy expressions that surrounded us. Several young women were staring holes through my back, wanting their turn in the prince's arms. I hoped that they did not draw any more attention to me. Luciana could not study me too closely and figure out who I was.

"You look lovely tonight," Prince Brendan said. His hand pressed lightly on my waist to guide my steps. I forgot the jealous women, but I could not forget my thoughts of Belle.

"And you look very handsome." The prince and I smiled at each other. "Thank you for the compliment. This dress belonged to my mother. That makes it one of my favorites."

"I am glad that you have something to remember her by." I was pleased that he did not apologize for my loss or fish awkwardly for a reply. Prince Brendan really was charming.

"You understand."

"He isn't dead, of course, but I carry my father's sword on patrol. He gave it to me when I was twelve. There were not many opportunities for him to use it anyway. It makes me feel connected to him."

"I heard that you were stationed at the Amendyrri border, along the Forest Pass."

The prince looked surprised at my interest in the subject. We paused as the orchestra changed to a waltz and began to dance again. "A lady, interested in a soldier's life? How shocking," he teased.

"You are not just any soldier. Besides, Amendyr itself interests me. I have never been afraid of magic."

"I wish I knew more about it," the prince admitted. "That's Cass and Cieran's job. But I never understood why my father and some of the nobles are so afraid of it. Magic can be very useful."

Although I was delighted that Prince Brendan seemed to have more progressive views about magic than his father, I saw an opening in the conversation and dove for it. "It can also be dangerous. Has anyone ever threatened you with magic?"

Prince Brendan looked thoughtful. "Not that I am aware. I suppose Cass or Cieran would head it off before I heard about it, unless it was serious. Why?"

"You are the prince." I nearly stumbled as we moved across the floor, but managed to correct myself in time. My slippers were beginning to pinch my feet. "I expect you are dealing with one assassination or another constantly."

Brendan laughed. "Not at all. Why, Ellie, you certainly have conversations about the strangest topics. I find it rather endearing." My stomach twisted unpleasantly at the affectionate comment. I knew it was necessary, but I could not dismiss the guilt I felt for lying to the prince.

The hours passed quickly, and we conversed easily. Occasionally, he gave a dance to another girl, but he always returned to me. Throughout the night, I kept careful watch for Luciana. I saw her out of the corner of my eye twice, watching Brendan and I dance, but the crowd always moved between us before she could recognize me from such a distance. I did not see Belle, and her absence left me lonely and sad beneath fake cheerfulness.

The third time I saw Luciana, she approached us in the middle of a quadrille, her face set and her hands clenched. I lowered my chin, tucked my shoulders, and flew out of the prince's arms without a goodbye, running awkwardly in my tight slippers. "Ah, I wondered if you would run again," Brendan called after me, pushing aside several startled bodies as he chased me.

Clutching my skirts, I ran for the front door, ducking and weaving through the partygoers faster than Brendan, who could not squeeze his larger figure by as easily. The cool night air shocked my skin as I shouldered my way through the door, ignoring the curious stares that followed me. Matthew was waiting for me, and the horses lifted their heads as I ran for the carriage.

As I hurried down the stairs, I felt resistance when I tried to lift my feet. I stopped and looked down, cringing as I noticed the black pitch that had been smeared over the bottom steps. The terrible smell filled my mouth and nose, and I wondered why I had not noticed it before. I tried to move, but one of my slippers was caught in the sticky mess. I finally pulled myself free and began hobbling to the carriage, both of my slippers covered in black goo.

As I threw myself into the carriage and slammed the door, still covering my nose and mouth with my hand, I saw Prince Brendan waving after me. Matthew ignored him. He clicked his tongue and urged the horses into a run.

CHAPTER 4

MATTHEW WAS HELPING me out of the carriage when I saw a large shadow flying up the road. It took me a few moments to make out the shape of a coach pulled by a team of white horses. Prince Brendan had followed me all the way from the palace. At first I was relieved, because it meant that he and Luciana were miles apart. Then I remembered all of the bad things that would happen if Prince Brendan found me. No sensible lady would want to be caught after running away from the prince.

I ran for the first hiding place I could think of—the chicken coop. Matthew or Cate usually fed the irritable birds in the morning, so I had never examined the small wooden box except in passing. As I crouched behind the damp smelling boards, straining the muscles of my back, the chickens inside stirred. "Clu-cah, clu-cah, nightstalker hides. Tuck beaks in wings, danger outside!"

"Shhh!" I hissed as loudly as I dared. "Be quiet! I'm not a fox, I'm a person."

The chickens grew louder, encouraged that I was speaking a language they understood. "Are you a friend? Come in! Come in!"

I groaned, covering my eyes with my hand. Songbirds were bad, but chickens were worse. "That doesn't even rhyme. Just please be quiet. Er...a nightstalker is coming."

That closed their beaks for a solid ten seconds, but then I heard a frantic scrabbling inside the coop interspersed with cries of

"Nightstalker! Nightstalker!" I regretted saying anything at all to the stupid creatures.

Silently, I lamented my position. Here I was, crouching behind a chicken coop in the middle of a night, hiding from a prince because my stepsister wanted to take over the kingdom, and trying to convince a bunch of excitable birds to be quiet. On top of all that, my slippers were still covered in pitch, and they smelled terrible. I was tempted to leave them behind when I made a run for the manor. *Oh mother, if you could see what kind of trouble your daughter has gotten herself into now,* I thought glumly.

My head rose as a twig snapped several yards away, and I nearly stopped breathing. The chickens were still babbling amongst themselves. "Oh no, I woke them," a deep voice said, and a few seconds later, someone cried out in surprise. From the groans of pain that followed, I guessed that whoever it was had fallen. Seizing my chance, I darted from the chicken coop to the back of the stables, clutching my skirts to keep them out of the way.

"Oi, stop!" a familiar voice called, and I halted mid step, nearly falling into the mud.

"Matthew!" I ran back to the chicken coop where the stableman was laying on the ground, clutching his knee. "What happened?"

"Saw you run back 'ere, girlie. Tried to find ya, tripped over a branch." I helped Matthew to his feet, brushing off his coat as he stood.

"Oh, I'm sorry, your shirt is ruined." His white shirt was covered in dirt, but the black overcoat seemed fine, at least in the dark.

"That dress ain't in great shape neither," he said, eyeing me. I must have looked a state with mussed hair, pitch on my shoes, and my mother's beautiful silver dress covered with mud. "His Highness went inside after he took a peek in the carriage. Your lady drove up seconds af'er he did. She saw the prince and headed him off, sayin' you were took sick and couldn't be seen."

"Belle is here? But what about Luciana?" I was shocked that Matthew had also figured out my secret, but decided not to say anything.

"She were alone when I saw her."

That meant that Luciana was stewing at the ball while the prince, Belle, and I were hours away at Baxstresse. If I had not been cold, dirty, and tired after my misadventures, I might have laughed. Someone would probably lend her a carriage, or she could hire one, but the mess would take a few hours to sort out, especially since most of the people in the palace would be searching for the absent Prince Brendan. I still could not believe that he had left his own birthday ball to follow me.

Matthew gestured with one hand, about to continue his explanation, when both of us heard voices. I grabbed his arm and helped him limp behind the chicken coop, where we crouched down shoulder to shoulder.

"Are you sure you would rather leave?" Belle asked, her voice floating up through the darkness.

"No. Honestly, I want to sneak back home before my parents throw themselves off of a rampart."

"I promise she will be at the ball tomorrow, Your Highness." I heard a slightly sour note in Belladonna's voice, but only a lover would have noticed it. She was obviously still a little jealous of Prince Brendan's interest in me.

"As long as I have your assurance that she is all right."

"Of course. My sister has been strange since her recovery .She meant no disrespect by running off."

I frowned in the shadow of the coop. Belle was not near enough to see, so I glared at the ground instead. We were going to have a serious talk once Prince Brendan left. Strange indeed!

"Of course. Now, if I...ah, here it comes." The sound of carriage wheels crunching on a gravel drive was audible from our hiding place. There were a few more quiet words exchanged between Belladonna and the prince. Less than a minute later, Matthew and I listened as the carriage drove off down the manor drive.

Once the prince was a safe distance away, Matthew and I crawled out from behind the chicken coop. The chickens had worn themselves out running around and squawking, and they gave us no parting comments. Belle caught sight of us picking our way around mud clods in the dark and hurried over to grip Matthew's arm when she saw that he was hurt.

After Matthew's ankle was wrapped and I cleaned myself up, Belle met me her room. I rested on the bed, watching as she undressed. I not bothered to dress again after my quick wash, and my greedy eyes took in every detail of her body. I watched as her careful hands undid her bracelets, necklace, and earrings and placed them in her jewelry box.

"So, I have been strange since my recovery?" I scolded as she closed the wooden lid, only sounding a little put out. Mostly, I was glad that Belle, the prince, and I had survived another night without injury.

"You were strange from the moment you were born, but I was too polite to tell the prince." Belle sniffed, pretending to sound offended. She had succeeded in peeling off her outer dress without assistance, but was struggling with her corset. My gaze fell on the lovely pair of breasts that stood out from her torso as she arched her back, fumbling with the laces.

"You are not polite at all. In fact, you're very rude. Here, let me help you." I got out of bed, hardly noticing the cold floor under my bare feet. I was too distracted by the sight of Belle in her corset and underskirts. I kissed the back of her neck as my fingers undid the hooks and eyelets, sighing into her warm skin. Belle took a large breath as the corset fell open, stretching her shoulders to enjoy the freedom of movement. I rested my head on her chest, and she wrapped her arm around my waist, pulling me tighter against her side.

"Are you going to help me with the rest of this?" she asked, tugging at her white underthings.

I smiled. Despite the problems with my wardrobe and my hurried departure from the ball, the night had ended on a positive note. "Maybe." I lifted my chin so that our lips were a breath apart. "But you have to apologize for implying that I was touched."

Belle laughed. "You are touched. I'm touching you right now." Her fingers walked along the curve of my naked hip and crept around to pinch the vulnerable swell of my backside.

I swallowed a soft cry as her warm hand tried to steal between my legs. "I think that both of us have already had enough excitement for one night," I said, halfheartedly attempting to leave her embrace.

Still smiling, she kissed my golden hair, trying to coax my legs apart. "You can never have enough excitement. Open for me?"

I closed my eyes as she began a soft line of kisses from my ear to the corner of my mouth. "We're not in bed yet," I protested, my last defense.

"Why do we need a bed?" Half-dressed and wild looking with her corset unlaced and her underskirts bunched together, Belle backed me up until I was pinned between her and the wall. "I want to have you right here." I recognized and accepted the look in Belladonna's eyes, the one that said she needed to reassert her claim to me. Privately, I was amused that someone so bold, so strong, so confident, constantly needed to reassure herself that I really did belong to her. It was rather endearing.

Too far gone to ask for permission, her eyes rolled back into her head as she cupped me—soft, wet, and vulnerable—with her hand. She joined our lips in a deep, probing kiss that stole my breath and set my head spinning almost as much as the fingers that slid effortlessly inside of me. We were motionless for one long, shared heartbeat.

"Mine." She growled into my neck, leaving two well-placed nips on the curve of my throat. "Tell me..."

"I'm yours, Belle," I whispered before our mouths sealed in another kiss.

Her hand drew away, leaving me empty, aching. *No.* My lips formed the word, but nothing came from my mouth. I lifted my hips, seeking purchase on something, any part of her, but Belle was too busy tearing at her skirts, trying to push them down to her ankles. I pulled at her unlaced corset until, by some miracle, I tugged it over her head and threw it aside.

Finally, with twin sighs, we pressed together again. Everything was warm, naked skin and frantic heartbeats, and there was nothing between us. My head rolled back against the wall as her fingers found me again, teasing my entrance before pushing inside. I hissed as I stretched to take her hand, but I spread my thighs wider, relishing the slight sting.

She began moving inside of me, curling her fingers forward to catch against my front wall as her thumb swiped in firm circles. Her thrusts were long and deep enough to lift me onto my toes. I was helpless to do anything but wrap my arms around her neck and cling to her while she had me.

Our cheeks brushed together as she pressed her forehead against the cold stone wall, panting heavily. With her lips beside my ear, I could hear every gasp, every shuddering cry. Even though I was the one being taken, I adored the noises she made as she touched me. They made her seem feral, unrestrained. "Come for me, Ellie. I want to feel you fill my hand."

My hips jerked with the first waves of release at her command. I fluttered wildly around her fingers, and spots danced before my eyes. Each pull of her fingers drew a flood of wetness from me, and I shuddered and cried out with each contraction. Belle had to support me by pressing me against the wall until I stopped trembling in her arms.

"I love you, Ellie mine," she said softly as I strained to catch my breath. I moved away from the wall and sank to my knees. "What are you doing?"

Instead of answering, I placed a kiss over the curve of her knee and gazed along the line of her legs, past her stomach and breasts, to smile up at her. I wrapped my arms around her hips, resting my cheek against her thigh as she eased her fingers into my hair. "Make me." I blushed furiously, unable to meet her eyes, but the words hung between us.

"What?"

"Make me," I repeated, murmuring against her skin.

With a sharp breath, Belle pulled me tight against her. I groaned as her thick, sweet taste spread over my tongue. There was no gentleness as she rolled her hips against my mouth, covering my cheeks and nose with her wetness. I let her guide me as I drank of her, giving her complete control. She arched toward me as I caught her sensitive bundle between my lips and sucked, her scream echoing in the empty room. I felt her fingers clenching and relaxing in my hair and grabbed one of her hands with mine, squeezing tight as she exploded for me in a surge of shuddering warmth.

After a moment of stillness, I kissed her soft belly, which was still twitching with the memory of her pleasure, and she helped pull me to my feet. Somehow we managed to stumble toward the bed and collapsed on top of the covers, still clinging to each other and placing soft kisses on tempting shoulders or cheeks. I fell asleep as I so often did, with my head tucked against her chest, listening to her steady heartbeat.

CHAPTER 5

ON THE MORNING of the third ball, I went to visit Brahms. To my surprise, there was no frost on the ground, and it felt like spring instead of almost winter. The strange weather was so nice that I felt comfortable enough to kick my shoes off by the door. The dew was cold, but my feet were grateful to be free of my shoes.

I was going to ask Brahms a favor. I needed a way to avoid the prince tonight, because he would surely follow me home this time. After all, he knew where I lived. My nose wrinkled as I recalled the pitch on the stairs. Tonight, I would be sure to exit the castle through a back door.

"You need a third dress," said a voice at my knee. I was so startled that I nearly tripped over Jessith as she wound between my ankles, unusually affectionate. She rarely ventured outside, and I was surprised to see her near the stables.

"There is no time to get a third dress. I will have to use the same one I wore on the first night." It would be a little embarrassing to use the same dress more than once, but there was nothing else to be done. I did not mention that the hemline of my mother's dress was still stained with the foul-smelling pitch.

Jessith's yellow eyes were illuminated in the soft morning sunlight. "If I could find you a dress, would you take it?"

"How would a cat find a dress?"

Jessith began grooming her tortoiseshell fur, looking unconcerned. Her eyes released me. "I asked you first."

"Yes, I would take it," I said, kneeling down to pick her up. She squirmed in my arms as I rose to my feet, going so far as to nip at my shoulder, although it did not hurt. "Do you want to get dew all over your paws?"

"I already walked out here, didn't I? Take me to the hazel tree."

Since so many birds enjoyed perching in my mother's hazel tree, I assumed Jessith wanted to watch them. She had taken to hunting spiders and rats since her bargain with the local birds prevented her from killing them, but she still enjoyed observing them. I did not understand why she tempted herself.

Feeling indulgent, I headed in the direction of the hazel tree with my arms full of cat. "You could have said please," I scolded her. Jessith's whiskers tickled my shoulder, and her muscles twitched as she turned her head to look at the tree. Even though this particular day was oddly warm, the hazel tree believed it was winter and was in full bloom. A cloud passed over the sun, casting a warm brown shadow over the field, and I saw two white birds dip toward us. Beneath them were several smaller birds, and in their claws, they were carrying...

"Jessith, did you do this?" I gasped, staring at the dress that had been dropped at my feet. I hurried to pick it up before the dew soaked into the fabric, setting Jessith down beside me. The dress was golden satin, with embroidery on the waist and neck. The material felt wonderfully soft in my hands. "Oh, thank you. It's beautiful!"

Jessith pawed at my foot. "I thought so."

"How did you get it?" I did not receive an answer, and I wondered if I truly wanted to know. Perhaps it, too, was stolen. The birds that had brought the dress to me hovered around my head. A particularly brave fellow began to pluck at my hair, and I lightly brushed him aside. With several strands in his beak, he flew out of reach, carrying his prize to the top of the hazel tree. I rubbed my scalp, keeping hold of the dress.

"If you come in with me, Jessith, maybe I can find you some cream. You deserve a reward."

If Jessith had not been a cat, she would have smiled. "I think that cream would be appropriate." It was as close as she would come to a conventional 'you're welcome'.

***

The rest of my morning was much less pleasant. After I visited Brahms and hid my surprise gift, Cate, Sarah, and I began sorting and airing out the upstairs storage rooms. It was an annual chore, but this was the first time I had participated. My concentration waned after a few minutes of digging through boxes, although we did laugh together over a ridiculous stuffed vulture perched on a feather hat.

It was not until we split up to work faster that I felt a presence behind me, in the darkest, gloomiest room in the upper corridor. A body, warm, pressed against me from behind. For a moment, I thought it was my lover and I leaned into her, but the shape felt wrong and I jerked away. Nails clutched my arm, leaving red half-moon crescents, and I realized it was Luciana.

"What do you want?"

Luciana gripped my shoulder and turned me to face her. "Have you wondered what the ball is like, staying here by yourself? Did you know you were invited?" My heart stopped beating. Had she seen me the night before? Was she taunting me? "Did you want to dance with your precious Belle? Wear a beautiful dress and impress everyone?"

I realized she was angry, but not at me. She was angry because she had not yet ensnared the prince, and she needed release. For a moment, I was grateful she had not chosen Cate to cast her fury upon. My punishment would be painful and degrading, but she would not force herself on me, if only because she wanted to prove herself capable of restraint. At least, I hoped she was capable of restraint.

"Well, you will dance with me now." She grabbed my waist with one hand, clutching her stone fingers tighter around my arm, and threw me into a painful dance. Luciana was an excellent dancer. I had seen her dance at my father's wedding. I had even seen her dance at the prince's ball. She had never danced like this. I felt like a doll being jerked on its strings, painfully twisted. She let go of my arm, which throbbed with relief, but grabbed onto my hair, which was covered by a kerchief to protect it from dust, and pulled. I cried out, and she pulled harder.

Luciana's body weight forced me down, twisting my ankle as I collapsed to my knees. I felt it bend unnaturally, the blood cut off and the muscles screaming. She heard my gasp of pain and trembled like a hunting dog. Her face leaned over me, an ugly smile spreading her cheeks. Her mouth was a breath away from mine, as though she was about to kiss me, but she did not.

I thought about resisting, pulling out of her strong grip and running as fast as I could, but my ankle throbbed and twitched with crippling bolts of pain. The sorcerer's chain was around her neck and she stank of magic. The pendant was twirling, watching me. If I ran, she would catch me. And maybe she would forget her promise to Belladonna.

My breath came in short, heavy gasps. "I will scream," I warned her. Fear and desperation gave me the courage to defy her, even though she could probably kill me.

"Scream then. She will not hear. Where is your guard dog now, you greedy little beggar?" she whispered fiercely in my ear. Her hand squeezed my neck, cutting off my breath. "Is she here to protect you?"

But it was not Belladonna who saved me this time. It was Cate who stood in the doorway with high shoulders. "No!"

One word, with only two letters, but coming from Cate's lips, it was monumental. Both of us nearly fell backwards with surprise. Shocked into silence, Luciana dropped me to the floorboards. I stayed down, ready to grab her ankles if she lunged for Cate, but she did not step forward or raise her hand. For the first time, I noticed Sarah standing beside her.

I saw the conflicting emotions pass through Luciana's body. Surprise as she dealt with the fact that Cate, her compliant little pet, had turned on her. Aggression as all her muscles coiled and her lips pulled back in an animal snarl. Finally, wariness, as she realized there were three of us, and only one of her. Even with magic, stopping all of us would be difficult. "Not tonight, not tonight," she said under her breath. I realized that if she had not been planning such important things for that evening, all three of us might have been killed.

She made her decision and swept out of the room, leaving behind only the ghostly pressure of her fingers on my throat. In a complete reversal of roles, I collapsed in to Cate's arms, my chest heaving with dry sobs, relieved to let her support me this once instead of supporting her.

"Ellie, did she..." Sarah and Cate said together, all in a rush. I shook my head, trying to catch my breath. Curiously, my cheeks were dry, but my chest shuddered terribly.

"My ankle, it hurts." The words scraped in my throat.

Cate peeled back the hem of my dress as Sarah patted my shoulder. My ankle was twisted and starting to turn an ugly purple color. "I can get some cold meat to put on it," Sarah offered. "Stay here, you shouldn't move yet." She hurried, not walking, but not quite running out of the door and down the hallway.

"Cate," I said, looking up into her concerned face. Her forehead was puckered and her hands flitted from one shoulder to the other, touching my hair, not sure where to rest. "You told Luciana no."

Cate's eyes widened with surprise. "Did I?"

"You did." I could tell that she was having more trouble believing this than I was, even though she had said the words herself.

"I did," she said, more confidently. "You know, she has...hurt me less. Luciana. The past few weeks. That is, she beat me. But there was less. Less of the other thing."

"Maybe she is distracted. Cate, is it wrong to hope Luciana does attack the prince?"

Cate considered that for a moment, her eyes losing focus as she thought deeply. She stared at her lap, where she had finally folded her busy hands. Her red hair hung around her face like drawn afternoon curtains. "No. It is not wrong to hope that she is caught. It would be wrong if you wanted the prince hurt."

"I've got it," Sarah panted as she rushed into the room with her prize and knelt beside me. "Here, put this on. We'll give it a chance to rest a bit and then see how to get you downstairs." I sighed with relief as I felt the numbness grow. Cate remained lost in thought. I wondered what she was thinking about, but decided not to ask.

Cate and Sarah held my upper arms to help support my weight as I navigated the treacherous stairs, and Mam gave me some cream to help with the swelling. I smiled. That woman had her own remedy for everything. I sat on one of the kitchen chairs, my foot propped on an unsteady stool supported by three uneven blocks of wood. The outside of my foot was warm to the touch, even through the bandaging, but my entire lower leg felt cold.

Cate and Sarah were still hovering around me when Belle came into the kitchen with fury in her eyes. "What did she do to you?" she snarled, trembling with unreleased energy and anger.

Cate gripped Sarah's wrist and dragged her from the room even as she protested. When we were alone, I considered Belle. "I am perfectly fine," I lied. "Please calm down."

"Do not lie to me. Why is there a bandage on your foot?"

"I fell." Belle gave me a look. "Luciana pushed me and I fell," I corrected, omitting as many details as possible. I did not want Belle to fly into a rage. Not now, when the situation was so delicate already.

"There are bruises on your arms." Belle winced as she took in the sight of them. I stared at my hands, which were folded in my lap. "She marked you."

"No," I protested, but Belle took two steps forward. She put a heavy hand on my arm and pulled up my sleeves to examine the bruising. I went limp and allowed her to search every inch of my body, running her hands over my belly, back, breasts, and even cupping gently between my legs, to reaffirm ownership. There was a quiet desperation in her face as she examined me. She pressed little kisses over my face, trying to reassure herself that I was all right, that I did not hate her for being unable to save me.

"Cate was there," I whispered as her soft hands stroked my arms. She rested her head on my chest, listening to the slow thump of my heart.

"I should have been there. Not Cate."

A river of tears streamed from her eyes and onto my working dress. I did not care. I wove my fingers through her raven hair. "You are here now. That is all I need to know you love me."

CHAPTER 6

MY MAGIC HAD NEVER given me the Sight before, but on the third night, I felt something that seemed like it. There was a constant twisting in my belly, a doubled pulse that could not be slowed, and a strange tightness in my breath. It probably was not magic, but the premonition weighed heavily on me anyway, a stone woven net about my shoulders. This was Luciana's final chance to snare Prince Brendan after two nights of careful observation, and I knew she would take it.

I arrived at the castle minutes after Belle and Luciana. My lips pulled into a tight line as I lifted my light golden dress and hurried up the stairs, the skirts rustling about my knees. I remembered the pitch that Prince Brendan had smeared over them the night before. This time, I would escape some back way. Matthew had been instructed to unhitch Brahms and tie him several yards away from my carriage. While the Prince ran to the empty carriage, I would run for the horse.

Corynne and Brahms were both very flattered by the idea when I had presented it to them that morning. Corynne assured me brightly that she could outrun the Prince's team, and Brahms was pleased that he had been given the important task of carrying me home. I was mostly worried about Corynne. Racehorses were not meant to do the work of draft horses, but I needed their speed.

I stood in the doorway of the entrance hall. In my fine golden dress, I was invisible in the bright, colorful crowd. My shoes were much more sensible this time, a pair of comfortable cloth slippers that were large enough to accommodate my swollen ankle. My dress was long enough to cover most of the shoes, and so my odd choice of footwear did not attract any attention.

I was fortunate to catch sight of Luciana right away. Belle was not with her, and I wondered where she was, but returned my attention to Luciana in time to watch her slip through a doorway near the entrance to the ballroom. I hurried after her, not wanting to let her out of my sight.

After several mumbled apologies and a few near dodges, I was at the door that Luciana had entered. I did not catch sight of Prince Brendan, and hoped that he was somewhere in the ballroom, far away from Luciana and the chain. Glancing over my shoulder, I made sure no one was watching me before I opened the door and entered a dimly lit hallway. This was obviously a section of the palace that should have been closed off from the party.

I closed the door behind me and waited a moment for my eyes to grow accustomed to the dark. There were several more doors along both sides of the hallway, but I had no idea whether Luciana had entered one of them or continued further into the darkness. I decided to listen for movement or voices, too cautious to venture into any of the rooms and alert Luciana to my presence. Passing a portrait of a courtier with a particularly large nose, I crept toward the first door and put my ear against it. Nothing. I walked to the next door and repeated the process.

As I was listening at the fourth room, one of the doors further down the hall clicked open, making my spine stiffen. Luciana entered the hallway again. Her hands were unclasped and relaxed at her sides and her forehead was smooth. The only sign of anger was her blazing eyes as they tightened on my face, but her control was not shaken. She would not lose herself to rage this time, not when things were so desperate, but I saw it gathering in her chest.

"You. I should have killed you when I had the chance." She spoke with a cold fury that was somehow more fearsome than the familiar hot madness. "I will not make the same mistake again."

She did not waste her time playing with me or insulting me. Instead, she gripped the glowing chain around her neck with white fingers and spoke words I did not recognize, letting them hang in the air between us. Pain exploded along my skin, eating away at my flesh. I screamed and looking down at my arms. The skin seemed untouched, but the pain did not end. I fell to my knees, aware only of the crawling, burning magic coating my flesh and Luciana's high laughter.

Suddenly, the pain was gone. I breathed in once through my dry lips, still tingling all over with the residue of Luciana's nasty spell. I was lying on the floor, half of my body pressed into cold stone, the other half sprawled on the edge of a rug. I heard a shout and the sound of something heavy crashing to the ground. Using the little bit of strength I had gathered, I looked up. Two blurred figures were grappling with each other, fingers tangled in hair and clutching at dresses. My vision cleared slightly and I screamed. Somehow, Belle had found me and come to my rescue just when I needed her.

I felt my strength returning and lifted myself up onto my knees. Luciana did not notice, too busy trying to keep Belle's hands away from her neck, where the golden chain still rested between the 'v' of her collarbone. The eye seemed to grow larger and larger, pulsing in the torchlight.

"I am awake. I see you," it said.

I watched helplessly as Belle's fingers grabbed hold of the chain, which was blindingly bright and shaking. The metal left red burn lines on Luciana's white neck. Belle screamed as she tried to tear it from Luciana's throat, but she could not bear to touch the metal. She collapsed to the floor at Luciana's feet, twitching and writhing as magic overpowered her body. Luciana gave her a look that was half panic and half disgust. She glared at me, and then deliberately turned away, vanishing down the hall.

I pushed myself to my feet, hurrying over to where Belle lay motionless on the stone floor. I do not know how long I spent by her side, helpless to do anything but cry against her too-warm skin. Occasionally, her body spasmed with cruel magical shocks, and I held her until they passed, powerless to stop them.

I finally looked up. Luciana and the chain were gone. Strangely, I did not care. Hardly sparing them a thought, I pressed a kiss against Belladonna's hot forehead. "Stay here. I'll be back, I promise. I'm going to get help." With one last glance at Belle's limp body on the ground, I hurried back down the hallway, hoping I could find someone to help me get her into the carriage.

I slipped into the ballroom as carefully as I could, not wanting anyone to notice my entrance. I eased the door into place behind me, holding my skirts with one hand as I glanced frantically from side to side, trying to decide what to do. I needed someone to help me return Belle to her carriage, but Luciana was still somewhere nearby. I looked through the crowd purposefully this time, trying to keep my breath even and resisting the temptation to cradle my swimming head in my hands. All I could think about was Belle lying back in the hallway, her face and skin burning while I did nothing...nothing.

"Are you all right?"

Prince Brendan's voice startled me, forcing Belle's tortured image out of my mind. Standing beside him was a man I did not recognize, but I sensed the magical energy coming from him immediately. Tears roll down my cheeks as I tried to explain what had happened. "My sister...Belle...back there. The hallway...She has taken ill. I need to get her to her carriage."

"Ellie, steady there. You look like you are about to fall over. What do you mean your sister has taken ill?"

"Belladonna, she's injured. I have to get her home."

Prince Brendan put his strong, square hand on my shoulder. "If she's injured, perhaps one of the palace physicians can take a look at her."

"No! I mean..." I could not let Luciana anywhere near Belle again, especially in her weakened state. "Please, help me get her home. I have to get her to Baxstresse right away."

"A physician cannot help her," said the strange man with Prince Brendan. "There is magic in her blood, and her body needs time to purge it. Taking her home is the best solution." I had been too frantic to study him earlier, but now I knew that he must be Cieran, the King's magical advisor. A small corner of my gnawing agony eased.

Prince Brendan looked thoughtful, but after realizing how frantic I was, he nodded his head once in agreement. "I could call a servant...no, I will carry her myself. It's not too far, and she needs to get home as quickly as possible. Show me where she is."

I led Prince Brendan and Cieran back down the hallway, anxious to return to Belle's side and make sure she was still breathing. When I saw her stretched out on the floor just as I had left her, I nearly collapsed. More tears flooded from my eyes and smeared down my chin as I wiped at them with my hand.

"She does look very ill," Brendan said, leaning down to feel Belladonna's forehead. "Are you sure you would not like me to fetch someone here?"

"Just get her home. Get her home, and she will be all right. She has to be all right." The thought of losing Belle was too terrible to consider.

Belle was tall for a woman, but Prince Brendan was larger, and with Cieran's help, he managed to lift her without too much trouble. My sleek, powerful Belle looked so pale and vulnerable as they carried her from the room. The muscles of Prince Brenda's back stretched with the effort of supporting her weight. I thought of Belle scooping me in her arms, calling me her sweet girl, cradling me, making love to me. The memories made me weep. My heart twisted, and I hurried to follow the prince.

Our journey through several more corridors and outside into the cool night was unmemorable. I was completely focused on Belle, wondering what she was feeling, hoping I could get her home in time. "Which carriage is yours, Ellie?" Prince Brendan asked, but Corynne spotted me and trotted over before I could answer his question.

Matthew was waiting faithfully on the box, and as soon as he saw Belle's limp body in the prince's arms, he hurried over to help Brendan and Cieran settle her across the carriage seat. "Saints above, Miss Ellie, what happened?" he asked as Corynne lipped at my hair. I patted her nose, but pushed her away.

"Fever," I lied. There was no time to explain. "She has to go home right away..." I turned to Corynne. "Cor," I whispered under my breath, "please...Get Belle to Mam as fast as you can. She is...everything."

Corynne looked at me with large brown eyes, understanding more than Prince Brendan. She shifted her hooves urgently in the dust of the road. "I promise, Ellie."

I thanked her with my eyes, focusing my attention back on Matthew. "Bring her to Baxstresse. I'll ride Brahms behind you. There's no time..."

Prince Brendan started to protest, but before any words passed his lips, a hot wave of bone-humming magic rattled through me. I almost lost my footing, but Prince Brendan and Matthew grabbed my arms to steady me. "Luciana," I screamed, not caring who else might be nearby. At the sound of her name, Matthew jumped back on the box, and Corynne was instantly running down the road, her precious cargo rolling behind her.

I whirled my head around, looking for Luciana. She was several yards away, running directly at me with unnatural speed. She did not slow as she neared me, reaching out her arms and spreading her fingers like cruel talons. Not bothering to use magic, she leapt on me, tearing at my hair and face with her fingers, clawing at my eyes. I must have screamed, but a strange white noise filled my head, and all I could feel was the vibration of boiling magic.

The eye hovered over my nose as her chain fell toward my face. My eyes were drawn to it like a pendulum. It was shaking, glowing with a magical light. ***I see you. You will die.*** Suddenly, the eye seemed to fly backwards. It took me several precious seconds to realize that Prince Brendan was pulling her off me. Luciana lifted her hand, palm forward, and barked a word in a language that made my throat scream with the heat of it. Prince Brendan collapsed to the ground. I watched, horrified, as he fell to the ground, much like Belladonna had. Cieran immediately said another word, and a glowing, oily coating appeared over the prince's skin. Sweat beaded on Cieran's forehead and ran in rivulets down his square cheeks as he knelt beside the prince, still keeping one hand raised in Luciana's direction.

To my surprise, and Luciana's, Prince Brendan shook his head, looking around him as if he were in a strange kingdom, but completely unharmed. He touched his forehead, and I saw that his hands were covered with a pair of fine velvet gloves. A wave of relief nearly made me lose my footing. The magic had dazed him, but when he had touched the chain, it had not gotten into his skin. Cieran must have done something to save him.

Luciana hurried away, vanishing as quickly as she appeared. Brendan tried to stand up and go after her, but Cieran put a hand on his shoulder, holding him down. "Go," he said to me. "Get away from here before she comes after you again. I'm going to speak with the King and make sure Prince Brendan wasn't injured. She'll be arrested for this, I assure you."

Part of me did not want to leave, and I opened my mouth to protest. Then, I remembered Belle's limp, lifeless form. I needed to be with her and make sure she was all right. Without another word, I turned and ran for the tree where I knew Brahms was waiting for me. I did not even stop when one of my slippers snapped at the heel and tugged from my uninjured foot.

CHAPTER 7

BRAHMS and I left the palace without attracting attention. He moved faster than a storm over the hills when I told him that Belle was in danger. I felt guilty for leaving Prince Brendan behind with Luciana, but I hoped she would not be able to harm him while he was in Cieran and Cassandra's protection. I needed to be with my lover. Nothing else—the prince, the chain, the kingdom—was as important to me in that moment as Belle.

Baxstresse was surprisingly peaceful when I arrived in the gray of early morning. Frost had returned to the fields, and Brahms and I breathed puffs of white air in the early cold. None of the servants were up but Matthew. He met me as I rode in to take Brahms back to the stables. "She's in 'er room," he told me as I dismounted, patting Brahms' heaving sides in gratitude. "Mam's tryin' ta get her ta take some water now. Go."

I left without another word, desperate for proof that Belle was, at least, still alive and breathing. Careless of my sore ankle, I rushed up the stairs and hurried past the library. I threw open the doors to her bedroom, and what I saw nearly stopped my heart. Belle was as still and pale as death, but when I hurried to her side and pressed a hand to her forehead, her skin nearly burned me. She let out a low groan, her head falling to one side as a strand of dark hair caught against her lip. She was unconscious.

I hovered at Belle's bedside for hours, stroking the soft underside of her wrist and brushing away the strands of hair that clung to her slick, fevered forehead. Mam and I did everything in our power to help her, but the hot magic that beat thickly in her blood had to run its course. Belladonna's endurance would determine her survival.

"You can't leave me, Belle," I whispered over her limp form, tugging the covers off her shoulders to try and cool her down. "I need you too much." Belle's lips parted as she took in another shuddering sip of air, but she did not answer. I stayed at her side, not even leaving to change out of my dress. The fabric was mud spattered and torn, and my one remaining slipper had been kicked into a corner. My arms ached and my sight was unsteady, but I did not dare rest while my lover stumbled along the precipice of death.

Instead, I remembered. I remembered how her arms felt around me, how the love in her eyes warmed my face, how her lean body felt against me, inside of me. I remembered, and the memories were a lovely and painful jumble of rawness. Belle had left her mark on my heart, and I could never escape her.

My sorrowful thoughts numbed slightly as the small servant's door opened and Mam crept in. The worry lines above her bright eyes were deep enough to coax me out of my chair. "You have to hide, Ellie," she whispered. "Luciana is coming."

I continued looking down at Belle. "Nothing can make me leave."

"She'll be killing you both."

"I don't care. My life is nothing without Belle in it."

Mam shook her head, sucking on her teeth. "You're a fool, then, child. Mistress Belladonna wouldn't be wanting you dead." Both of our heads jerked towards the door as the scraping of heels on the hallway floorstones filtered into the room. It would only be a matter of moments.

Mam scurried back through the servant's door, reaching her hand out to me for a brief moment. I did not take it. She left me hovering over Belladonna as I waited for Luciana to arrive. The wait was short. Luciana flung the doors open less than a minute after Mam had crept out of the room, wet hair clinging to her bare shoulders. Her face was drained of its usual sadistic, toying arrogance, but she was beautiful even in her fury. The chain still hung around her neck. Inwardly, I cursed myself. I should have thought to grab the chain instead of rushing for Belle...but Luciana could have overpowered me and taken it back, and I might not have been able to help Belle. I knew I would make the same choice again.

Luciana looked between me and Belladonna, narrowing her eyes. Her fingers stroked over the gold and silver pendant. "Did you really think I wouldn't come back to finish what I started?" she asked, stepping closer to the bed. "Your precious lover is lying there for nothing, and your prince is unable to remember a thing that happened last night."

"What did you do to him?" I stood up from my chair, positioning myself between her and Belle. I would not let Luciana hurt her a second time.

"Does it matter? Cieran and Cassandra are petitioning the King to have me arrested, but by the time he gets here, it will be too late. I'll already have what I want." She snarled at me, pulling her lips back over her teeth. "I should have pushed you out of the window when I had the chance. You would have been much less of a bother if an accidental fall had snapped your pretty neck."

I knew Luciana was going to kill me. Belladonna was not there to shield me from her wrath this time, but even as she dangled between life and death, she gave me strength. "She will recover," I said with a certainty I did not feel.

"I doubt it. Love affairs—and people—so often find themselves dead before their time." Luciana stepped forward and wrapped her fingers around my throat, squeezing with inhuman strength. *Magic,* I thought as my muscles jerked, trying to free themselves from Luciana's chokehold. Blots of color exploded behind my eyes. I could not breathe.

And then I was on the ground, air exploding into my lungs as Luciana ran toward the doors and threw them back open. Mam was braced in the entrance to the room. She peered over Luciana's shoulder at me and Belladonna, but did not speak to us. "The prince is here," she said.

Luciana instantly forgot about killing me. She bolted from the room without another word, too focused on ensnaring the prince to remember her revenge. If I had not thought so before, now I was convinced that she was mad. Mam helped me to my feet, steadying my balance and leaning me against a wall.

"We have to stop her," I gasped, my throat lighting with pain around my words.

"How?"

I pushed myself away from the wall and rushed to the door. "No idea. But we have to do something."

I sprinted out into the hallway and took the servant's stairs, not wanting to run into Luciana on my way. I limped a little on my injured ankle, but I arrived off to the side of the entrance hall just as Luciana was making her curtsy. She had her best smile painted on her face. "...honor to have you at Baxstresse," she said, the tail end of her greeting drifting to the back of the hall where I stood listening. I ducked behind a stone doorframe, hiding myself just as Luciana tossed a glance in my direction.

My heel dug into something soft, and I winced as bone needle teeth bit the skin of my ankle. "Watch where you're hiding," Jessith yowled. "I'm trying to see."

"Sorry." I peered back through the doorway, trying to be as discreet as I could. A large group of servants had gathered at the edges of the entrance hall, eagerly watching Prince Brendan and his attendants. Cate was among them, but she quickly moved out of sight. I saw Sarah gripping her loose skirts with small hands and gazing at the prince with a mixture of fear and wonder. Jamison was at the front of the group, tugging importantly at his brass buttons.

Prince Brendan did not seem to notice any of them. "Lady Luciana, is Ellie here? Is she all right?"

To her credit, Luciana held her calm expression. "Ellie? Of course, where else would she be?"

"I was helping your sisters into their carriage last night, but I must have fallen, because I forget..." His face tightened as he searched for a memory. "When I awoke, I found Ellie's...Lady Eleanor's slipper beside me, but she was gone. Cieran and Cassandra went to see my father and left me in my room, but I escaped and found my carriage to go after her. Could I see her? I want to make sure that she and Lady Belladonna are all right. From what Cieran was saying, there was an attack, but I'm afraid I cannot remember all of the details. I must have injured myself somehow."

"Ellie's health has been in such a fragile state since her illness, Your Grace. I really must insist that she not be disturbed." I had to admit that it took courage for Luciana to deny the prince a request, but she was probably also insane.

As she shifted to one side, I caught a glint of brilliant silver gold, and I strained forward to see. Settled on purple cushion was the slipper I had lost. I realized what I needed to do. "Jessith," I hissed, "go to Belladonna's room and get my other slipper."

"Playing fetch like a common dog," Jessith muttered, but did not bother arguing. She slipped into the patchwork shadows at the edges of the hallway as I turned back to watch Prince Brendan and Luciana.

The prince looked thoughtful, running a large, nervous hand through his hair. "I know that Lady Eleanor is ill, but I must insist on seeing her."

Instead of protesting as I expected, Luciana nodded her head in assent. Her fingers stroked over the golden links of the chain around her throat. "I understand, Your Grace. I will tell her to come down, if you will wait here." She turned and walked up the tall, curling staircase, leaving the prince, the servants, and me waiting.

A minute passed, perhaps two. I did not dare to move. I had no idea when Luciana would return, or what she might do. Finally, I heard the soft scrape of something being dropped at my feet. "I hope you appreciate this. I had to carry it in my mouth. Disgusting," Jessith said.

I bent down to pick up the slipper, my mouth half open to call for Prince Brendan, but stopped short. I looked up just in time to watch myself descend the curved stairway, my hand outstretched. I touched the wall, making sure I was still hidden behind the stone doorframe. "Jessith! If I am hiding here, then who in all of Seria is that?"

"It's Luciana, you twit. I can smell magic all over her."

"Luciana?" My thoughts were frozen, numb with shock. How could I be in two places at the same time? Where was Luciana? "But...Oh!"

"Be quiet and watch!" Jessith hissed, flexing her claws against the vulnerable skin of my calf as a warning. "You are SO slow sometimes."

I gripped the slipper in my hand and stood, studying myself—no, Luciana—as she reached the bottom of the stairs. She drew closer to Prince Brendan and curtsied weakly, and I realized we were not a perfect match. This version of me was thinner, paler, with yellowish skin, as though I had not eaten in days. Or as though I had been sick for several months...

"Your Highness." Luciana-as-me curtsied. "I apologize for wearing my nightgown." It was incredibly eerie hearing my own voice, but not forming the words myself.

"Ellie, you look terrible!" Prince Brendan hurried forward, offering my imitator his arm. "Where is Lady Luciana?"

"With Belladonna." I noticed that Luciana could not take all of the bitterness out of my voice as she spoke Belladonna's name. I had whispered Belle's name in daydreams, rolled it in an invitation, offered it as a joyful greeting, sobbed it into her shoulder as she made love to me, but I had never used it so venomously. Luciana's name was the one my voice hated.

The prince studied Luciana's magical face. "You look much thinner and paler than last night. Maybe you should go back to bed after all..." I smiled coldly. Luciana had done her job too well. The prince had seen me fresh and healthy for three nights in a row, even though my face had been contorted with grief the last time that he had looked.

"I am feeling much better now," Luciana said with my voice, still holding onto Prince Brendan's arm. "I see that you have my slipper. I was afraid I had lost it."

The prince knelt, reaching for her left foot. It was bare, and he slid the slipper onto it easily. Even the feet looked like mine—or, at least, like they had been before the scars and swelling. The slippers had pinched my feet terribly the night before thanks to my swollen ankle, but the left shoe was slightly loose on Luciana.

Giving him a charming smile that I never would have imagined on my own face, she thanked him. Jessith pawed urgently at my leg. "Ellie! Do something!"

I gripped the right slipper so tightly that the blood drained from my hand. "Like what?"

Before Jessith could reply, two things happened that sent the hall into chaos. The double front doors swung open, and I saw Cate nearly fall over as a swarm of songbirds flew into the entrance hall, all of them heading straight for Luciana. She screamed as a hundred tiny beaks tore at her skin, her hair, and the fabric of her clothes. At the same time, Lady Kingsclere appeared at the top of the stairs, wearing one of her nicest blue dresses and looking perfectly sane. She clutched the banister and stopped, her mouth falling open as she stared, horror struck, at Luciana. The servants were in a similar state of mute terror. Half of them had noticed Lady Kingsclere and tore their eyes away from the birds every few seconds to study her.

I stared down at Jessith, who was watching the entire scene and looking very pleased with herself. "You didn't!"

"I most certainly did. I'm glad Cate let them in. Otherwise, they might have flown down the chimneys. No, go! You have a chain to break."

Jessith's voice was drowned out as all of the birds began to sing in verse. "Turn and peep! Turn and peep! There's blood within the shoe. The shoe, it is too small for her, the true bride waits for you!" Confused, I looked at the slipper on Luciana's left foot. Rivulets of blood were streaming out of the shoe, and she was screaming. It took a second look for me to realize that she was changing before my eyes, shedding her magical disguise and returning to her natural shape. The edges of the shoe had cut through the flesh of her foot as it grew to its normal size.

"Enough!" I shouted, brandishing the right slipper like a weapon as I stormed out from behind the stone doorway. At the sight of me, the birds stopped attacking Luciana and flocked to me, singing excitedly as they flew over my outstretched hand. One of them, a fat sparrow, dropped something silver into the slipper. I recognized it immediately: the sorcerer's chain. The chain had been broken again by dozens of sharp beaks, but the pendant was still pulsing with magical light. I picked it up, fingering the eye. It did not burn me this time. I took the thin metal discs in between my fingers and snapped them in half.

A great wind rushed up from the floor, and a high-pitched scream echoed through the hall. Magic rolled over my skin, and the force nearly shook my bones apart. With a sharp cracking sound, the two halves of the pendant disintegrated, leaving my hands filled with a fine white powder. After the wind was gone, the birds continued singing and circling the shoe, flying into one another and scattering feathers everywhere. "Turn and peep! Turn and peep! No blood is in the shoe! The shoe is not too small for her, the true brid—"

"No! Stop singing," I yelled. The birds stopped. "Prince Brendan, arrest my sister for treason."

To his credit, Prince Brendan regained his composure quickly. He approached Luciana, who had fallen to the floor in the middle of her skirts. She was wearing her dress again instead of the nightgown, and her body was her own. Kneeling beside her, he gripped her shoulder firmly with one hand, and her arm with the other. Luciana hung limply in his grip. As she turned toward me, I saw why she did not fight him. Both of her eyes, the cold eyes that I hated so well, had been pecked and scratched out. Horrible, bloody chunks of flesh were all that remained.

Prince Brendan noticed her face at the same time I did. He paled and nearly fell over, but did not let go. "Ellie! How are you...there? Never mind. Heavens, get someone here...No one should be left with their eyes hanging out."

"It would serve her right." All of us turned to Lady Kingsclere, who had reached the bottom of the stairs. "She has kept me in agony for months. I only just came back to myself a few hours ago." That made sense, I thought. Luciana had not had time to re-cast whatever spell she had used on her mother.

"No," another voice said from nearby. All of us turned back in the other direction, where Cate was standing proudly despite her tousled red curls and the feather caught near her ear. "No," she repeated, walking forward. Luciana twitched, life returning to her body as she writhed in Prince Brendan's grip. He held her steady. "That death is too kind for her. Let her live. And I hope that it is the most wretched life she can possibly imagine."

"If anyone deserves to decide, it's you," I said. "Brendan." He lowered his eyes to me. "As a personal favor, let my friend Cate choose Luciana's punishment."

"Of course. But will you explain this whole mess to me first?"

"Yes, I will. And thank you."

I looked at Cate, expecting to see anger, joy, or triumph on her face. Instead, her expression was frighteningly blank. She leaned close, so only Prince Brendan and I heard what she whispered in Luciana's ear. "The last word you utter on this earth will be my name. I will be listening to you scream it when the wolf kills you."

Cate turned to me, and I watched her dilated eyes snap shut as she, too, collapsed to the stone floor.

CHAPTER 8

AFTER THE BIRDS were sent away and Cate was tucked into bed, I entertained Brendan in the kitchen. It did not take long to explain the details. With Seria's prince as a witness against her, there was no question of Luciana's guilt. At least something had gone right in this affair.

"I wish the situation had not escalated this far," Brendan told me, looking sympathetic. I was rather proud of the fact that the prince was sitting in my kitchen. I thought of the kitchen as mine—ours, including Mam, Cate, and Sarah—after all the work that we had done in it.

"So do I. But what could we tell you? We did warn Cieran, but accusing Luciana outright without proof would have been useless."

Brendan gave a tired laugh. "There was nothing more you could have done, considering my father's attitudes toward magic, but I can't help feeling a little like bait."

"You were bait. I suppose you have a right to be upset." I should have been relieved that the prince was safe and Luciana was no longer a threat, but my thoughts were still with Belle in her upstairs room, unconscious, hovering in the twilight world between life and death.

Brendan must have seen my distraction. He placed his hand over mine. "I think I already know your answer after last night, but I am going to ask anyway. Ellie, I am quite taken with you. Seeing the way you handled this affair has only made me admire you more. Would you permit me to court you? I know you have no parents to ask."

My heart sank to my shoes. "I am honored by your interest, Your Grace, but...I already belong to someone." I would belong to Belle for the rest of my life and after, even if she did not wake from her magically induced sleep.

He gave a slightly disappointed but understanding nod of his head and removed his large hand from mine. In many ways, he did remind me of Belle. They were both tall, strong, kind, and full of interesting conversation. "I thought so. Go to her, Ellie. That is where you should be right now. I will get statements from the rest of the household and give you some time."

For a moment, my chest felt heavy and thick with fear. Prince Brendan knew. How had he figured it out? But his smile was reassuring, if slightly forced, and I knew he would not do anything to separate me from Belle. With a lighter heart, I gave Prince Brendan a quick, grateful hug. He returned it, holding on for a moment, and then let me go. "Thank you," I called over my shoulder as I hurried to the place where my heart was waiting for me.

My throat hardened and my chest ached as I opened the door to Belle's room. The sleek, strong creature that had been my lover was weak as a kitten, shivering even though she was buried deep beneath her covers. Only her thin, yellow face remained visible.

I touched her forehead, remembering how my mother had rested her cool hands on my face whenever I was ill as a child. This time, I needed to be caretaker. "Belle, I'm here. I will always be here." Her eyes remained fastened shut. I kissed her forehead, the gray shadows beneath the sharp cheekbones, her dry lips. I wanted to collapse onto the bed next to her and sob myself empty, but I stayed sitting. Before, Belle had always been my strength. This time, I needed to be the strong one.

A noise at the door startled me and I raised my head. Lady Kingsclere stood at the door, her hair tucked into a neat bun. "How is she?" she whispered, joining me beside the bed. As I had done moments before, she rested her hand on Belladonna's forehead. She looked like she had just come out of the sickbed herself, but her tight, tired shoulders were still held proudly.

I stroked Belladonna's cheek with my own hand. "Not well. She needs time." Both of us were silent for a long stretch, joined by our fear and longing.

"Prince Brendan told me everything. I knew Luciana wanted her inheritance, but I never imagined...and now, my daughter..." She gazed sadly at Belladonna. Lady Kingsclere was coming back in to herself.

Belladonna's breathing seemed easier with both of us watching over her, and her shivering stopped. "I'm not ready to let her go." My voice sounded small and terrified to my own ears. "Not after I just found her."

Lady Kingsclere stepped over to the window. She pulled aside the dark drapes, allowing pale sunlight into the room. "I doubt that she is ready to let you go either," she said, staring out of the window and across the yellow fields.

I knew then that Lady Kingsclere knew. And I was not afraid. "I love her more than life. Where she goes, I will follow."

Lady Kingsclere turned to me, looking much older and much wiser than I felt. "You are a stronger woman than I am. If you lose her, wait. You will find her. When I lost my husband, I lost myself. But I am not ready for death yet. I am content to wait and enjoy living for both of us. Besides..." She gave me a sly look from the corner of her eye. "Baxstresse needs an heir, and I need grandchildren from you two."

I blushed. Getting children the traditional way was out of the question, but I was sure that would not stop Belle from trying if...when...she recovered. "I love children, but if you expect me, or Belle, to share each other with some man, then I will have to refuse.

"Of course not," said our mother. I could think of her as my mother now. Not a stepmother, but a mother-in-law; not a replacement, but an addition. It was a much more comfortable relationship.

***

Five slow days passed. I remained sluggish, unmoved by constant appeals to leave Belladonna. I would not be forced from the room. Sarah, Cate, Mam, and even Lady Kingsclere tried to tempt me with food, but I ate two or three mouthfuls and pushed the plates away. I washed my arms and face at the small basin in the corner, but that was my only concession.

Jessith remained in the room with me, only rarely slipping through the partially open doorway to check on the rest of the house. She spent most of the time sleeping, but her warm weight on my lap grounded me when I thought I would spiral out of control. Occasionally, she curled around Belladonna's feet or pressed her cold nose to one of the limp, pale hands.

"She won't die," Jessith told me.

"How do you know?" I asked her, desperate for any kind of reassurance.

"She does not smell like death. She does not look like death. But she is very sick."

I disagreed. I could smell death in the room, an old, hard smell that burned my eyes. It hid in the dark, almost black wood of the grandfather clock that called out the hour, waiting through the seconds. And Belladonna certainly looked like death, with her yellow skin and the sharp planes of her face and shoulders jutting out like spikes. I felt the urge to cover a mirror with black cloth, but could not bring myself to do it. That would be admitting Belle's condition was worsening.

However, Jessith was not prone to lying, and animals often saw things that humans did not. I accepted her opinion and tried to believe in it. My faith in the world and in goodness had been shaken. Not my mother's death, not my father's death, not even Luciana's torture had prepared me for this emptiness and despair. Surely, no light could exist in the world if Belladonna's candle burnt itself out.

Night was the worst. The cold, pale starlight from the window cast ghoulish yellow faces on the walls, mouths stretched open into black gaping holes. My loose hair made shadow paintings over the tossed covers as I hung my head over the bed, listening for the slow, shallow breaths that meant Belladonna had not crossed into death. Her face and forehead were warm under my hands, but her fingers were ice cold when I held them. I tried to give her water, but she would not take it. I whispered to her that she needed to come back to me, that I was waiting for her, that Luciana was gone. Her imprisonment and sentence were meaningless now.

At seven in the morning by the ticking clock, Belle opened her eyes at last. Their jewel blue was pale, faded and washed out, but she was alive. She could not see for the first minute, but I held her hand so tightly that she whispered my name. "Ellie..."

I pressed kisses over her face, making small sounds between them. "Belle..." Her yellow paper skin flushed with red warmth under my lips. I kissed the life back into her.

She only stayed awake for a few moments, long enough to accept the cup that I pressed against her lips and remind me that she loved me. Her eyes blinked, then lowered. Sleep reclaimed her, and it was no longer a death sleep, but a healing rest. Her breathing was easy and deep. Now that the stiff layer of frost constricting my chest had begun to melt, so was mine.

Belle regained consciousness again later that evening. This time, she was much more alert and her robin's egg eyes had regained some of their brightness. "Darling," she greeted me, lifting her hand since she could not pull me into her arms. I pulled her into mine instead, kissing her hair. "How long has it been?"

"Six days." She felt so good in my arms that I wanted to cry. "Luciana is in prison. We are all safe." Belle tried to lift herself up and prop her weight on a pillow, but I eased her back down. "I promise to tell you about it later. Everything is all right." Now that Belle was awake, looking at me, speaking to me, everything really was all right.

After a few more soft questions, "Is mother all right? Have you eaten?" Belle allowed me to wash her with a cold cloth and change her nightgown. She only submitted to the care because I was her lover. Since the constant fear of death had faded, my attraction to her could come forward again. Lying naked before me, Belle was the most magnificent creature in the world. She was thin as a branch and she had lost color, but her wiry muscle had not disappeared. To me, she was just as lovely as ever.

I was too tired to do anything more than to enjoy looking, and Belle was in no condition for physical activity. Instead, I washed her and helped comb her hair, thanking God, Fate, or whatever had spared my lover with each stroke. "That feels good," Belle murmured, sounding like a purring Jessith.

With pink in her skin and looking considerably more comfortable, Belle returned to her bed. I joined her, curling up beside her and leaving the covers off so we could enjoy the warm spring air.

CHAPTER 9

OF COURSE, NEWS of Luciana's arrest, my recovery, Belle's illness, and the Prince's involvement spread like a pox through the upper classes. Baxstresse became a madhouse. Everybody and their second cousins had to come see what had happened, offer insincere condolences and strongly worded opinions, and generally act as nuisances.

Thankfully, Lady Kingsclere's health had improved rapidly, and she was more than well enough to entertain guests. I learned a great deal by watching her gently deflect inquiries and politely rebuff the busybodies. I found myself playing lady of the house again instead of helping Mam, Sarah, and Cate in the kitchen. To my great satisfaction, one of Lady Kingsclere's first acts after returning to her station was to reimburse the pay discrepancy for all of the Baxstresse servants and dismiss Jamison on my advice. I also convinced her to begin looking at blueprints for extending the servants' quarters.

Although my evenings were spent at hastily thrown together dinners with the nobles, I spent my mornings hard at work. Cooking and cleaning, I had discovered, became habits that were not easily dismissed.

My nights were spent in Belle's room. Everyone knew, but no one thought anything of it. I acted the doting sister, not wanting to leave Belle alone at night in case she took ill again. Although she and I had shared several pleasant kisses and soft touches, I was hesitant to make love with her while she was still recovering, especially since we had so many guests.

On one of these nights, around a week-and-a-half into Belle's recovery, I stood outside the bedroom, preparing to greet her. When I reached for the knob, I heard two voices float underneath the crack in the door. "...crawling back now that Luciana's gone, but another part of me remembers how, when I was small, you held my hand and walked me outside to see the horses..." Belladonna's voice sounded tight, as though she held tears in her throat. Absorbed in the conversation, I held my left hand suspended over the doorknob.

I heard a deep sigh, and then sound of the mattress shifting. "I remember." It was Lady Kingsclere. Her voice sounded similar to Belles, but with a tired sort of maturity. There was a long pause and I considered backing away from the door or even knocking, but my feet were frozen to the floor.

"You could have done more." Belle spoke again, angrier this time. "Sent her away, threatened her, punished her, something. But you just watched."

My chest seemed to shrink, and I almost stopped breathing. Belle had never said much to me about her relationship with Lady Kingsclere. Now that I thought about it, my lover's behavior struck me as strange. Belle was loyal to her last breath. Why hadn't this loyalty extended to her own mother? She had not seemed as concerned about Lady Kingsclere's weak, mentally vulnerable condition as I would have expected.

"I was selfish," Lady Kingsclere admitted in a low voice. I could picture her face, eyes lowered, hands clasped in the folds of her skirts, chin bent, but not tucked in shame. Lady Kingsclere was not pretentious, but she was proud. "I wanted what was best for my daughter. Both of my daughters."

"That **thing** is not your daughter." I almost staggered backward, as if struck by the venom in Belle's words. "I hardly consider her human at all. She is a murderous, sadistic, power-hungry snake. That is the daughter you defended."

"She isn't my daughter, not anymore." Lady Kingsclere paused. "I was wrong. I should have been with you. I was too consumed with a wife's grief to remember that I was a mother, too. I was not strong enough. Maybe if I had not let you feel so alone, none of this would have..."

More rustling and the sound of a choked sob through the door. I could hardly believe it. Crying was so unlike Belle, especially in front of someone else. "Do you know what it is like to lose both of your parents at the same time? Oh, you were still breathing, but you were not alive. And to have your sister, who should have been your comfort, following you, telling you that you were worthless, that you would never get the money. I didn't care about the money." Her words were frantic, desperate. I wanted to open the door, but could not find the strength.

"Mocking me, torturing and raping servants...and I could do nothing. I was fourteen. Who would listen to me? It made me sick. But I survived. She didn't kill me. She enjoyed watching my conscience do the tormenting for her. I hated myself for letting her. It grew to be a habit, doing nothing. I had nothing left to care about. I doubted human goodness. And then..."

And then there was me. The thought came to me so suddenly that I was sure it did not belong in my mind, but in Belle's. *And then there was me.* I realized why Belle had found me so fascinating, had fallen in love with me. What I had considered to be my naïve foolishness, my embarrassing innocence, had been Belle's salvation. Talking about books. Doting on Jessith. Smiling at the servants. How long had Belle spent wandering the manor halls like a wraith without seeing a single spark of happiness?

I was far from a perfect person, I knew, but I was untouched, a small piece of the regular world that had not been swallowed by Luciana's shadow. And when Luciana had tried to consume me, I had survived. Suddenly, I felt less like a shy, silly girl, and much more like a woman.

I opened the door. Belle and Lady Kingsclere started. Both of them were sitting on the bed. The image fastened itself in my mind; a smaller, brown-haired woman with wisps of gray about her cheeks reaching for her daughter, pale skinned and trembling. Both of them were crying. I walked between them, placing a hand on each of their shoulders. I imagined the gaping, soul-sucking emptiness I would have felt without Belle, and could not hate Lady Kingsclere for abandoning her daughter. After all, she was trying to find her way back.

"Sometimes," I said, "you have to cry before you can smile again." Not as poetic as some of Belle's secret verses, but I thought it was appropriate enough. Belle stared up at me with helpless, glassy blue eyes, and I wanted to weep, too. "Belle, she is your mother, and she loves you." That set off another round of hot tears. They spilled onto my hands as I cradled her chin.

And then, in what I consider to be no less than a minor miracle, I let Belle go and she turned her crying face to our mother. She opened her arms and Belle collapsed into them, her lean body falling slack like a puppet with broken strings. I kept a steadying hand on her back and let them cry together.

***

It was a wonderful, strange dream...*Belladonna and I were lying on a blanket, watching white-streaked clouds blow past on the high wind. The lonely call of a bird and the whispering of leaves were the only sounds in our ears. Short, trellised walls with climbing ivy surrounded us on all four sides. The sun was a gleaming golden coin, and it shone warm upon our faces. We smiled at each other. The breeze was at our backs, tossing my light hair and strands of Belle's thick, dark curls.*

In Belladonna's clasped hands were two roses, one red and one completely white. She offered the white rose to me, and as I took it with my left hand, a forgotten thorn pricked my finger, the fourth one from my thumb. One drop of blood rolled off of my fingertip and fell onto the rose, staining one of the white petals, a bead of red clinging to the flower's pale curve.

I put the rose in my right hand, careful of thorns this time, and held out my pricked finger. Belle pressed her lips to the small purple mark and I felt new skin grow over it. She kissed the center of my hand and the pulse in my wrist. Her soft lips found mine and the sweet ache in my chest swelled until I had to kiss her back.

Her dress came undone at the back under my quick fingers and soft skin poured out into my hands as I tried to fill myself with all of her. Her purple-black hair was plastered to her neck and shoulders, soft ropes of it spilling over onto me, warm under the sunlight. We pressed close, two lovers with one skin, her lips mapping the freckles scattered across my cheeks and the bridge of my nose as my hands roamed over her corded back.

And then it was a dream no longer. Belle's comfortable weight settled over me in our bed as she kissed me over and over again. And of course, I kissed her back. So, this was what had inspired my dream. Her thumbs stroked my neck, the undersides of my wrists, finding the softest places. I trembled, and she cradled my face in her hands. Those blue eyes begged me to let her take, claim, possess.

A strange urge tugged at my heartstrings, and I shifted beneath her, turning onto my side, and then my belly. I tossed Belle a smile over my shoulder, the tips of my cheeks burning with twin spots of pink. I did not know why I wanted her to make love to me this way, but the idea was somehow irresistible.

Belle's forehead lifted as surprise, but pleasure shone in her handsome face. She hurried to fold her body over mine. Her hands stroked my hips as her teeth caught and held my neck. "Who would believe me if I told them my sweet, innocent Ellie let me have her from behind?" she purred between bites and kisses to my vulnerable throat. "But I would never tell...you belong to me."

She drew my thighs apart a little too quickly, claimed me a little too roughly. Her fingers slid deep inside of me, filling me with one hard stroke. She twisted and curled until she hit the right angle, and I gasped to let her know when she had found it. I raised myself higher, breathing heavily as she kissed the back of my neck. I felt incredibly exposed and vulnerable in this position, but there was something intoxicating about being taken this way.

Still quivering and stretched tight around her fingers, I felt Belle's hips begin to push against mine, using them to aid the thrusts of her hand. I let out a delighted cry and buried my face in the pillow as she took me, our warmth running together over her hand and my thighs. The hardened tips of my breasts dragged over the mattress as Belle and I rocked together, and I felt hers pressed tight against my shoulder blades.

"Mm, smooth, so warm...Ellie, you're all soft velvet around me." She coaxed me to raise my hips higher, holding me just so. With a sigh, she pressed her warmth into the swell of my backside, and I hissed as I felt wetness against my skin.

Belle flicked lazily over my sensitive bud. It was straining at its hood, a hard little point against her thumbpad. Knowing that she felt every pulse of the tiny bundle, every flutter of my muscles, embarrassed and excited me. Held under her thumb, with her other fingers stretching me, she knew all of my secrets.

Belle paused for a moment, hovering over me, leaving me empty with a deep ache. I knew what she expected without words. She wanted me to beg for her.

"Love, please, touch me..." I pleaded, rocking back into her hand.

"Oh, you mean here?" Her firm strokes had me arching until the muscles in my back screamed.

"Harder..." Her thrusts came harder, faster, and her teeth latched on to the line of my shoulder. Her thumb swiped over me again and again, grinding in tight circles, and I screamed.

Waves of pleasure swelled and crashed inside me. I clutched down around her fingers, pulling impossibly tight before I broke down in a series of shivers. My entire body pulsed, and more wetness spilled out from deep inside of me, slipping over Belladonna's fingers. She groaned and came with me, her hips jerking unevenly as she rode through her own release.

My crest seemed to last for an eternity, and I rocked into her hand until I had nothing left to give. I felt Belle tremble against me as I sobbed her name. We held still, breathing heavily, both of us overcome. I could hardly look at her as she tenderly reclaimed her fingers. My muscles clung to them greedily, unwilling to let her go, but with a few whispered words and a soft kiss to each eyelid, I relaxed for her. Sensing my feelings as only a lover could, she tilted my chin and gazed into my eyes, her hand still covered in my wetness. "Shy, dear heart?" she asked, kissing my nose.

Hiding my embarrassment, I dipped my head and began cleaning her hand with my tongue. With my head bent, I could not see Belladonna's face, but I knew she was smiling. "Not too shy." She sounded more than a little smug. It did not bother me. She deserved to be smug.

When I determined that her hand and lips were clean, I told her about my dream. She looked thoughtful as I described the roses, the trellis, and the golden sun. "It was wonderful. I almost wish I could go back. But since you gave me something even better than my dream, I'll forgive you."

"I suppose you'll want an outdoor wedding, then. I thought so before, but I never remembered to ask."

I was mute and still as a stone. Belle looked at me strangely, only just noticing my expression of surprise. "I said that I suppose you'll want an outdoor wedding..."

"An outdoor wedding," I repeated. A wedding? For us? I could hardly imagine it. Well, I had wanted to imagine it, but could not bear to dwell on an event that I had dreamed of since childhood, but would never experience. Belle had called me her wife, but I had assumed it was a private endearment between us.

"You didn't think I would marry you?" Belle looked almost hurt, and I hurried to kiss her frown away.

"No, I want to marry you. But you said we could never let the world know we were married."

"I wasn't planning on putting out an announcement. I just thought it would be nice to invite some of the people who already know and have a small ceremony, even if it isn't legal."

The idea instantly appealed to me. "I want to have an outdoor wedding, and I want it to be by my mother's hazel tree. Cate and Sarah can be my bridesmaids, and—"

"Ellie, I love you, adore you, and want to marry you so that I can spend the rest of my life with you, but if you start planning the wedding now, I will go mad from lack of sleep and exhaustion."

"You're exhausted?" I feigned disappointment as my hand crept down her smooth belly and stole between her legs. "Too exhausted for this?"

"Yes, too exhausted," Belle said in a strained voice. But of course she was pretending, and I got to show her my enthusiasm for her idea after all.

CHAPTER 10

CATE HAD A ROUNDABOUT way of letting me know that we needed to talk. She could not come right out and say it. She had a habit of pausing in her work, staring at me with her wide doe eyes and pale cheeks. She would not say anything, and I would not say anything, until one of us shook our head and looked away, hunching the line of our shoulders.

We were in her room the third time this happened, and Cate was the one who turned away first. I was growing frustrated with her games. "Are you going to tell me?" I asked, not caring if I was pushing.

I saw Cate's throat bob nervously, and she took a breath of preparation. "I'm leaving Baxstresse," she said, still turned to face the opposite wall.

I abandoned the stool I was sitting on and rose to my feet. "Leaving?" It was a single word, but there were a thousand unspoken questions straining behind it, bursting in my mouth.

"I have to leave," Cate said. It was a firm, unwavering answer, and I should have been proud of her decision, but I could not help feeling hurt. I wanted her to stay. "I am not leaving you, Ellie. I'm just leaving Baxstresse."

"There's a difference?" Cate's back flinched visibly at my sharp tone, and I felt guilty for snapping at her. "I'm sorry. You're free to do whatever you wish with your life now. I just don't want you to go. Can't I change your mind?"

Cate pushed herself off the wall. She glanced over her shoulder out at the rest of the room, gazing past the fiery line of hair against her cheek. Her face was set firmly, but not harshly. She had made up her mind. "Ellie, I came to Baxstresse as a child to pay a family debt. When I started to become a woman, Luciana noticed me. I was never happy here until I met you. There are too many ghosts in this manor. I need to find my own place, my own way—"

"You can't leave yet," I interrupted, using the only excuse I had left. "You have to stand with me at my wedding."

Cate smiled at me, her cheeks flushed with pleasure. "Ellie, I would be honored to stand with you at your wedding. But I'm still leaving."

"Will you come back?" As proud as I was of Cate's newfound confidence, I did not want to lose her forever.

"Yes. And I'm not going to leave this very moment."

"I can't keep you here, can I?" I said softly.

Cate turned toward me fully and took me in her arms, giving me a fierce hug. "No, you can't. You are my dearest friend, but not my mistress." And neither, I realized, was Luciana. That thought made me so happy that losing Cate did not seem quite as horrible.

Another thought struck me. "Cate, did you have a vision telling you to go?" Although a seer's visions were not written in stone, the seer usually sensed how likely the occurrence was. They were rarely wrong.

There was a moment of silence, and I wondered if Cate would answer my question at all. "Yes, I did. I saw a dark wolf running through the high trees." Her voice took on a strange, deeper timbre, and she sounded much older. "I need to leave. I need to find...something."

I knew she was holding something back from me, but I did not press her this time. "I know you will find it, Cate. And I will do whatever I can to help you, as long as you come back to me. If you forget, I will go out looking for you."

"Oh, Ellie, how could I ever forget?"

I kissed her cheek and let her go.

***

Once again, I found myself looking for a dress. "I wonder why clothes seem to take up so much of my time," I complained to Belle, crossing my arms over my breasts. "First the three-night ball, and now a wedding dress..."

Belle rolled her eyes and turned the page of her book. "Wear one of those three."

"Belle, you should know better. Those are party dresses, not wedding dresses."

"Why does it matter? We are only inviting a few people, and none of them will care if you are not wearing a proper wedding dress." Belle must have sensed my growing irritation, because she closed the book. "I meant that I think you will look beautiful in anything you wear." She sounded so sincere that I could not stay mad at her even though I knew she was just trying to get out of trouble.

"I want our wedding to be perfect."

"It will be, because you are the one I am marrying."

"That was a little too much flattery, dear heart," I said, but I was secretly pleased and forgot how sore I was about the dress. "I would have worn my mother's wedding dress, if..." I let my voice trail off. By mutual consent, Belle and I did not mention Luciana's name if we could avoid it. Not because we were afraid of her, but because it was unpleasant to think about her or talk about her.

"Stop worrying about the dress." Belle patted my hand and opened her book to the page she had saved. "I will figure something out for you."

The next day, Lady Kingsclere asked me up to her room after lunch. Curious, but not particularly worried, I made my way up the stairs to her suite of rooms, taking the servants' hallway out of habit. I opened the door to her study to find Lady Kingsclere sitting at her desk, catching up on correspondences. "Just a moment, dear." She finished her letter and signed it with a flourish.

I waited, my weight shifted to one hip in a very unladylike fashion, hands clasped behind my back. Lady Kingsclere gave me a slightly disapproving look and I straightened, but it was followed by a smile. Strangely, it reminded me of something my mother would have done. "Belle tells me that you need to borrow a wedding dress," she said, standing up and pushing the chair behind her desk back in place.

My forehead wrinkled. Lady Kingsclere and I were the same size, but I really did not want to wear the dress she had used at my father's wedding. There were too many convoluted emotions attached to that memory. Lady Kingsclere, like Belle, was very perceptive to my facial expressions. "Not that dress. Come, I'll show you."

Realizing for the first time how much mother and daughter had in common, I followed Lady Kingsclere into her bedroom, and over to the large wooden wardrobe where I had found the blue dress. Feeling slightly guilty, even though Lady Kingsclere had been made aware of the "borrowing" I had done and had not objected, I watched as she pulled a white box from the back of the wardrobe. "Here," she said, handing it to me. I opened it.

Inside of the box was the most beautiful wedding dress I had ever seen. It was light blue silk, with a flipped v of white from waist to hemline. The same white color covered the neck and shoulders. The blue section of the dress was embroidered with silver thread, and the white section with gold. It was obviously not just a wedding dress, but a noble heirloom that had been passed down through several generations.

"Did you wear this at your first wedding?" I gasped, still admiring the dress. "It's beautiful."

Lady Kingsclere smiled, and though I knew she was remembering, she did not look crushed or despondent. Instead she appeared almost nostalgic, even happy. "Yes, I did. That was one of the happiest days of my life. I want your wedding to be just as happy."

With a wave of joy and affection, I gave Lady Kingsclere a light hug, not wanting to crush the dress box, and he returned the embrace. She seemed to understand all that I could not say. I finally managed, "Thank you. Thank you so much..."

"There is only one stipulation," she said, lowering her eyebrows seriously.

"What?"

"You must pass the dress on to my granddaughter, provided it fits." I had the decency to blush.

***

Our wedding was not at all like my childhood fantasies. It was infinitely better. Having been a guest at several weddings, including my father's second marriage; I had expected my own to take place in a large cathedral with several hundred onlookers. I was titled, even though I had not been born into it, and I was a curiosity, if nothing else.

Instead, the small ceremony took place outside, in the open air. A steady, gentle wind blew from the north. We gathered beneath my mother's hazel tree, and I knew she could see how happy her daughter was. There was color everywhere, the blue of the sky and the green of the leaves, and the sun was strong and warm on our smiling faces.

Cate and Sarah stood with me. Belle, after many sleepless nights of soul searching, had asked her mother to stand with her, and I could not have been prouder of her choice. Mam, Matthew, and even Brahms, Corynne, Jessith, and the rest of the cats were invited, although Trugel slept through most of the ceremony. Because it was such a tiny gathering, no one thought it strange that I wanted two horses and several cats to attend my wedding, or that wild birds attempted to perch on my shoulders as I said my vows, wanting to be included.

The Honorable Father Matthias, a very sweet but slightly forgetful old man, presided. He had known me when I was a child growing up at

Sandleford, and when I discreetly inquired his opinion about a "nontraditional" ceremony, he revealed that he had performed such services before. I was surprised and a little relieved to hear that Belle and I were not the only nobility joined in a secret marriage. Of course, dear old Father Matthias did not give me the names of the people in question and I was too polite to ask, even though I was dreadfully curious.

I wore Lady Kingsclere's beautiful dress and a traditional crown of orange blossoms, but at the very front, just above my forehead, I had tucked a white rose, one of the same blooms that grew at Sandleford. The beautiful roses were thriving in Baxstresse's new garden, which Belle was helping me plant. A gold linked necklace with white jasper rested around my throat, another gift from Lady Kingsclere. My hair hung loose around my shoulders and I felt beautiful because Belle loved me enough to marry me.

Years later, I cannot remember exactly what we said as we recited, in Old Serian, our vows of faithfulness, love, and honor. What I do remember is the loving way Belle smiled at me, the softness and warmth of her hand as it held mine, and her sure, steady breaths as she stood beside me. I remember the tears in Cate's eyes that she tried to blink away and Sarah's secret wink. I remember Lady Kingsclere looking at Belle, her daughter, and me, her daughter's wife, with a youthful happiness that transcended time and memory. I was sure she was thinking of Alastair, but not with feelings of loss or regret.

And so when I said those two words that bound my lover and I forever—"I do"—and she kissed me, I knew we would live happily ever after.

> I would have picked you daffodils,
> But with a smile, you took my hand.
> You kissed me where the river ran
> And called me lady fair.
> Instead I picked you bluebells, dear,
> And with a smile, you led me through
> The ivy trellised garden gate,
> A white rose in my hair.

The Marriage poem of Lady Eleanor Kingsclere To her wife, Lady Belladonna Kingsclere.

Here ends the First diary of Eleanor of Sandleford, wife of Lady Belladonna Kingsclere. Preserved in the Royal Library by Princess Rowena of Seria, granddaughter of King Brendan and his wife, Queen Sarah.

The End

About **Rae D. Magdon**

Rae D. Magdon is a writer living and working in the state of Alaska. Over the past few years, she has written several lesbian-themed novels, including *Dark Horizons*, *The Second Sister*, and her first published work, *All The Pretty Things* coauthored with Michelle Magly. She enjoys writing fantasy and science fiction, in addition to modern-day romances. When she is not writing original fiction, she ~~wastes~~ spends her time dabbling in ~~unapologetically smutty~~ romantic lesbian fanfiction. Her favorite fandoms are Law & Order: SVU and Mass Effect. In her free moments, which are few and far between, she enjoys spending time with Tory, her *fiancée* of ten years, and their two cats.

Connect with Rae online

Website - http://raedmagdon.com/
Facebook - https://www.facebook.com/RaeDMagdon
Tumblr - http://raedmagdon.tumblr.com/
Email - rdmagdon@desertpalmpress.com

Cover Design By : Rachel George
www.rachelgeorgeillustration.com

Other books from Desert Palm Press

The Guardian Series by Stein Willard
A Guardian's Touch – Book 1
A Guardian's Love – Book 2
A Guardian's Passion – Book 3

The Friends Series by AJ Adaire
Sunset Island – Book 1
The Interim (novelette)
Awaiting My Assignment – Book 2
Anything Your Heart Desires – Book 3

Scarred for Life by SL Kassidy

Coming soon
One Day Longer Than Forever by AJ Adaire
A Guardian's Salvation – Guardian Series Book 4 by Stein Willard
Please Baby by S.L. Kassidy
Chronicles of Osota - Warrior

Desert Palm Press

www.desertpalmpress.com

Printed in Great Britain
by Amazon.co.uk, Ltd.,
Marston Gate.